KenKarta

Battle of the Onoxmon

By Alison Kartevold

The Artists' Orchard, LLC

Text and Illustrations copyright © 2011 Alison Kartevold
www.kenkarta.com

The Artists' Orchard, LLC
P.O. Box 113317
Pittsburgh, PA 15241
www.theartistsorchard.com

ISBN: 978-0-9843166-3-2

Library of Congress Control Number: 2010916296

Printed in the United States of America

Illustrations by Les Polinko
Jacket Paintings by Les Polinko
Jacket Design by Jodi Lesniakowski

Table of Contents

Prologue: Alone in the Dark   9

Chapter One: Where to begin?   12

Chapter Two: The Sisters   14

Chapter Three: Lay of the Land   25

Chapter Four: The Departure   31

Chapter Five: Taken   38

Chapter Six: What Comes in Dreams   40

Chapter Seven: Sound the Alarm   48

Chapter Eight: The Declaration   55

Chapter Nine: The Plan   59

Chapter Ten: Finding a Gift in the Dark   65

Chapter Eleven: Veronica and the Stable Boy   67

Chapter Twelve: Fairies are the Best   73

Chapter Thirteen: Back at the Barn   78

Chapter Fourteen: Sophia and the Dragon   82

Chapter Fifteen: Accidental Betrayal   87

Chapter Sixteen: I So Believe in Fairies   95

Chapter Seventeen: To Valleyridge   98

Chapter Eighteen: In the Shine of Day   106

Chapter Nineteen: In a Battle's Wake   112

Chapter Twenty: To Scratch an Itch   117

Chapter Twenty-One: The Unicornubelluacomis   124

Chapter Twenty-Two: The Kangamou   134

Chapter Twenty-Three: Crossing the Palousoa   139

Chapter Twenty-Four: The Fairy Princess   144

Chapter Twenty-Five: Cascade in the Glen   151

Chapter Twenty-Six: Trapped on Dragontier   163

Chapter Twenty-Seven: Tiers in the Sky   164

Chapter Twenty-Eight: The Battle at Casglen   168

Chapter Twenty-Nine: The Dragon and the Fairy Queen   177

Chapter Thirty: The Mitigo Plains   185

Chapter Thirty-One: Moldea   192

Chapter Thirty-Two: Crossing the Mitigo   199

Chapter Thirty-Three: Unwanted Visitors   204

Chapter Thirty-Four: Bitter Farewell   208

Chapter Thirty-Five: The Rescue   211

Chapter Thirty-Six: A Master's Bidding   215

Chapter Thirty-Seven: From Joy to War   217

Chapter Thirty-Eight: To Face Your Fears   222

Chapter Thirty-Nine: No, Not Yet   227

Chapter Forty: Into the Fight   235

Chapter Forty-One: Back on the Ledge   241

Chapter Forty-Two: Achieving the Arch   246

Chapter Forty-Three: Empty Space   251

Chapter Forty-Four: Preparing the Allies   254

Chapter Forty-Five: Don't Cry, Try   259

Chapter Forty-Six: Into Harm's Way   266

Chapter Forty-Seven: The Onoxmon   269

Chapter Forty-Eight: The Dark Lord's Descent   274

Chapter Forty-Nine: Drowning on Dry Land   277

Chapter Fifty: Fairytier   279

Chapter Fifty-One: Sophia and Daddy   281

Chapter Fifty-Two: Open Your Eyes   287

Epilogue: The Dark Crystal   292

Glossary   294

To my Angel Babies with Eyes of Blue

Sophia scampered down the worn stone steps and onto the flat of the flagstone road. In the dark, she could just make out her mother surrounded by the glow of crystal lanterns held aloft by her guards. The Queen glided elegantly along the far edge of the bridge that spanned the crevasse between the back of the castle and the mountain behind. The monarch's dress shimmered in the lantern's shine and before her rose a massive set of ornate arched doors carved into the mountain-side. The door on the right had a smaller arch mounted into it. When opened, it was just large enough for people to pass through. The Queen began to speak. Sophia couldn't hear what she said but knew her mother's incantation would open the smaller door. Her mother would step through that door into Mount Grace and be gone.

If she could just have one more hug and kiss before Mommy left, then she would be all right. She'd get in trouble for being out of bed and for sneaking out of the castle, but it would be worth it. The hug and kiss that would follow the scolding would sustain her until her mother was once again home. Sophia had just reached the bridge's leading edge. She'd have to yell to catch Mommy now.

The Princess opened her mouth to speak, but a shadow swooped down through the dark night sky. She gasped as the light from the crystal lanterns disappeared. Then came a smothering darkness.

Sophia jerked awake. Fear pumped into her veins. She shook, more afraid than she had ever been in her young life. Unable to see, she searched her mind for an explanation. She remembered her slippered feet padding silently across the stone path approaching the bridge. With her favorite blanket in hand, she had seen her mother getting ready to open the door to Mount Grace. Next came a strange whooshing from above, then a breeze through her thin nightgown. Then... nothing.

Now the world was dark and desperate. Something was wrapped about her that she could not get out of, and beyond this silk cocoon she felt a presence she had never known before. She thought she knew hurt- she had skinned her knees plenty. She thought she knew anger- she had screamed about not getting her way more than once. But all those emotions were nothing compared to this, this presence now around her, somewhere in the dark. The fear was paralyzing. Was this evil?

Tears wet her cheeks. Why had she disobeyed her mother? Why had she snuck off the castle grounds trying to follow where she should not? Because she didn't want to be left behind, to be left alone was why. Couldn't her mother see that? Now Mommy was gone, and Sophia was more alone than she could ever have imagined. No one would even know she was missing, would they? Her mother had sent Julia on a run, and by the time anyone else realized that Sophia wasn't in her bed it would be morning. She could be Lands away by then.

Then who would save her?

Chapter One
Where to begin?

Ah, we have been joined by a latecomer. Greetings earthling, fear not. Ha! I've always wanted to say that. But seriously now- I do not know what brought you here, but I do know it is rare for anyone from your world to come. Your arrival is really quite exciting. As your guide, *you can call me Yorgide,* I wonder if you must be rather special. You see, most in my world believe earth to be nothing more than myth, but Yorgide knows it to be true, for I am one of the privileged few from my realm who has actually been there. To earth that is, yes I have.

Yorgide also knows that if you ever hope to find the path back home, there are things you must first learn, yes indeed. What those things are exactly has yet to be revealed to me, so knowing where to begin, so as to help you on this journey, is a bit... awkward. However, given the timing of your arrival, I assume you need to know something of the story Yorgide was just showing. If you are to truly understand though, I should probably start at the beginning. But as they say, the beginning is anywhere you start. So, what must you know? Well, first, you're not in Kansas anymore! See, I know your world. It is you who needs to learn of mine.

My world, the Tiers, is filled with power and lore that abandoned the confines of earth long ago. Some of its ways and creatures will seem familiar to you, others will be completely foreign. Unlike on earth, here on the Tiers, people still rely on their Gifts.

Gifts are something you are born with. They usually run in the bloodlines of certain families, but that is not always the case. They vary in strength and importance. Some Gifts are downright

12

magical, while others are more intuitive. They just help you do normal things better. You know, such as, your pie always tastes best even though everyone uses the same recipe, or when everyone else is lost in the woods you just know which way to go. Gifts can be as simple as that, or they can be much more. Except in exceptional cases, the more magical Gifts do not usually begin to develop in humans until they reach their double-digits.

Speaking of exceptional Gifts, I think it's time for Yorgide to give you a peek at the first family of KenKarta. Let me see, where to begin? We must go back before the abduction of course, but how far? I think to— shortly before the King's departure...

Veronica pushed the door open and entered without a sound. Her heart raced. She squeezed Sophia's hand and tugged the smaller child into the chamber behind her. Eyes wide, her sister's ridged body bumped against her own. They lurched forward into an armoire. Veronica struggled to right herself and shot a sideways glance of warning.

Jaw clenched, Sophia mouthed, "Sorry!"

Veronica shook her head in disgust. What was Sophia doing? They were so close. But the slightest noise now would bring defeat. Just a few more steps and they could strike...

Before them rose a massive bed. The foot and headboards of the rich inlaid-wood frame were wrapped in supple chocolate-brown-crocodile leather. There beneath the plush down comforters lay their prey. The sisters crept across the room through angled rays of shine. Dawn was a good time to attack, to catch your opponent unaware.

Finally, they slid into position. Veronica held up one finger to Sophia, then two, then three. As she raised her last finger, Sophia let out a high-pitched battle cry and launched into the air. As Veronica vaulted above the bed behind her, a growl rose from beneath the piles of pillows below. Before she could land, two strong arms shot out from under the covers and snagged the girls in midair. They were flung to the middle of the bed and pinned.

Veronica closed her eyes. They had failed, and would now suffer the consequences. Sophia squealed below.

Veronica opened her eyes and saw a sleepy face on the

pillow next to her. She whispered, "Help?"

"Help your father tickle you? Well, if I must," replied her mother.

The next few minutes were a blur of squirming torment and laughter. Until finally, completely spent, they all four flopped back into the soft bedding.

Sophia produced a heavy old book from just beyond the bed and plopped it onto their father's chest.

"What's this?" her dad asked.

"You know what it is," Sophia said. "Read it."

Veronica knew what was in the book. They all did. It was a story passed down from one generation to the next on their father's side of the family. The story in this book was once used as their great grandmother's second-annual reader. She liked it so much that she would often read it to her children and then to her grandchildren.

Dad said, "You know, when I was a little boy, this story always scared me."

"Yeah," Sophia said, "but when your grandma finished reading you'd always say, 'Read it again, Grandma!' And she would."

Since their great grandmother died before they were born, their father had carried on the tradition by reading the story to Veronica and Sophia. They would crawl up on either side of him, preferably in the middle of their parents' giant bed, which was their favorite place to cuddle, and listen intently to the story. Just like now.

The fable tells of a farmer, his wife, and their little dog Turpie. The fact that the drawings of Turpie looked remarkably like a black version of their own dog, Scoobee, never failed to delight the girls.

Veronica knew the story well and didn't really need to listen closely to the words. What was more important was the time they spent together while her dad read it, when it was just the four of them and the world and its troubles outside didn't exist. She cherished these moments. They all did.

She snuggled under her daddy's arm as he said, "Each night the large child-sized, deformed, elf-like hobyahs would come creeping through the woods and tall grass, sneaking up on the farmer's small home. Turpie would bark loudly and scare them away. Not knowing the hobyahs were looming in the dark, the racket made the farmer angry for he could neither slumber or sleep."

"Kind of like you and Scoobee, huh Daddy?" Sophia said.

They all laughed. Scoobee's barking did make her father angry. Veronica knew the story would go on like this while the farmer kept taking off Turpie's parts (first his tail, then his legs, and finally his head) until poor little Turpie could bark no more.

Her father continued, "The very next night, without the protection of Turpie, the skinny, long-limbed, pointed-eared, nasty-looking hobyahs came sneak, sneak, sneaking through the old woods. And skip, skip, skipping through the tall grass. They attacked the farmer and stole his wife. They hung her in a big sack in the middle of their lair and danced around her chanting, 'Poke you, poke you.' Realizing his error, the farmer put Turpie back together so he could save the day. He did of course by rescuing the farmer's wife and eating up all the hobyahs. And that's why there are no hobyahs today."

In a way-too-innocent voice, Sophia asked, "Daddy, are hobyahs real?"

16

"Now Sophia, we all know that this story is a fairytale. But yes, hobyahs are real. They used to roam Virtier at night, causing all kinds of trouble, but they were banished to a Lower Tier ages ago."

"The Lower Tiers?" Sophia said, eyes big as saucers.

"Yes, the Lower Tiers," Father replied.

Veronica turned over to face her mother. She rolled her

eyes, exasperated. Sophia knew what the Lower Tiers were. Everyone on Virtier knew. That's where you find all manner of evil, despicable creatures. Some were spawned there, while others (human and magical creatures alike) were banished to those Lands for their misdeeds. Recently however, rumors abounded that hobyahs had somehow escaped the Lower Tiers and now once again roamed the remote countryside. Educated people didn't believe it could be true though. Everyone knew that the Arches that allow travel through Empty Space from one Tier to another only work one way on the Lower Tiers. You can arrive through them, but you cannot leave.

Sophia kept pelting their dad with questions that she already knew the answers to. Their mother just smiled at V and stroked her hair. Without a word, Mom reminded her it didn't matter what they talked about as long as they just stayed in the big comfy bed together. When they got up, V's dad would be leaving on a journey and her mom would become busy helping others. Right now it was all about them. So Veronica burrowed closer to her mother, received a big hug, and breathed in the moment.

"I've done it!" Veronica proclaimed, grinning with glee as she bounded into the room. Though she had been told many times in her past eleven annuals not to use her weapons anywhere but the practice arena when inside, she couldn't help herself. She sliced at the air with her sword. "Sophia, didn't you hear me? I've done it!"

"What did you do?" Sophia asked, looking up only briefly from the stones, gems, and various other elemental items she had gathered off the shelves from around the large formal room. The young Princess had been busy spreading and arranging an assortment of them across the carpeted floor.

"I've advanced to the next training level in sword craft!" Veronica said as she flipped her thick blonde braid over her shoulder.

"That's great, Veronica!" Sophia hopped up to give her sister a big hug. "I'm so proud of you." Sophia encircled Veronica's chest with her arms and, although smaller in size, she lifted her big sister slightly off the floor with the strength of someone older.

"All right, all right, let me breathe now please. And ouch, Sophia, now you're pulling my hair." Veronica tugged at her braid. When undone, her waist-long blonde hair created an image against her fair skin and lean stature of the sort that poets write about. At least, that's what Mother said. Yet, Veronica preferred it pulled back in one sort of braid or another.

Some of her friends said she should wear it down because boys would like it, but boys were forbidden by her father. Besides, Veronica was far too busy shooting her bow, wielding her sword, or writing in journals to worry about interference from wayward tresses or admirers. Comfort and function always won over fashion, as did right over wrong. Her moral compass and incredible fighting skills were but two of her Gifts.

Reluctantly, Sophia released her sister from her iron grip. The younger sister appeared to be every bit the Princess. Sophia's olive complexion and silky, honey-brown mane made her blue eyes all the more vivid. Her beauty, sweetness, and infectious laughter drew people to her.

Looking down at the mess surrounding her sister, Veronica laughed. As always, Sophia had been playing with items containing Imperium Pieces.

Pieces are very important to how life is lived on the Tiers. So like all children her age, Veronica knew that power could be found in almost any object, but only those with the proper Gift could tap into and draw that power out. Most humans with Gifts can manage a few things, like drawing out a bit of light from refined crystals or drawing heat and/or fire from stones that contain the proper elements. But Veronica knew she and her sister were expected to be able to do much more. The Gifts ran strong in their family so expectations were high. In KenKarta, all with a strong Gift were encouraged, expected even, to develop it. Most who exhibited a particular aptitude learned to be fabricators, or to draw energy from special Pieces to power things like a cascade, loom, kiln, or even a weapon. In some cases, people actually became the weapon, navitas energy blasted right out of their bodies. Veronica couldn't wait to be old enough to try, but that was annuals away. Those who could do it spent annual after annual training to specialize and enhance their abilities. Plus, they had to have the necessary Gift to begin with.

Though young, Veronica already showed more skill with the Imperium Pieces than did some adults. So, while she giggled at her sister, Veronica knew that within the Pieces Sophia saw the mysteries that most could not. When left to her own devices, Sophia spent countless hours studying the Imperium Pieces. She sorted and stacked, arranged and examined every set she could get her hands on. If no proper set was available, she made her own out of any small items on hand. Indeed, Veronica had no doubt that someday Sophia would learn to unlock the power of legends, but right now she was barely eight, and had yet to master a single Piece.

Veronica asked, "Have you had any luck making the crystal Piece shine yet?"

"No."

"Well, that's all right, someday you will, but right now you'd better put everything back, 'cause Mom won't be happy if she sees this mess." Veronica waved her hand over Sophia's piles.

"No, not yet, not until I get one of them to glow."

"Well here, let me help then." Veronica snatched a small block with a red ruby embedded in it up off of the floor. "All you have to do is focus. And then..." Veronica concentrated her thoughts and gaze at the Piece in her hand. The small stone began to shine.

"Veronica, stop! Why do you always have to *do* that?"

"Do what?"

"Everything, everything in the whole entire tier- you're always first." Tears welled up in Sophia's steely blue eyes. "I want to be first! But that makes me into not a very nice person, to want that." Frustrated, the younger Princess stomped her foot, balled her fists, and then just cried.

"Nuh-ah Sophia, quit crying every time you don't get your way. I was just trying to help."

"I don't want your help! You think I can't do *anything*." Sophia bawled.

Having just turned eleven, Veronica didn't fully understand what she'd done, so she couldn't help but yell, "You're such a brat!"

"I hope the hobyahs get you!" Sophia screamed back.

"Sophia, hobyahs aren't even real," Veronica snapped.

"Yes they *aaarre*!" Sophia shrieked tightening her fists until her knuckles turned white.

Veronica said, "Not here on Virtier."

"Enough." Their mother walked into the cascade room where they really shouldn't be. This room was not part of the residence. But the cascade screen covered the entire wall and there were lots of decorative items here within arm's reach. The fact that many of those items were now on the floor did not escape the Queen, but at the moment she had other things on her mind.

"I could hear you clear down in the ballroom. I think the two of you have been spending a bit too much time together in your studies. I'd tell you to go play separately, but I have something important I need to discuss with you both. You're not going to like it, but there is nothing I can do. So save your protests."

Veronica asked, "What is it, Mom?"

Sophia wiped her tears and moved to her mother as the Queen sat down on the floor between them and crossed her legs. The Queen knew that Sophia loved this, for now her lap formed a perfect little nest for her youngest to cuddle up in. She gazed at her two daughters and sighed. To look at them was to look at day and night, different, yet somehow familiar and eternally connected.

"You both know that it is Mommy's and Daddy's job to keep the Lands safe. Right? Well, it's a big job that takes us away from you far too often, and for that I'm sorry. Girls, I don't know how much you realize it. Your daddy and I don't want you to worry about such things, but there is danger in the Land. Dangers to the people we are sworn to protect, dangers to people in all the Lands on Virtier, and if we don't stop them, dangers to you."

Veronica asked, "What's wrong? Is Daddy, okay?"

"He's fine. He just needs my help." The Queen closed her eyes for a moment. Lying was not something that came naturally for her, but she did not want to upset her girls. Besides, she really didn't know the answer to Veronica's question. All communications concerning the King indicated that negotiations were going surprisingly well on Dragontier. This was good news because of its importance to peace in the various Lands on Virtier and also because the journey to the Upper Tier had taken some time to arrange. They expected negotiations with the other Lands involved to be difficult.

The Upper Tiers were inhabited by those Mythical peoples and creatures, such as dragons, fairies, and equidae, whose Gifts had advanced beyond the normal human realm. Each Tier along this upper level had only one Land under one rule and was surrounded by Empty Space. The Kingdom of KenKarta was on Virtier, the Center Tier where most humans lived. To reach any other Tier from Virtier, the King, or anyone, must pass through an Arch.

Due to the distance of Empty Space that separated Dragontier and KenKarta, the King chose to first travel to Bedforda, a Center Land closer in proximity to the homeland of dragons, and then pass through an Arch. Tier-jumping was not the King's strongest suit, and he truly hated the feeling of Empty Space around him. Stepping through an Arch felt like stepping off a high cliff, your stomach jumps into your throat and your skin crawls with energy as you are pulled along a path to an adjoining Arch. The Queen found the sensation exhilarating. The King did not.

Anything the King could do to make that experience shorter, he would, even if it meant days of extra travel over-land. But part of the reason he was traveling over-land to Bedforda before tier-jumping was that it would give him a chance to visit his old friend Cletus along the way. The pair had been friends since childhood, and there was no telling what kind of trouble those two could find, even in the middle of Pringer Forest where Clet lived. That thought brought a slight smile to the Queen, but it didn't last.

She couldn't keep at bay the feeling that something was wrong, that her husband Dale, the King of KenKarta, needed her help and needed it now. The feeling had been with her for days, ever since the first report that things were going well. Neither of them had expected that. Chinja had been a very uneasy neighbor of late. The large reclusive Kingdom to the west felt that KenKarta's approach to commerce and social standings was far too progressive. The Chinjana preferred a strict class structure where only those of the Demogeron class are encouraged to develop their Gifts. So strangely, with each reassuring report, her dread had grown. And now she had made a decision.

Chapter Three
Lay of the Land

It has been revealed to Yorgide that you need to learn a bit more about life on the Tiers, the lay of the land, if you will.

Understand that our civilizations are not without advanced capabilities. To you we may appear a bit, "old fashioned," but you should look closer, yes indeed. In places where many with Gifts gather, and those Gifts are nurtured, life is far from primitive. Look at Karta. Here in KenKarta's capital, many amenities make life easier, much like in the cities on earth. For instance, most buildings have controlled climates, running water with drains for waste, and the means to prepare food with a controlled heat source. However, unlike earth, here in the world of Tiers, we do not have all your stinky pollution. Nor do we have what you call technology.

On the Tiers things are much more organic. Energy and power must be generated from within. Take for example this cascade you've been watching, or cas as it is called, and compare it to tel-e-vision, a device with which your world is indeed obsessed. Not that I blame you, really, with so many channels and all. And some of those programs really are hypnotic. Once on earth, I began watching this marathon where they were playing one episode after another about these brothers fighting evil. Before I knew it, the entire day was gone. And don't get me started on the video games. Wow! What a time-sucker! I have to admit it though, I do love to shoot those zombies. Really, it amazes me that you ever get anything done.

Anyway, as I was saying, both our cas and your television have the means to project images, but this result is arrived at quite differently. While television is achieved by the use of electronics,

25

a cas is powered by a person's Gift, his mind energy if you will. The cascade helps to harness and transfer the images and sounds a person sees, hears, or feels. Most people are lucky if they can merely project the actual activities and surroundings they are in at the time (like your video conferencing), but there are a few of us who can actually influence, or even create, what is seen. Those who are very Gifted at this can create and capture images and sounds in a charged geode, making a geode image or ge-im that others can watch later. This is the closest thing we have to your movies. Not to brag, but I myself am considered to be a ge-im master. Not entirely unlike your Spielberg. The difference of course being that I have to rely on the power of my mind to create and capture the images. It can be so draining! I'll likely need to sleep for a week when we're done here. I do hope you're worth it. This is why it is far more common for cascades to be used as a means to communicate and educate, rather than for entertainment. You see, without a charged Piece, and sometimes even with, an operator or cascader as we call them, needs to be in physical contact with the geode and the liquid that cascades down across the viewing screen to make it function.

When I say a Piece, I am, of course, referring to Imperium Pieces. Exactly what they are might be hard for you to wrap your mind around. Perhaps for comparison sake you should think of batteries or power generators, though Imperium Pieces are much more. Even found in their natural state, most Pieces hold energy, but the Piece has to be charged to allow the energy to be released. Pieces with the most potential are "refined and charged," but let me tell you, charging a Piece is a feat in and of itself. I mean can you charge a battery with your mind? No, I don't think so. It is amazing how many school children flunk out of the Mythscola when it comes time to take this test! You must be able to channel

enough Gifted energy through the Piece to activate, or w(
the natural energy stored within. Once this is done, most (
with the proper Gift can draw upon the Piece as needed, a. .cust
for a time. If the Piece is not very strong, meaning it doesn't
naturally hold a lot of energy on its own, then it must be charged
fairly often by someone with the Gift and training to do so. On the
other hand, if it is a strong Piece, used by someone very Gifted,
then the more it is used the more charged it becomes.

This is why Pieces of stone or gems that contain the most
natural energy are highly sought after on the Tiers, and that's
putting it mildly. There are people who hunt for these things like
treasure. Some mine them. The unscrupulous steal them, and
sometimes Lands even go to war over them. The more energy an
object has to begin with, the more a Gifted person can draw from
it, thus the more valuable it is. One of the most highly prized Pieces
on all of Virtier is the Onoxmon. All wish to possess it. It matters
not that they cannot wield it. For legend states, that in the right
hands- or depending how you look at it, the wrong- this stone of
ancient and mysterious origin can destroy... no, no, I would tell too
much. Just know this: Be its power true or not, as is common with
all things perceived powerful, the Onoxmon has served causes
both wicked and just.

Oh, and another thing. You must not assume that just
because a Piece is powerful it can be made to do just anything
by anyone, because it doesn't work that way. Some elements are
just better at providing one kind of energy over another, and the
person drawing on it, again, say it with me now, has to have the
corresponding Gift to effectively utilize it. For instance, a Piece of
moonstone can be called on to make a room cold, whereas most
would need a Piece of fire opal to provide heat for that room. The
Gift to utilize either of these Pieces is not rare, so most people,

even those with limited Gifts, can use them if they are already charged.

This is why sets that contain basic elements are refined into charged Pieces that people carry with them or place in their homes. While the Gifts required to perform simple household chores are fairly common, many are more elusive, and others are outright rare. Like the Gift to wield the Onoxmon. Sometimes generations pass without anyone being born who can control it.

Yorgide hopes you're getting all this because you will be quizzed on it later. Well, not really, but I don't want to be interrupted while I'm showing you the rest of the tale. So hear this: Those people who can master the Pieces (or call on many different types to achieve the desired effect) are considered truly Gifted. Those who can draw from unrefined pieces as they are found in nature are truly Magical.

Though there is some debate, most who retain the good sense Deus gave them consider the Queen of KenKarta to be Magical. I of course do. You see, she has Gifts that allow her to use not just one or two, but many Pieces. And unlike the majority of people who must clench a Piece in their fist in order to draw power from it, the Queen's abilities are so advanced that usually the appropriate Piece needs merely to be close in order for her to tap the strength inside. The power is then hers to command. This is why you would have to be a complete fool to challenge her inside KenKarta Castle. There is much too much power for her to draw upon there.

The elegant stone complex that is KenKarta Castle sits atop a plateau carved from a ridge of Mount Grace and overlooks the capital city of Karta. The layout is straightforward. The more important the office is to the function of the entire Land of KenKarta, the higher up the mountain foothills it is located. The main grounds and lower floors of the main castle are where all official governmental functions take place. It is here in the official offices of the King and Queen that dignitaries are entertained, negotiations are held, plots are foiled, and policies decided. By design, the beauty, grace, history, and strength displayed in this part of the castle inspires awe.

Now, above all this hustle, bustle, and intrigue, in a lovely, yet less-ornate section of the castle, is the private residence of the Royal Family. If you were granted access to this part of the castle- which is soooo not likely, no offense, but only those with a close personal connection to the family are allowed in. Of course I, Yorgide, have been there, but you, they don't even know you. I don't say that to be unkind. I'm just stating that if they did know you, and you were allowed inside, you'd be surprised. It does not look like a palace. It looks more like the house of any number of KenKarta's citizens. It's nice, very nice indeed, but not very fancy. It is here that Alison and Dale are Mom and Dad, not Queen and King, and it is here that Veronica and Sophia are daughters and sisters, not Princesses. It is here that their family is not royal, they are simply at home. Let me show you...

Chapter Four
The Departure

While Veronica got ready for bed, the Queen looked out one of the many arch-shaped windows in KenKarta Castle. From her vantage above, the city of Karta was clearly laid out in the shape of a triangle. Two rivers, the Aly to the west and the Don to the east, flowed from either side of the mountain behind her and came together at the southern tip of Karta to form the mighty AlyDon. Shine from the glowing crystal street lamps reflected off the dark smooth water and outlined the great public park that occupied the triangle's southern point.

Tonight the park was quiet, but when the Queen closed her eyes she could see banners of blue and black, tents of red and purple, the yellow shine from the Pinnacle sun and a carpet of green grass, all deep, rich colors of a festival. Minstrels' strumming mingled with laughter in her ears. The scent of sweet cinnamon and meat lightly charred over open flame both lingered in her nose. She breathed it in, pleasant memories of unburdened times. Reluctantly, the Queen opened her eyes to the present.

She scanned the city at the triangle's center and was overcome with a sense of pride. Unlike the park, buildings and streets here were awash with the bluish-white light of activated crystals. Under this progressive shine, she could clearly identify the diverse architecture of commerce, housing, education, religion, and recreation all gracefully intertwined at the heart of her city. Closer to her, where the ground began to slope upward, though their windows were all dark, she could just make out the tops of the local governmental offices that began on the northern edge of the city right outside the first castle wall. Right inside the outer castle gates, though they too were mostly dark, she recognized the stone silhouettes of offices that dealt with the workings of various regions throughout the Lands.

The Queen's gaze drifted up to the spiraled light of a Tier that shone in the night sky outside the window of Veronica's room, her thoughts passing over the reasons why she would travel at night. This would be a difficult jump. The Empty Space to be crossed was vast, and she would be doing it unassisted through the largest Arch on Virtier.

The larger the Arch, the more energy it took to operate. Having a shorter distance to travel would be helpful. While Virtier's large elongated mass remained stationary in Empty Space, the Upper Tiers rotated on their axis. Only the relatively flat side of each Tier was livable, the side that reflected light. During the day, the side inhabited by the chosen Mythical creatures was turned toward the shine of the Pinnacle. At night the livable area of the Upper Tiers turned away from the Pinn toward Virtier. In short, the distance between the Tiers was shorter at night.

In addition, fewer people would miss the Queen if she left at night, meaning fewer would question what she was doing. However, perhaps most importantly, she could tuck her girls into bed and sing them their songs, the ones she had made up for them at birth and still sang every night at bedtime. She had already sung Sophia's, and it was now Veronica's turn. So while her oldest climbed into bed, the Queen began the lullaby:

"Your eyes are turning blue
they come from us to you
and with them comes our very hearts and souls.
You also have my love
and your daddy's too
no matter what you'll always be
our baby with eyes of blue.

As the world comes into view
we'll be right next to you
to guide you through the ups and downs of life.
We'll share your happiness
and your sorrows too
no matter what you'll always be
our baby with eyes of blue.

Many annuals from now
you'll understand just how
you change our lives with every breath you take.
The realization will come
when you become a mom
and your heart will melt at merely a coo
from your baby with eyes of blue."

As the last note hung in the air, the Queen kissed
Veronica's forehead then reminded her of their previous
conversation. "Stay within the castle grounds."

"But Mom-"

"No buts, the protection stones located throughout
the castle will keep you safe while I'm away." Alison hugged
Veronica and went for one last peek at her youngest who lay

in her bed playing with some Pieces by the soft glow of her night crystal.

"Mommy, where's Julia?" Sophia fussed.

Alison stroked her daughter's hair and sighed. Sophia simply loved the large brown cat-like creature with her soft coat of purple spots lightly ringed in red. Julia had served the Queen, using her incredible speed as a royal messenger, since her coronation. Cheetatarah could have had a Land of their own in the Upper Tiers, as did other Mythical creatures, but they had not yet given up on humans. Instead they chose to live on the Mitigo Plains or serve as official messengers of Virtier's Royal Households.

Julia was a beauty, and a kinder heart could not be found in any of the Lands. From the time of Sophia's birth, Julia was drawn to her. If the toddler went missing, the Queen would often find the pair curled up together somewhere in the castle or out in the gardens napping. Sophia's nanny, Ashley, would toss her hands in the air with exasperation upon finding them, but the Queen would just smile. Her child would always be safe with Julia.

The Queen chuckled lightly at her wandering thoughts. For Sophia, dressing up and holding court with her many friends often included tying ribbons in Julia's fur and bows around her neck and tail. The other magical animals in the royal court would scold Julia and tell her this behavior was undignified for someone of her stature. But neither Julia nor the Queen cared; they loved making their little Princess happy and longed for the day when Sophia could actually speak with the Mythical creature. It takes a Gifted mind to hear what magical animals are saying. And ordinarily that mind needs to develop for at least a decade before such a Gift is revealed.

Sophia first heard Julia when she was five. Of course, Julia could always understand Sophia. She and those like her can understand human speech just like anyone else, as long as it is spoken in a language they know. Most just can't verbalize it.

Regrettably, on this night the Queen had sent the elegantly masked Julia with a very important message to her sister-in-law, Lady Leanne in Medius.

"Julia isn't here, Sophia. I had to send her on a run." Sophia's lower lip was already turned down. She was about to howl, but Alison cut her off. "But, but... there is good news. I sent Julia with a message to your Aunt Leanne and she will be coming to visit along with your cousins, Davis and Jaye, in a matter of days."

Veronica and Sophia always loved it when family came to visit, and they all wished it could happen more often.

"Will our cousins Colton and McKenna be coming for a visit too?" Sophia asked.

Since Dale's brother and family lived a long distance away in the far west, the Queen's answer to that question was, "Unfortunately, no. However, Julia will be back tomorrow, long before bedtime."

"Promise?" Sophia asked.

"Promise," Alison answered, leaning down to give Sophia a kiss and pull up the blankets, tucking them tightly around her youngest once more. The songs had long since faded, the stalling had gone on long enough. As she rose and left the room, she tried to soften the sour mood of her departure by singing out light heartedly over her shoulder, "Good night, my Princesses of KenKarta."

In unison, two little voices chimed from their adjoining rooms, "Good night, Queen of KenKarta." Their buoyant giggles echoed after the Queen as she walked across the catwalk that lead from their quarters to hers.

Silently her personal guards escorted the Queen through the back gate and down the dimly lit stone path. There was no formality or fan fare, nothing to draw attention to the fact that the Queen was leaving home. The only clue came from her rather ornate clothes and jewelry. Even with little tier shine, the cloth still shimmered silver with a hint of pink as the rays reflected off the spun yttrium threads woven throughout. Yttrium was the best element to help one tier-jump. Holding a Piece in your hand, like people did when using other Imperium Pieces, helped, but wearing yttrium around your entire body made it easier to draw from its power. That was why those who could afford it had special garments made just for tier-travel.

Pardon the interruption, but I feel I must interject. Tier-jumping, as we call it, can be dangerous to be sure. If you don't know what you're doing, you can end up trapped in Empty Space drifting around for all time, or at least until you get pulled in by another Arch. Strangely, you won't die out there, in Empty Space, but you will surely lose your mind.

Yorgide once had a cousin who drifted off the path. He was in Empty Space for five annuals before he finally came close enough to an open Arch to escape. Let me tell you, he was never quite right after that. A little loose in the noodle, if you know what I mean. He was lucky though. Most people who get lost in Empty Space are never seen again.

All right, that's getting a bit off track, and I realize I keep interrupting, but just one last thing, then Yorgide will editorialize no more. On my honor, yes indeed. I'll just show you the story. First I just feel compelled to stress that tier-jumping is not a normal human activity. Only those with advanced Gifts can accomplish it unharmed. There, I'm done. Now where was I? Ah, Yes, the Queen and her travel attire.

While many people carried their Imperium Pieces loose in a bag, the Queen has entire sets of Advanced Pieces set into her jewelry. So besides her long creamy cloak and form-fitting garments beneath with the yttrium weave, tonight the Queen wore a delicate crown tucked into the loose spiraled curls of her hair, a necklace with a large blue sapphire that brought out the color of her eyes. Earrings framed her angled face, bracelets draped each slender wrist, and several rings graced her long fingers. Though elegant in appearance, the function each Piece mounted in that jewelry could provide was far more important than its outright beauty. For while most of the castle would go to sleep this night thinking that she was in the family residence, in reality, she felt as if she were going off to war. She did indeed.

Chapter Five

Taken

"Now, My Lord?" came a low rumble from the darkness. "She is almost beyond our reach."

"Even when she has been close enough for me to feel her breath, she has been beyond my reach," the creature's master said. "Tonight I will take by force that which I once was sure would be given me willingly."

"It will not be easy. Even in ambush the Queen will not be taken without struggle," the beast rumbled from his perch high on the mountain beyond the reach of mortal eyes.

"Tis true, a struggle that might be our last," Lord Leamoldae said before his attention was drawn away from the Queen, to a movement on the road opposite his prey. As he strained to see, his lips thinned into a malicious sneer. "Ah, do you believe in fate, Daelkay? There... tell me, what do your ancient eyes see in the gloom?"

"A child, my Lord."

"No, not just *a* child, *their* child. That child is the embodiment of the hearts I seek. With it, I will break them both."

Lord Leamoldae vaulted to straddle his steed's back. The dragon unfolded his wings and pushed off the rocky outcrop. Their descent was silent, and the distance between the winged giant and the little girl on the flagstone path closed quickly. Right before he reached her, Daelkay flapped his wings to slow and control his approach. The air whooshed over his wings' leathery surface and the child began to turn toward the sound. If she screamed, the Queen's guards, still within ear shot, would be alerted. So before she saw the terror above, he whispered an old word filled with magic, "Sopor." The girl's small body went limp and was encased in the dragon's talons before it could crumple to the ground. With several powerful thrusts from his immense wingspan, their altitude was restored to the protective darkness of the night sky above KenKarta Castle.

They were gone before anyone even knew they were there.

Chapter Six
What Comes in Dreams

Sleep was not coming easy for Veronica. It never did. Every night she read until her eyes fell shut, book in hand. Normally her mom or dad would then slip in, extinguish her light crystal, and slide the book from her fingers while she slumbered. That could not happen tonight. She took a deep breath to fill the hollowness within, but it remained. This wasn't the first time her parents had both been away from home, but it didn't happen as often as one might think. Despite the demands of their jobs, Veronica knew her parents went to great lengths to make sure at least one of them was with her and Sophia each night, but that only made it harder when they were gone.

Veronica looked at the wall mural. Numerous palace artists could have made her feel as if she were on an actual beach, but artists did not paint the whimsical dolphins jumping from the waves. These, plus the palm trees, red flowers, and dragonflies were all created by the hand of a novice, as were the sun, moon, bees, and flowers that adorned the light purple walls of Sophia's room. Their mother had painted all these things, and they would not have it any other way. Their mother had made something special for them with her own hands.

Veronica imagined she was on the beach with those dolphins on her wall. The residence was quiet. Surprisingly, Sophia was even leaving her alone. She must already be asleep. Usually V had to chase Phia back to her own room several times each night. Tonight it had only taken once. Veronica's tone and choice of words had been particularly harsh when Sophia came in to announce once again that she thought she had seen fairies. Sophia was always saying that. Though she had never really seen one, Sophia loved fairies and liked to pretend that her room was Fairytier. She was certain that one day she'd get to go. Veronica didn't have the heart to tell Sophie it was never going to happen. First, no one was allowed to go there. And second, even if they were, Sophia was terrified of tier-jumping! Made a huge scene the last time their mom took them to Equitier. It was *so* embarrassing.

"Sophia, get out of my room," Veronica had said earlier. Sophia was flitting about on tiptoes singing a nonsensical melody. "Arrrgh!" V yelled in exasperation as she threw a pillow at her annoying little sister and proclaimed, "You are such a pain. I wish you were never born."

She shouldn't have said it. Mom would definitely not approve, but her mother was gone. Veronica's mood was foul, and Sophia really knew how to irritate her.

"Aahhh!" Sophia squealed. "You're mean, Veronica!" She turned and penguin waddled back through the bath that connected their rooms like a secret passageway.

That had been some time ago. Now the hour was late. Veronica's eyes had grown heavy, and the open book in her hand slipped.

The dream began like many she had had before. She stood at the bottom of a low hill covered with large flowers. The flowers, a rich royal red with deep purple centers, swayed on a breeze against a sky of brilliant blue. She whistled, high and shrill, and then over the hill trotted Dalminyo, the equidae who had Bonded to her less than two annuals ago.

Veronica's dream shifted back to that fateful day on

Equitier. The whole incident had created quite a stir amongst the Equitier Council, not to mention how upset Mom and Dad had been. At nine, Veronica was far too young to offer herself for Bonding.

A human cannot choose to own one of these Mythical horse-like creatures, for alas they cannot be owned. Rider and steed are bonded in a lifelong partnership, and it is the equidae that chooses the person, not the other way around. Choosing who will be allowed to ride you for the rest of your life is not a decision the equidae take lightly. So to offer oneself up for Bonding too early would likely result in failure, bringing not only disgrace on one's house, but also the possibility of bodily harm. Tradition states you must first reach your thirteenth annual before even visiting their Land for the purpose of Bonding, but since the only way to Equitier is through an Arch and most still lack the ability to tier-jump at that age, nearly all must wait even longer.

Veronica was on this tier only because she was traveling with the Queen, whose advanced powers allowed her to guide more than one person through an Arch at a time.

They had arrived astride her mother's equidae, Gallantae, the noblest steed Veronica had ever seen. Her entire life she had watched her mother ride atop his massive white and gray dappled frame, which was regally trimmed with dark gray mane, tail, and socks. She loved to see them together and longed for the day that she would be old enough to seek an equidae of her own. How royal and noble they always looked, which was fitting, as indeed without question, both were. The pair's noble nature was confirmed by the fact that they were Bonded. One of the Gifts these animals possessed was the ability to see beyond external appearances into one's heart of hearts. If one's intentions were not worthy, no equidae would freely choose them. There was no question as to their royal natures either. Veronica's mother was of course Queen Alison of KenKarta. Gallantae was a Prince of the Equidae.

So, while her mother and Gallantae saw to royal business, Princess Veronica wandered and took in the pastoral beauty of Equitier.

Looking across the land of rolling emerald green hills dotted with giant shade trees and traversed by cool clean streams, Veronica could see how any equine would view this place as heavenly. To protect the equidae from any who would do them harm or try to force them into unwanted, or worse yet, dark service, their kind were brought to this Upper Tier many ages ago by Deus as a reward for unwavering service and nobility.

At the center of an enormous open field, the Arch jutted up from the ground. Its gothic frame silhouetted against the skyline like a lone tree in the field struck her. Odd, Arches were usually found in more protected settings. The grandeur of this placement was magnificent. Set in the stone frame, the four Arch stones and the Alistone at its peak glistened lazily in the shine.

The eruptive entity that streaked before her in the field took Veronica by surprise. Dalminyo. She could just make out his white coat with medium black spots. His long black mane and tail blurred like the trail of a comet as he ran with zeal across the field. The blur turned toward her. Before she could comprehend, he was standing directly in front of her. She should have been scared; an equidae moving at full speed was startling. However, this was not the first time Veronica had witnessed such a feat. She did arrive here after all on the back of Gallantae.

Dalminyo was young. Having just reached the minimum age of Bonding, his spirit was strong, and known to be a bit reckless among his kind. Later he told Veronica he was utterly taken in by the seemly fragile, yet fearless, form before him. Afterward, when the council asked whether he knew what he was doing he had to say yes, but it had felt like a dream. He was drawn to her. He had never ventured so close or quickly to a human. He couldn't help himself. He took several steps forward while she stood absolutely still. He lowered his head and looked directly into her eyes.

Instinctively, she raised her diminutive hands and placed them on either side of his massive head. Light glowed from within him. It radiated outward and engulfed Veronica. Not until then did he even know who she was. In that moment, he knew everything about her and she, everything about him. At the delicate age of nine, Veronica, a Royal Princess of KenKarta, had just been Bonded to Dalminyo of the Equidae. Given that the Princess's young age was unprecedented and the ritual done without ceremony, the Bonding should not have worked. If it hadn't, it could have permanently injured Veronica's mind. Powerful magic, the kind required for Bonding, was not meant to pass through one so young. Miraculously though, both Veronica and Dalminyo were fine. What was done was done and could not be undone.

Her dream turned black. Veronica could hear her sister's voice calling out to her. Sophia's hoarse whispers sounded far away and afraid. Veronica's initial irritation at this intrusion turned to concern as she slipped deeper into her sister's nightmare.

Flashes of the back of the castle, their mother before Mount Grace, a strange flapping sound, all assaulted her senses at once. The vision of her sister cloaked in darkness and consumed by fear crept into Veronica's mind with horrific detail. And now Veronica could feel it. Some sort of fine cloth enveloped her, slick like silk. She struggled hard to breath. Stale air, like under the covers of your bed, barely relieved the hunger in her lungs. And then, the ground, hard and cold lay beneath her body.

Sophia wanted to scream but could not. So instead she strained her ears to listen. Voices were speaking close by. One was deep and sounded profoundly sad. The other had a crisp and proper ring to it, but really scared her. In her whole young life she had never understood what the word evil meant; now she felt as if she did. An airiness to this voice made it seem cold and detached from everything around it.

"Take the child and hide her."

"Where, my Lord?"

"I cannot know. I go now to see her father. Even in bondage, I cannot fully contain his mind, at least not yet. Before I speak a word, he will know I have something he values greatly. He will know I have possession of something that he loves. The sense of joy he'll sense in me will horrify him more than any words I will speak or physical pain I'll inflict." His voice sounded like a malicious smile as he said, "Oh, I'll continue to torture him, but his physical pain will be mainly for my pleasure. The mental anguish of not knowing the fate of his loved ones will be the true torture. I will not chance giving him the advantage of learning where his daughter is being held. Not until he tells me what I want to know."

"How long, my Lord?"

"Riding Hellantae will shorten the over-land journey, but from here at the Valleyridge the nearest Arch at my disposal is a long day away at Bedforda. Do not open your mind to my calls for at least five days. That should give me enough time to break him and return."

Sophia felt sluggish, but tried to shake off the deep sleep that numbed her. So odd. The more she tried to focus on what the voices were saying, the more her head hurt. Sleep was winning. Sophia drew herself up into a ball. She clutched the blanket she had been carrying back at the castle. How long ago was that? Where was that from here? Oh, she should have stayed in bed like Veronica! If only her sister were here. She would never get mad at Veronica for being bossy again! No matter what, Veronica always seemed to have a plan. She always knew what to do and didn't mind telling others how to do it. For once Sophia wished her older sibling could tell her what to do. Sophia envisioned Veronica asleep in her bed, and as the strange sleep came over her, she whispered, "Veronica, please, help me!"

With Sophia's voice ringing in her ears, Veronica sat up in bed and shouted her sister's name. Scoobee, who as usual was sleeping on the Princess's bed, jumped directly to his feet. The golden terrier's tail and ears went erect. The goatee on his face was pushed up on one side, and his eyes remained unfocused. He barked blindly in alarm. The sound echoed off the walls of Veronica's room and into that of her sister's, but the bed there was empty! Sophia's abduction had played in Veronica's dream as clear as a cas.

Only, it had been no dream.

Chapter Seven
Sound the Alarm

"Good morning, Princess," the young guard said as Veronica entered the outer chamber.

She couldn't help but notice the way he looked at her, but wasn't sure what it meant. Did his eyes narrow in suspicion, or confusion at her presence in a secured area wearing only night clothes? The why did not really matter. It only mattered that he might try to keep her from her goal. "Is the General still speaking to my mother?"

"Yes, but the General asked not to be disturbed-"

The lieutenant raised his hands to ward her off, but Veronica didn't even break stride. He began to step into her path, then hesitated, apparently uncertain whether he should touch a royal. She pushed past him and burst into the darkened room behind. There the Queen's face filled most of the giant cascade that filled most of the wall in the dimly lit, windowless cas-room. Her mother's blonde hair cradled the crown on her head and spiraled down in loose looping curls on either side of her face and came to rest on her shoulders. Her eyes, a smidge more gray than usual, glistened, touched by fatigue within the golden frame. In addition, the rest of her mother's features seemed a bit more drawn as well. However, the cas was fully charged, and its strength helped make her image radiant, as if she might float right off the screen. In front of it, hands clasped behind his back, stood General Fooney, one of the King's most trusted advisors on both the commerce and political fronts. He listened silently as the Queen no doubt filled him in on what she had learned overnight.

"Mom!"

Now it was the General's almond-shaped eyes that narrowed. His jaw locked beneath his round face as he maneuvered his stout frame to block her path. Veronica knew he thought kids should be rarely seen and never heard, so she'd have to speak quickly and hope the gravity of what she had to say would halt his advance. Unlike the young guard outside, she didn't think he would mind laying hands on a royal, especially one who was just a kid.

"Mommy, Sophia is gone! She's been taken!" Veronica said with a gasp, voice cracking as she ran up to the stone slab that reflected her mother's image.

"*What*?" escaped the Queen's lips.

Veronica knew her mom thought she had a tendency to be a bit dramatic, but the sound of her voice must have conveyed the truth. The Queen's brow creased and her eyes filled with concern.

"Mommy she's *gone*. I had a dream she had been taken, and when I woke up she was gone."

General Fooney began, "Princess, I'm sure she's around-"

"General, find my daughter," the Queen said. With the slightest bow the General hurried to speak to the troops outside the room as the Queen turned to her daughter. "Veronica, Honey, are you all right?"

"Yeah, but Mom, when are you coming home?"

"Oh baby, I'd be there now if I could, but the Arch is damaged, and I'm trapped here."

"*What?* Where's Daddy?"

Hand outstretched, tears in her eyes, Mom said, "I

don't know."

"*What?*" Veronica stiffened. The world she knew, one of safety and love, dissolved. She longed to be swept up in her mother's arms and feel her protective embrace. That couldn't happen. Instead panic reached out to hug her. How could she ever break its grip and control the swell of emotions rising up to drown her?

Her mother's voice reached out like a lifeline, pulling her to calmer waters. "Veronica, listen to me, look into my eyes."

With tears beginning to spill from her own, Veronica did as her mother requested.

"Veronica, I'm not going to lie to you. I believe someone is preparing to attack KenKarta. Right now I'm not exactly sure what's going on, but I will figure it out. Your father is not here on Dragontier. I'm not sure where he is, but I know he is going to be all right. I can feel it. I need you to keep that a secret, though. If anyone asks, tell them Daddy is here with me. Do you understand?"

"Yes, but what about *Sophia*?"

"The General will find her." The Queen gave a hopeful look to General Fooney as he returned to the room with another officer in tow.

"Your Majesty, the staff has already been searching the grounds, and there is no sign of her."

"Mom, in the dream, Sophia followed you off the inner grounds, toward Mount Grace, and then, just as she got to the bridge, something swooped out of the darkness and took her."

"*Swooped?*" asked the General and Queen in unison.

Veronica continued, "You know, out of the air, like, like flying down from the mountain."

"General-"

"We'll investigate," the General said,

"In the meantime, General Fooney, you lock down the city. No one goes in or out."

The cas began to ripple a bit and fade.

"Your majesty, do you need to rest?"

"I need to speak to the people, find out if anyone saw anything, prepare them for what is to come!" The edge of emotion came sharp in her mother's voice. It was unlike her to sound like that when she was working. Her mom paused. She lightly cleared her throat. When she continued, the Queen's tone was even, controlled, and filled with authority. "If I break the connection now it will be hours before I have the strength to reestablish it. I'm operating my end alone, for currently I can not trust anyone here to help. Bring in cascaders to help boost the signal on your end. I want to connect to every cascade in Karta. Do it *now*. While we wait, I will bring you up to date on what has happened here."

General Fooney made eye contact with the man standing next to him. Without a word the officer turned on his heels and crisply left the room to set the Queen's commands in motion. Veronica stood stark still before the cas screen and watched her mother be Queen.

V learned that upon her mother's arrival on Dragontier, the Queen discovered that the King's delegation had never arrived. In fact, none of the delegations had shown, each had been told the event was postponed. The cascades KenKarta had received were fakes. The Dragon council now believed they came from Bedforda, so the Queen gave instructions to send the Hunters there to see what was happening.

The Hunters were led by Veronica's uncle, Sir Mark,

the Queen's brother by marriage to her sister Karol. Aunt Karol and Uncle Mark's union took place when V's mom was quite young, and her mom seemed as close to him as any blood relative. In fact, it had been decided long ago that if anything ever befell the King and Queen, Lady Karol and Sir Mark would be entrusted to care for their girls. While his wife served in the very public role as Administrator of Kief, Sir Mark held a more subtle position of importance in KenKarta. The Hunters did as their name implied, they hunted things, often dangerous things. Sir Mark and his men were already in the general area of Bedforda investigating reports of hobyah sightings, so naturally they would now be dispatched at once to Bedforda.

The Queen also indicated that her husband's friend Cletus should be contacted in Pringer Forest as soon as possible in an effort to determine if the King had ever made it there.

Veronica's heart pulsed in her ears as Queen Alison informed General Fooney why she could not return home—the Center Arch on Dragontier was sabotaged mere moments before the Queen was to enter for her return jump.

Someone tried to kill Mom! Why? The only thing that kept V's panic at bay was the glimmering image before her and the reassuring sound of her mother's voice. She was right there, she was okay, but this development meant her mom was truly trapped.

Two annuals ago a rogue dragon had destroyed Dragontier's Secondary Arch and its stones before disappearing. No one knew exactly why he had done it, but since replacement Arch Stones had yet to be found, the crazed dragon's actions had left the Tier with only one operating

Arch.

The General said, "Sabotaged how?"

"It appears an overcharged Imperium Piece was used to form a navitas-bomb. The explosion of energy caused one pillar of the Arch to collapse," the Queen replied, "but thankfully all the stones are still intact."

"Was anyone hurt?"

"Two Arch minders, they were preparing to help me come home. General, they're dead, and several others are injured. One of them was newly assigned here from Moldea, and there is speculation that he is to blame, but any one of them is likely Gifted enough to be the saboteur. That's why I'm operating the cas alone. Until the dragons sort it out, it is unclear whom I should trust, and I am stranded here until the Arch can be repaired. In addition, I fear the King has somehow most certainly been compromised."

"Your Majesty, from what you've just told me, I feel we must proceed as if KenKarta is at war."

"Yes," the Queen said almost to herself, "but with whom exactly?"

The General gave a sideways glance to a guard standing utterly still in the gloom. He opened the door allowing a beam of shine to cut across the shadowy cas room. People filed in and sprang into action around its edges. This room was designed to utilize the Gifts of many in order to communicate with large numbers of cascades at once. Everyone was well trained and knew what to do.

"Veronica, I want to hear all about your dream, but right now I have to be Queen. Okay?"

Veronica nodded knowingly; this was a phrase they used among themselves often. The girls would ask their parents if they had to be King or Queen when they didn't want them to go to work.

Veronica's mom pressed the first two fingers of her right hand to her lips, then extended them toward V. Her blue eyes glistened, and the smile was forced. "Good. I love you, baby!"

"I love you too, Mom," Veronica said after kissing and raising her own fingers in response.

"Being Queen and helping the Kingdom is the best way for me to help Sophia. Okay?"

"Okay, Mom," Veronica whispered and stepped back toward the door. Her mother's facade might fool others, but V knew that Queen was the last thing her mom wanted to be right now. If her mom had a choice, she'd be here looking for Sophia herself. She recognized the pain hidden just beneath the surface of her mother's smile. It wouldn't have been the first time her mom had put her girls before the Kingdom. She'd been criticized for this in the past.

That being said, plenty of times the Lands had come first. This would be the biggest, but it was by no means the only crisis Veronica had seen her mother handle. There was nothing for her to do now but get out of the way. The fact both reassured and infuriated her.

Chapter Eight
The Declaration

In private homes and public squares, cascades all around the city of Karta rippled to life. Veronica sighed, the appearance of a well-known cascader from the castle's office of information announcing that the Queen requested everyone's attention was unusual enough to pique most people's curiosity.

Appearing on multiple cascades at the same time was a difficult and draining task for all under the best of circumstances. What the Queen did now was complicated by the facts that she had no preparation time and was off tier and operating her cascade alone. All were details the public at large would hopefully remain unaware of.

Veronica also knew that the Queen had instructed the cascade operators to focus on her image and not the background; this would cause it to be blurred, or lack details. She wanted people to assume she was in Karta, in the castle, at least for now.

The Queen sat perfectly still, eyes lowered, as her image trickled down to fill the entire surface of cascade screens both large and small throughout the city. Then she looked up and began to speak:

"Good people of KenKarta, I appear before you at an hour of great need. Recent events have convinced us that forces outside our Lands are preparing to invade.

As you know, for some time now there

have been those outside of KenKarta that have feared us. They've feared our strength and our strides to expand the opportunity of wealth and education beyond the Demogeron. Despite our best efforts to alleviate these fears, I believe someone is using this atmosphere of anxiety to plot a path of true evil.

"I say this because only one whose soul is damned would attack us as we are now being attacked. Last night, while you slept, my daughter, your Princess Sophia, was stolen from us. In taking Sophia, they strike at our very hearts. In my heart, I know she is in grave danger, alone and afraid, but in my heart I also know she is still alive. Someone hopes to use Princess Sophia to crush us. I tell you now, we will crush any and all behind her abduction first.

"To do this I need the help of each of you. There can be no panic. Panic and fear will only serve our enemy. Instead, you need to reach out in support to each other and prepare yourselves for war. For though it is not what we seek, war is most surely upon us. Those who bring it still hide in the shadows, because they fear to face the strength of KenKarta in the shine of day. When our enemy finally does show itself, we must already be prepared.

"As of now the city of Karta is closed. No one will cross the rivers until we can be absolutely sure that Sophia is not here. We fear she is not, but we must be sure and your assistance and cooperation will help the process go faster. Report any suspicious happenings to the castle. In the meantime, you must begin to determine how your Gifts can best serve your Land in this time of need. Let the spirit of Deus flow through you, and your answers will come. Be vigilant, take nothing for granted, and use your own strengths to strengthen us all."

The cas screen flickered then went blank, plunging the room into a pit of darkness.

Veronica held her breath and felt for a handhold. The silence tore at her, threatened to pull her under. Panic reached out through the gloom to seize her completely, until someone ignited a crystal. Its first rays revealed that many around the room were feeling much the same as she did. But panic retreated from the shine. Specialists, their gaping blank stares were quickly blinked away, replaced instead with the furrowed foreheads and clenched jaws of determination. The silence broke like a collective exhale as their training took hold. Those in the cas room burst into action.

From the back wall near the door where she had stood to watch her mother, Veronica tried to get the General's attention. She wanted to tell him more about her dream. Not that she was sure he would listen. He didn't seem to like kids much, and he didn't put much faith in other people's Gifts. Her mom said it was because he only believed in the ones that he himself had. The General glanced her way, his lips pursed and brow crumpled, before he broke eye contact and busied himself in conversation with the lieutenant at his side. He would make no time for her now.

Veronica turned, walked out the door, and headed toward the royal residence. The wave of activity was spreading both across the entire castle and the city of Karta below. An energy, a sense of urgency, coursed so strong she could feel and actually hear it in the air. Horns blew deep and long on the rivers below.

Veronica stopped on a high open-air walkway long enough to see that the many bridges that crossed the rivers that framed the city of Karta were all being drawn and blocked. Those working and traveling out in the fields beyond would not be sleeping at home this night.

For foe and friend alike, the city of Karta was now closed.

It would be hours before her mother could even try to reestablish a connection on the cas. As V walked, she mumbled, "Sophia is not in the city, yet all the soldiers are going to be wasting time searching the city. Where's this Valleyridge the evil man who took Sophia spoke of?" She would have to find it herself.

Scoobee had fallen into step beside Veronica as soon as she left the cas room, listening. His nails clicked out an upbeat cadence on the stone flooring as his short legs moved quickly to keep up. The red jewel hanging from his royal purple collar swayed in rhythm beneath his bearded chin. The bushy goatee and eyebrows struck a stark contrast to his well-trimmed coat. Growling his dislike of the General, he said, "In my opinion, old Fooney is an arrogant windbag. I'll show you where the Valleyridge is, V. I've seen your father point it out on the map in his study."

"Scoobee, have you been eavesdropping on Daddy?"

"Why do you think I sleep on that old chair he has in his study? It's not nearly as comfortable as your mom's chair of many colors."

Her mother's chair of many colors was definitely Scoobee's favorite place to nap, other than V's bed at night, of course. Veronica swore she could see an extra spring in her little dog's step as he trotted down the hall. It felt good to have him near. Then she thought guardedly so Scoobee couldn't hear, too bad she was going to have to leave him behind.

Veronica loved Scoobee. He was the first magical

present she and her sister had ever received, given on the day halfway between Sophia's third and Veronica's sixth birthdays. However, Scoobee wasn't really all that magical. With his short legs, stout chest, and pert triangle ears, their wheaten-colored terrier was pretty much like any other dog, except for the fact that he could make his thoughts known to Veronica and Sophia. Veronica suspected that he could probably talk to other Gifted people, but he didn't even try. He preferred to make his needs recognized the old-fashioned way. He barked and whined and barked some more, until the nearest human figured out what it was he wanted. He was particularly fond of doing this to Ashley, the girls' nanny, who was not naturally fond of dogs. Instead of talking to her, he chose to grate on her nerves with verbal demands, knowing full well that she was stuck with him simply because he was always with the girls. If he would just talk to her, things would be so much easier. Instead he insisted on making the girls translate his needs to her, or worse yet, just whined at her. As with people, Gifts possessed by magical creatures came in different strengths. Plus, it was up to the individual to cultivate them, make their Gifts grow stronger, or let them fade away un-harvested.

As he got older Scoobee did begin to communicate with other magical creatures in the castle, but aside from the girls, never any humans. At least that was what he claimed. Veronica suspected that recently he'd snuck a thought or two to her mom, but neither would admit it.

Scoobee's early inability to speak was why Veronica's parents weren't sure what to think when, at the young age of six, Veronica first told them things like, "Scoobee says he needs another treat," or when he wasn't on his best behavior, "Scoobee says that it's really not necessary for you to threaten him with bodily harm, Daddy." At first they weren't sure if this was an imaginary game or if she were really channeling a Gift. It was the latter.

Veronica's Gift of speaking with magical creatures became perfectly clear when she told her parents a story that had first been told to her by a hawken. She described a meadow in the woods part way up the mountain that loomed large behind the castle. Though her parents knew the meadow on Mount Grace well, Veronica had never been there. It was outside the castle grounds and not easy to reach. When the King and Queen asked Veronica how she knew the place, she replied, "A magnificent red bird with a mask, whose feathers look like flames of a fire, visited my window sill and told me all about it. Her name is Ember. She lives in the forest, and she is my friend."

Veronica smiled now at Scoobee as they neared her dad's study. Despite his small size, she had no doubt that her self-appointed protector would take on anything he thought was trying to hurt his girls. He did have his faults though, like barking at even the slightest shadow. He claimed to be barking at evil, no matter what form it might take, but everyone else thought he just liked the sound of his own voice. But he loved her as much as she loved him.

Scoobee showed Veronica the location of the Valley-ridge on the map in her dad's study. The geologic structure ran through the Palousoa region to the southeast of KenKarta. If they rode hard with few breaks, she could make it to the northern tip of the Valleyridge in a day and half on Dalminyo. At a conventional pace the trip would take most travelers on horseback at least three days.

Veronica felt Scoobee's stare and looked over from the

map to the chair where he sat. His warm brown eyes were narrowed, and his head was cocked to the side. Had she let her mental guard down? Did he know what she planned to do?

Scoobee's eyes widened, and he jumped to his feet. "Veronica, are you thinking about going to this place yourself?"

"I have to, Scoobee. The guards are looking for Sophia in the wrong place, and the longer we wait the harder it will be to find her."

"But your mother and father-"

"Are not here. Mom is trapped on Dragontier and Dad... no one knows where he is. I saw Sophia in my sleep, Scoobee. *I'm* the one who can find her, and I'm the one who has to save her."

"Then where you go, I go, my Princess. We will find her together. There is an outpost at the Crossroads that I've heard your father and his men speak of. They often stop there when traveling. If we hurry we can make it by nightfall."

Veronica went to her room and gathered her bow, quiver, dagger, and sword. She packed clothes and her two favorite blankets in a long bag that would tie across the back of Dalminyo's saddle, for she'd likely have to sleep outdoors.

Good thing she liked camping.

She went into her mother's closet and collected an Advanced Set of Imperium Pieces. Given to the Queen as a gift, it had never been used. She placed the set in a leather pouch and tied the pouch to her belt. She put on the ruby necklace her parents had given her. Then on her left wrist she donned a bracelet with a large stone that came into direct contact with her skin. When properly provoked by the wearer, the stone could form a protective shield of energy. She didn't know how to use all these things completely yet, but best to have them along. Her clothes beneath her riding cloak were layered yet form fitting and moved with her body. She didn't want to be wearing anything bulky if she got into a fight.

Scoobee watched in silence as Veronica led Dalminyo from the stable. She had not yet told the equidae her plan, at least not with words. She was now in close enough proximity that she simply left her mind open, unguarded. There Dalminyo could see for himself. Verbally V told the stable page that they were going out for some air on the lower slope of Mount Grace, an area she went to often on her own. Of course Dalminyo felt that wasn't true, but even if the page doubted her, he didn't dare voice that doubt. After all, Veronica was his Princess, and he was sworn to serve her.

Before leaving the residence, Scoobee had begged Veronica to let him come with her. She refused. She told him that when the time came he would have to let someone know that she and Dalminyo were all right and had not been kidnapped like her sister. She did not want to cause undo worry, or have the soldiers waste time looking for her. Scoobee argued that he could not talk to other people. Veronica just smiled. That was probably more by choice than anything else. Instead of arguing, she simply told Scoobee to talk to Gallantae when he got back from Equitier. He had traveled there on holiday while her mother was to be gone. Given what had happened, it would not be long before he got the news and returned home. No one would dare deny passage to the Queen's equidae. Gallantae, V told Scoobee, would know whom to tell.

Veronica and Dalminyo would slip off the castle grounds and be on their way without anyone being the wiser. Even though no one was to leave the city, Veronica knew a little-used passage that led to the lower slopes of Mount Grace, where guards would not yet be in place. Plus, that high up the river was shallow enough that Dalminyo could easily cross without having to slow down to swim. At full speed, he'd be hard to see. Especially if they tried to pass unnoticed.

With a tear in her eye, Veronica gave Scoobee a big hug and then climbed onto Dalminyo's back. As they headed toward a back gate on the northeast side of the castle, Scoobee couldn't help but let out a mournful howl of good-bye.

Chapter Ten

Finding a Gift in the Dark

Her eyes were open, but Sophia still couldn't see. The darkness was thick and the air, dank. She could feel bare ground beneath her. Mere inches in front of her, she touched stone. It was cold and damp. She rolled over. The floor beneath her had a slight incline so she decided to follow it upward. On hands and knees she crawled, slowly, probing the darkness in front of her with one hand then the other.

Was this all just a nightmare? The longest and worst one imaginable? At least the evil presence was gone.

In front of her, she sensed something close. She sat up on her knees and gingerly reached out her hand. Her fingers touched something hard like stone, but not. She swept her fingertips sideways. The stones were flexible; they overlapped and at the same time fit together perfectly. She had felt this before. They were not stone. Dragon scales? Was this just some wall or... could it be a *real* dragon blocking her path?

She jerked her hands back and sat on them. If only she could see! She clawed the dirt floor beneath her. Her fingers came across a rock. She clenched it tight in her hands before her. On the verge of throwing a fit, with one fist wrapped around the other, she rocked back and forth. A wail escaped her lips and tears streaked her face. The rock in Sophia's hand began to glow. It was not a refined Piece, but it contained a large amount of crystal. Amazingly Sophia had managed to bring it to life.

Her crying abruptly stopped. She had tried many times to make a refined piece of crystal light up, but had never been

65

able to do so. Now here in this horribly dark cave she held a glimmer of hope in her hand.

Chapter Eleven
Veronica and the Stable Boy

Darkness had almost completely drawn when Julia caught up with Veronica and Dalminyo. The cheetatarah was furious, relieved, and exhausted all at once. As expected, Scoobee had told all to the great cat before she could even enter the residence. Instead of resting as she should have after her two-day run to and from Medius to inform the King's sister Lady Leanne of the Queen's fears, Julia immediately began to track Dalminyo and Veronica. Good thing too. A steady stream of large rain drops had begun right after she made it through the farmland outside the city, so following their trail had become ever more difficult. She had found them, but her muscles quivered in complaint. Her fatigue was so utterly complete that it was all the cheetatarah could do to stand up.

With Veronica clinging low to his saddle, Dalminyo had run cross-country, avoiding roads and people. Riding an equidae at top speed was exciting, but hard work too. The pair's stamina was not that of adults. Still, Veronica was proud that they had made it as far in one afternoon as the regular cavalry could have in an entire day. The Crossroads was just ahead. On its northern side stood an outpost where soldiers of KenKarta and other travelers often stopped when passing through.

The day's events, both emotional and physical, had left Veronica, Dalminyo, and Julia exhausted. Julia wanted to take Veronica home, but the Princess refused. The only thing they agreed on was that they needed rest. Beyond the wooded area where they argued in hiding stood a stable. Up a small hill beyond that was the outpost. Smoke billowed out of the chimneys, and the windows glowed with warmth. Yet no matter how inviting it appeared, or how cold and wet Veronica felt, going into the outpost was out of the question. Anyone who saw her would likely want to send her back. Plus, Julia had expressed concern that enemies of the realm might actually be about, willing to do Veronica harm. Tired as she was, Julia admitted she would be hard pressed to protect Veronica out in the open. They needed the cover and protection of an enclosed space, and the stable looked like the best spot.

Veronica insisted that Julia rest while she snuck in to check it out. V unsheathed her dagger and darted across the open ground between her and the back of the stable. As she tried to slow down at the edge of the barn, she slipped on the slick soil and fell, right on her backside, into a large mud puddle.

"Oh, great!" Veronica swore under her breath as she got up completely splattered with mud. A faint nicker came from the woods. Dalminyo was having a good laugh at her expense. "He's such a snot," Veronica said. Glancing toward the trees where she knew he hid, V stuck out her tongue, then turned her attention to climbing through the window above her.

The shine in the stable was dim. Inside the large, long building, shoulder-high stalls lined both sides. The ceiling was high, supported by heavy beams, with haylofts at either end. Several horses lazily munched in stalls at the far end of the building. Otherwise, it appeared empty. On the end closest to her, several stalls with fresh straw would make acceptable beds. Julia was in desperate need of rest, but Dalminyo and she needed it too. It wasn't home, but it was out of the rain.

As Veronica turned back toward the window to inform the others all was clear, a soft rustle came from behind her. She spun toward the noise, raising her dagger. Someone wrenched the blade from her grip! Her feet flew out from beneath her. She lay pinned to the straw-strewn floor, confronted by the tip of her own weapon.

Staring down at her was a boy, about her age, possibly a

bit older, jaw clenched, blue eyes hard.

How in the world could this have happened? She sparred and held her own with full-grown men in her father's personal guard. This mere boy disarmed her...

"How?" muttered Veronica mostly to herself.

"What? How did I disarm a dirty little urchin up to no good?" the boy snarled. "I wouldn't be much of a warrior if I couldn't manage that, now would I."

"You're no warrior," Veronica said as the shock began to wear off.

"Quiet, thief! Tell me, what were you up to? Are you in league with those hobyahs?"

"How dare you-"

A deep rumble reached her ears and sent a chill down her spine. The low growl came from behind the boy, from the window Veronica had used to enter the stable.

"Are you all right?" asked the great cat as she gracefully jumped from the sill and onto the stable floor.

The boy spun around. His mouth dropped open as he jumped up and pointed Veronica's dagger at the cheetatarah. Julia bared her teeth menacingly and began to slink forward.

"Easy, Julia," Dalminyo said as he entered the stable through a door behind her. "I don't think he's dangerous. The kid looks more scared than anything. You're not that hungry, are you?"

Julia purred deeply, "Well, if he doesn't stop pointing that dagger, I'll be cleaning my teeth with his bones before breakfast."

To everyone's surprise, the boy dropped the dagger. With eyes wide and skin pale, he looked like a statue frozen in disbelief. Veronica snatched her dagger and jumped up to stand beside Julia. Still he didn't move.

"What's wrong with him?" Veronica asked.

"I think he can hear us," Julia said as his eyes shifted to hers.

"No way," Dalminyo said, tossing his head arrogantly. "That scrawny serf isn't *Gifted*. He's just a stable boy."

"Dalminyo!" Veronica said. "Don't talk like that! That's not nice, or true, it's just prejudice. Like Mom says, everyone has Gifts, they just have to learn how to use them."

"So she *says*," Dalminyo mocked.

"You're such a snob!" Veronica said.

"Children," Julia stated. They fell silent, and she returned her gaze to the boy who still hadn't moved. "Boy, can you hear me?"

He nodded slightly.

"Tell us, what is your name?"

"My name? My name is Zane. Zane Slayer."

"Slayer? That's a pretty pompous name, especially for a-"

"Quiet, Dalminyo," Julia said. "Is this the first time you have spoken with a magical creature?"

The stable boy's brow furrowed slightly, and he gnawed a bit on his lower lip. "Yes. Well, I think so. The truth is I'm not sure. A few days ago there was an equidae here and I thought maybe he was trying to talk to me, but then I wasn't sure."

"I'm sure he was *not*," Dalminyo snorted, arching his neck and raising his tail. "Why would an equidae talk to the likes of you?"

"I don't know," Zane replied. "Why are *you* talking to me?"

Dalminyo swished his tail so that the end of it hit the boy in the back of his shoulders and wrapped around to rest on his neck and face.

"Dalminyo!" Veronica said, pursing her lips and raising her finger at him.

Pushing away the long thick strands of black hair, Zane turned to her. "Who are you?"

"No one, just an urchin looking for a place to sleep."

"An urchin who travels with a cheetatarah and an arrogant equidae? I don't think so."

Dalminyo said, "Don't let him talk to you that way, Veronica."

Veronica scolded, "Dalminyo, where are your manners?"

"Veronica? *Veronica*! As in, Veronica, Royal Princess of KenKarta, Veronica?" Zane spat it out as if to say, oh great, can my life get any worse. "Oh, that's just spectacular!"

The shine from the crystal stone was dim, but with it she could explore her dank surroundings. Sophia edged quietly away from what must be a dragon blocking the entrance to a cave.

Her hoarse whisper pierced the heavy air. "I'm in a cave. Why am I in a cave? And why is there a dragon blocking my way?"

The surreal nature of it was the only thing that kept her from crying again. That, and the voice of her mother in her head saying, 'Don't cry; try!'

The cave, at least the part she could see, was shaped like a V and got narrower the further back she went. As it narrowed, the dirt on the floor got smoother. Holding her light crystal in one hand she wiped her other across the floor. To her surprise the dirt was really just a thin layer of dust that wiped away. Beneath it was an inlaid floor made up of thousands of tiny little tiles. She held the crystal closer to the floor and could swear it looked deep purple, almost plum.

"What is this place?"

She sat back and looked up into the darkness. Instead of seeing nothing, she saw what could have been the dimmest version of a tiery sky, the smallest of points catching the reflection of her crystal.

"Oh, if they were only brighter," she whispered as she raised her arms toward them. As they appeared to do just what she asked, she closed her eyes tight in disbelief. Then opened them slowly, hoping that what she thought she saw was really there. She could see! Not just by the shine of her little stone but by hundreds of delicate little brilliant crystals attached to the roof of the cave. For a moment she sat still, basking in their shine, then a little giggle escaped her lips. She had never been able to do anything like this before!

She slowly examined her surroundings and began to feel as if she sat in a giant dollhouse, one that had been split in half and pushed to the walls on either side of the cave. Between the two halves was a big and open tiled floor that ran to the back of the cave, right into the smallest Arch Sophia had ever seen. Compared to the size of the buildings that flanked it, it was huge, but compared to Sophia and all the real Arches she had seen, it was tiny. Sophia would just be

able to pass through it without ducking. It looked like a real one, but while the four Arch Stones that outlined the lower rectangle of the Arch were in place, the Alistone was missing. Without an Alistone placed into the top of the Arch, it wouldn't operate, even if it were real. Nonetheless, she caught her breath. The entire scene was just as she imagined Fairytier would be.

"Fairytier, is that where the dragon has taken me?" But dragons couldn't go to Fairytier, nor could anyone else for that matter. The fairies closed their Arch to outsiders annuals ago. She knew this because she had asked her parents to take her there countless times. Of course, that was before she discovered what tier-jumping felt like. Then she decided that they needed to come to her.

Fairies looked so delicate, yet were fast and strong. The stories said they were funny too, and Sophia liked funny. The colors (purple being her favorite of course) and designs of fairy folk drew Sophia in like water to a fall. Veronica often referred to Sophia's room as Fairytier because it looked like what they both imagined the real place would be like, all lilac, bright and airy with plenty of flowers and big fat blue and yellow bees.

Sophia also loved dollhouses. Now she found herself in the middle of a giant one, a castle-sized one. She peeked in. It was completely furnished! She reached out to touch it. Her hand passed right through the wall! The portion immediately surrounding her arm turned transparent so that she could easily see whatever room her hand was in. She moved her hand back and forth through the wall from one room to another, and the result was the same. The internal walls and furnishings were solid, but the exterior wall that faced the castle's courtyard was an illusion, complete with windows and balconies. No doors though. The fairies must fly in and out wherever they pleased!

She went across to the building's mirror image on the opposite side of the cave and discovered that its external wall was the same. Tension in her body eased as she examined the beautiful furnishings inside the castle's many rooms. Her fear melted away, and in its place she felt thirst and hunger!

She would have to keep looking for a way out. A way that didn't take her past that dragon whose back blocked the other end of the cave. She could see it clearly now that the crystal ceiling was lit, an impenetrable wall of dark scales. But she wouldn't think about what might happen when it moved. That made her stomach hurt. First she'd find food, then a way out.

Fairies were famous for their celebrations, and Sophia had heard stories about them hosting elaborate feasts for creatures of all varieties. This looked like the place where such an event would be held, not just for fairies but for perhaps human guests as well. The castle's design implied that at least at one time it was meant to welcome guests both large and small. So Sophia went to the area she guessed to be the kitchen. On the shelves were miniature tins and bottles. She placed a box-like tin on the floor in front of her and then pulled the cork from a tiny bottle.

"I hope the stories are true," Sophia said, "I'm starving." She held the bottle over the little box and let the liquid dribble into it.

At first it did nothing, and Sophia frowned. Then multi-colored light swirled around the tin, and as she watched she wished for a large piece of chicken, some steamed broccoli, a slice of watermelon, and a glass of water. When the light dimmed, that was exactly what was waiting for her on a silver platter and in a silver goblet. Sophia smiled. Other kids may not like them, but these foods were some of her favorites. Her mom always said she was a good eater, not nearly as picky as her sister. Sophia dug in. It was good, but when she finished, she might just have to try and swirl up something sweet for dessert.

"Fairies are the best!"

Chapter Thirteen
Back at the Barn

"Eyes on me, child." Julia spoke to Zane in a soothing yet stern tone. The tenor told Veronica that the cat didn't want to frighten the boy further, yet Julia wanted to leave no doubt of who was in charge. "So, which is it? Have you been able to talk to Mythical creatures before, or is this your first time?"

"Well, animals have always liked me-"

"Oh please!" Dalminyo snorted. "I find *that* hard to believe!"

"Well, it was true, at least until you came along," Zane fired back. "Then a few days ago, an equidae was here. There was something wrong with him though."

Julia's purple outlined eyes narrowed. "What do you mean?"

"I mean he was different. There was a darkness about him and a sadness, not like any equidae I've met before."

"And met a *lot* of them have you?" Dalminyo asked.

"More than you'd think, jug-head, this is a stable you know, but none of them were as lame as you."

Stomping a rear hoof into the dirt, Dalminyo said, "Why I ought to kick you through the wall, you little-"

"Now boys," Julia interrupted. "Zane, was it? Tell me about this equidae."

"He was big and black as a tierless night. It was hard to understand him. I thought it was me, but I can hear you guys just fine, so now I don't know. I think he said his name was Hellantae."

"Now I know you're just lying," Dalminyo said. "Hellantae, twin brother of the Queen's steed Gallantae, died as a colt on Equitier. They tell the story of how he was playing too close and got sucked through the Arch into Empty Space as a way to scare all the little foals."

Zane widened his stance and crossed his arms. "I don't know, jug-head. I'm just telling you what he said."

"Do you have any other Gifts?" Veronica asked, trying to defuse the growing tension.

"I don't know, I've always had a really good sense of direction, like I can just see where to go in my head, but my stepfather says it's not a Gift. He's always said we aren't Gifted folk."

Dalminyo snorted a laugh.

"You seem to be a skilled fighter," Julia said.

"Oh yeah, I'm the best," Zane said, pulling his shoulders back. "But that's just because I practice a lot, not because of some Gift."

"Well, you're a great bragger that's for sure," Veronica retorted, still feeling the sting from when he disarmed her. "You were lucky I didn't hear you sneak up on me. Otherwise I might have hurt you."

"Yeah, right! Like that would have happened. I wouldn't be much of a warrior if I couldn't disarm a mere girl."

Veronica bristled. "I have you know that I train with and can best many of my father's personal guards."

"His guards? I doubt it. I've sparred with them when they stay here. They're the Pinn, and if you bested them, it's only because they let you."

"*What?*"

"You know, let the boss's daughter win, duh."

It was an option Veronica had frankly never entertained. The thought of her father's men letting her win both hurt and angered her. As her hand settled on the hilt of her sword, Dalminyo, ears laid back, lowered his head toward the boy and muttered, "You disrespectful-"

Julia stepped forward and said, "Are you not a loyal citizen of KenKarta?"

"Of course I am. I pledged my allegiance to the King himself," Zane said, again straightening his posture to that of a soldier's. "He's always been really kind to me and my mom when he stays here. He even offered to let me attend school in KenKarta."

"And this is how you display that allegiance?" Julia growled. "By insulting his daughter, your Princess? You should know that I have bitten off appendages for less."

With her hand on Dalminyo's head to settle him, Veronica said, "I have half a mind to let you eat him, but the other half is too tired. Let it go, Julia." Then to Zane she said, "Look, we just need a place to spend the night and some food if you have it."

"Of course, my Lady," Zane said, bowing a bit too deep to be completely sincere. "Please forgive my offense. I forgot my place. I've been told it's a bad habit of mine. I'll have my mother make a room ready for you right away."

"No!" Veronica said. "This stall will do just fine."

"What? I can't let a Princess sleep in a *stall*."

Veronica's fist clenched at her side. Man, this kid made her mad. She was about to let him have it when she heard her mother's words in her head: 'If you don't have anything nice to say, then say nothing at all.' "Please," Veronica said quietly, the day's events catching up with her all at once. She reached

80

out and gently clasped the boy's hand. His skin sent warmth to her rain-soaked fingers as she looked directly into his cool, hard eyes. "Please, you can't tell anyone that we're here."

The lines around Zane's eyes and lips softened and she could hear a catch in his breathing. Then without moving he said, "Of course, my Lady."

Dalminyo whinnied deep in his throat, and the trance was broken. In the back of her mind Veronica could hear her equidae think, 'Excuse me! Can you believe the nerve of this little peasant brat? What is he thinking making eyes at *My Princess* that way, like she'd ever be interested in the likes of him.'

"Ah, there is a wash room at the end there," Zane said and turned to go. "I'll be back with some food as soon as I can."

"Thank you," Veronica said as he left, then she turned to Dalminyo. "I'm sure you misread him. But rest assured, the only thing I'm interested in is finding my sister."

"Oh, I'm sorry- did I think that 'out loud'?"

"Like you'd have to, you snob. You know I'm close enough to hear your private thoughts if you want me to, and anyway, why don't you give me some credit, Dalminyo? He's a selfish, bragging, annoying, ornery, jerk... boy."

'However, I do have to admit he's a cute one!' she thought, leaving her mind wide open so Dalminyo could pick up on it.

"Hey!" warned the equidae.

Veronica flipped her braid at him as she turned to walk down the alleyway. "Oh, did I think that *out loud*?"

Chapter Fourteen
Sophia and the Dragon

Sophia had eaten and drank her fill of fairy food, then looked for a way out. There was none, except for the opening that was currently sealed tight by dragon armor. She didn't want to think about what that meant, so she played house with the fairy castle and its furnishings. For a few blissful hours she had completely forgotten where she was. Far from her mind was the fact that she had been stolen from her home, flown to Pinnacle only knew where, and was now locked in a cave- a cave guarded by what she feared to be a real live dragon.

All these facts came rushing back when the scales of the beast scraped across the cave floor. The dragon was repositioning itself, turning its massive body, making room for its head to move back into the cave right toward Sophia. The ceiling was not high enough for it to stand completely upright so it had to crouch and move along with its belly low to the ground.

Hide! With that thought the crystal lights above her all went dark. She clutched the crystal rock she had found on the floor. At her touch, it began to glow. In that low glow she could now see the reflection of huge eyes looking down at her. They were indeed the eyes of a dragon. They should have scared her, but instead she felt somehow drawn to them. They looked like two big blue sapphires with black diamonds set in their centers.

She walked slowly toward them. "Who are you?"

The dragon answered in a low rumbling, "My name is Daelkay." Not with his mind but in an audible voice, for dragons could do either.

"Why are we here?"

"It is my master's wish."

"Master, who's your master?"

"Lord Leamoldae." The dragon paused, waiting for a response. When there was none he continued, "Are you not afraid?"

"Sure, I'm scared. I'm in a cave instead of my room, but I don't know any Lea-moldy," the little Princess stated. "Is he the evil man who took me?"

"Yes."

"If he's evil, how can he be your master?"

"I too am evil."

Frowning Sophia wondered, "But you're a dragon? You're not supposed to be evil. Your kind are the keepers of secrets and lore. That kind of job doesn't get entrusted to evil ones. Besides, you don't feel evil, not like your Lord Moldy."

"It's Lea-mol-dae, and what do you know of evil? You're nothing but a spoiled little child."

"I'm not spoiled. And my birthday was just two weeks ago so Mommy says I'm not so little anymore. I'm eight." But her voice cracked, and she began to sob loudly.

"Why does that make you cry?" the dragon asked.

"Because, I don't want to grow up too fast!" Sophia wailed.

Daelkay snorted, blowing Sophia's hair back. "Stop that nonsense this instant, or I'll eat you here and now."

Eyes wide, Sophia choked off her sobs.

"That's better. Now go to sleep."

"If I do, will you let me go home?"

"If I say yes, will you go to sleep?"

Sophia cocked her head and pursed her lips to one side. "Yes."

"Go to sleep."

Sophia picked up her blanket and the slick cloak she had been bound up in the night before, and then looked for a place to lie down. The floor was dirt, cold stone, or tile. By the light of the little crystal she held, she could see a nice nook where Daelkay's back leg met his body. She tentatively crawled up his scales and snuggled up to the dragon. He wasn't very soft, but he was definitely warmer than the floor.

Without lifting his massive head the dragon said, "Do you not fear I will eat you?"

"No silly, if you ate me you couldn't take me home, now could you."

"That is true, now sleep."

Sophia tried to comply, but she was restless. She tossed and turned, poking at the dragon, rearranging the cloak under her, trying to get comfortable.

"Why do you *fidget* so?" the dragon asked.

"It's just, I can't sleep without my song," Sophia said.

"Your song?"

"The song my mommy sings to me each night when I go to bed."

"What is this song?" Daelkay asked. "I know thousands of songs, all of the songs worth knowing."

"It's my song."

"'My song,' I don't think I know it."

"No, it's not called 'My Song,' it's called 'Angel Baby.'"

"I know no song by that name either; it is most definitely not a classic."

"No, silly dragon, my mommy made it up for me."

Daelkay grunted then added, "Let me hear this song."

"What?"

"Sing it to me."

"But..."

"You said she sings it every night, do you not know it then?"

"Yes, I guess."

"Then sing it."

Tentatively she began to sing in a small angelic voice that grew stronger as she went:

"Angel, Angel baby
you are the best that your mommy and daddy could
hope for combined.
Angel, Angel baby
I see the light of the world when I look into your eyes.
Angel, darling Angel
with your patience of Job and your heart made of gold
you're our girl.

Angel, Angel baby
my heart swells with joy every time I see you smile.
Angel, Angel baby
no song's quite as sweet as the sound of your sighs.
Angel, darling angel
it fills us with pride just to be by your side, Angel girl.

Oh yes you're our little Angel sent straight from heaven
above."

Though he still sounded gruff, there was softness to the dragon's voice that wasn't there before. "The Queen sings this every night?"

"Yep, I can't sleep until I hear it."

"Well, now you've heard it, so go to sleep."

Chapter Fifteen
Accidental Betrayal

When Zane returned to the barn, he brought food, a bedroll, a set of clean clothes, and a sword- a sword that looked exactly like Veronica's. She had to check the one lying in the straw at her side to make sure that it was still there.

"Where did you get that?" she asked.

"It was a gift from the King," Zane said, placing the sword gently across both hands, presenting it for her examination. "He said I needed to practice with a sword that fit me if I'm going to be in his guard someday."

"Oh." Veronica hadn't realized her sword was but one of a matching set.

Seeing that his sword was a perfect match to Veronica's Zane said, "Whoa, the only difference is that your hilt stone is red, and mine is blue. I had no idea that mine was one of a set."

"Nor did I." Then anxious to move on and at the same time curious to learn more about this boy she added, "You said my dad offered to let you go to Karta for schooling?"

"Yeah, this coming fall. I'll turn twelve during winter season. He said he would be my sponsor so I could attend the Mythscola, so I could learn about and develop my Gifts, but I said no."

"Why?"

"My mom didn't like the idea, she needs me here to run things for her."

"What about your dad?"

"He's my step-dad. He doesn't think much of Gifts. Besides, I don't need to go to some snobby elitist school. I can learn everything I need to right here."

Dalminyo said, "That is absolutely true, especially since *all* you need to know is how to bring me some more food and water."

Veronica shot her equidae a wicked glance then said, "You really should be honored you know; going to the Mythscola is a big deal. Lots of kids who apply are not accepted. Especially those who are not yet twelve."

"Veronica will begin in the fall, though she is not yet twelve," Dalminyo said. "It used to be that only the Demogeron, the nobles, were allowed to attend the Mythscola-"

"Until my mom changed it," Veronica quickly added, giving Dalminyo another sideways frown. "Now, it doesn't matter who your parents are, just what your Gifts are."

"Yes, well, that is the Queen's will." Dalminyo snorted through a mouth full of oats.

"Still," Veronica said aloud to cut Dalminyo off, then in her head added, 'Enough! Don't speak with your mouth full!' Snapping his tail in her direction, Dalminyo rolled his eyes at V and thrust his head down in the trough to sulk. Then to Zane she continued, "You have to compete to get in, and I've never heard of my father wanting to sponsor anyone before."

"Oh, don't get me wrong; I'm honored. The King is a great man. I pledged my allegiance to him with this very sword because of his kindness."

"Why do you have it here now?" Veronica asked, still wondering why her father would give a sword just like hers to a stable boy she had never heard of.

"Well, if you insist on staying here in the stables, then I'll need it to protect you. The hobyahs have been getting bolder and bolder these days."

Veronica was admittedly a bit flattered but said, "I assure you, I do not need your protection, especially from a storybook creature."

"Hobyahs aren't just in storybooks."

"Well, yes, that's true, but they are trapped in the Lower Tiers."

"Not anymore, I've seen them."

"You've *seen* them?" Veronica hopped up, leaving the partially eaten plate of food Zane had brought her lying askew on the straw.

"Well, I've heard them, and I've seen their handiwork, and it isn't pretty. They've been tearing up our chickens and geese for more than a month. Even stole one of our calves."

"Don't be silly. Foxes and wolves do such things all the time."

"Foxes and wolves don't leave little sickles behind." He grabbed a curved blade with a short handle from a workbench in the barn. "Take a look at this. I tell you, there is evil creeping around the tier, and it's getting braver."

Veronica recognized that farm implements of this type were used to harvest tall grass or grain by the un-gifted. But upon closer examination she also saw how razor sharp this one was and that it had strange markings etched into its blade and handle. Still.

"Don't be ridiculous," Veronica stated in her best Princess-at-court voice, trying to disguise her concern. "The Lands are perfectly safe."

Zane's face scrunched slightly on one side. "Oh yeah, then tell me, Princess, why are you hiding in my barn? And why did your father carry the Onoxmon with him when he came through here last week?"

"I doubt my father had the Onoxmon with him," Veronica said warily, seeing Julia look up from her food.

"Yes, he did. It was in his sword. Usually there's an oval hole in the hilt of it, but this time the hole was filled with a huge black stone. It fit perfectly. And it had the mark of the pinnacle sun etched into each side. I asked to touch it, but your father said absolutely not. Hey, does it really do what lore says it can do? Lay waste to entire cities and stuff?"

"Of course not," Veronica said, though in her heart she felt sure legends of the Onoxmon's immense power would someday prove true.

"Oh, is that because your dad can't make it work, or because the Onoxmon is a fake."

"My dad can make it work! He's-"

"Veronica," Julia said, "you really should finish eating and get some rest. We have a long journey ahead of us in the morning."

"Where are you going, anyway?" Zane asked.

Julia replied, "Back to Karta."

"No, we're going to the Valleyridge," Veronica stated.

"I've seen that place," Zane said, "I dreamt about it the other night." Then almost to himself he said, "Same night when I was talking to Ember."

"Ember?" Veronica asked. How would Zane know Ember?

"Yeah, she's my hawken," Zane answered, raising his chin and resting his hands on his hips.

"*Your* hawken?"

"Well, more like a friend. She is a magnificent bird. Long feathers around her face look like some kind of mask. And I'd never seen an orange-ish red like that before I met her. It's like her feathers were dipped in fire or something."

"How do you know her name? I thought you hadn't talked to magical creatures before now."

"Well, that's just what I call her. Wait, is that really her name? I thought it had just come to me... she must have told me. Maybe it was her who showed me the Valleyridge too? I thought it was just a dream, but maybe the place was real. I dreamt of it the night that crazy equidae ran off."

"What do you mean?" Julia asked. She had left her bone and was now on the same side of the stable as Zane and Veronica.

Dalminyo's ears were up and turned slightly toward them, listening, but his head remained down in the trough, making a show of greedily eating the additional oats Zane had given him.

"Well, it was the evening after the King and his men had left. I was cleaning up the stalls and talking to Ember. She had shown up earlier in the day. I really couldn't understand her, but she always listens to my stories and keeps me company while I work. I was telling her about the King's visit, how he must be off on some really important and dangerous mission because he had the Onoxmon with him. She started to act kind of funny, squawking and shaking her wings, and then I said I heard one of the King's men say they would be traveling by way of Bellafons, which is at the tip of the Valleyridge, on their way to the Arch at Bedforda. That's when that crazy equidae, Hellantae, busted down the barn door and ran off into the night. And then Ember flew off too. It was biz-arre." Zane fanned both hands out to his sides for emphasis, then added, "Later that night I had the wildest dream."

"What was it?" Julia asked.

"I dreamt that I was flying over the Valleyridge. I was banking and skimming right across the tree tops at the leading edge of it. Then I shot up high over a big meadow. Below I could see that the King and his men were under attack. They'd been ambushed. The King had leapt from his horse and was now sitting on top of a dragon. It was spec! At first, it looked like he was going to ride it. Then he raised his sword up in both hands like he was going to slay it. But before he could slam down his blade, this really weird green bolt of light hit him in the back and took him out. I think it was navitas. The light came from this guy who was riding the crazy equidae, Hellantae. When the guy looked up, it was the same man who had left Hellantae here at my stable a few days before. Next thing I knew the green-light stuff was headed right up at me. That's when I woke up, and man, was I glad it was just a dream."

Veronica waited numbly for him to continue, but that was where Zane finished, utterly unaware of the horror that now threatened to completely overwhelm her.

"Have you seen Ember since that night?" Julia asked.

"No, she comes and goes all the time. Sometimes I don't see her for weeks." Zane glanced from Julia to Veronica. During his story she had collapsed onto her blankets previously laid out in a clean stall. As he looked down at her, his face darkened. The twinkle of excitement that danced in his eyes during the telling of his tale was now replaced with concern. "Wait, this was just a dream, right? Nothing has really happened to the King has it? Has it?"

The stable was silent as Veronica choked back tears.

"We don't know what has happened to my dad, but I do know that my sister has been kidnapped, and I'm going to get her back." Veronica rolled away. Just in time to hide the hot tears that spilled onto her face. She shifted her head back toward the alleyway, but rather than face him, she peeked out undetected from under the arms now folded around her head.

Turning to Julia, Zane asked, "My dream was real? Well, was it?"

"It might have been a vision through Ember's eyes. Hawken are known for being able to align with the minds of Gifted ones and let them see through their eyes, but perhaps not."

"But if it was real, that means that equidae heard me. I told him where the King would be." He bit his lower lip as his head began to shake ever so slightly. His hands slid along each temple and knotted into fists in his wavy black hair. "What have I done?"

He made a step toward Veronica, but Julia blocked his path. "It's time to sleep now, Master Slayer."

The cheetatarah moved to lie down protectively in the hay at Veronica's back, leaving Zane to stand alone in the middle of the stable. He bowed his head and a wavy black lock fell across his face. For eleven going on twelve, he was taller than most. His frame was still that of a boy, but clearly, a life of manual labor had made him strong. It was also clear that

Zane liked to think of himself as being older than his annuals, both mentally and physically. Tonight however, the solitary figure Veronica saw standing in the barn was still a mere boy, a boy suddenly set adrift in the world of men. She knew how he felt.

Chapter Sixteen
I So Believe in Fairies

The dragon's leg was warm and soft enough, so why was she awake? Sophia blinked hard, trying to clear her head. Then she saw a flicker in the dark. It darted from one part of the fairy castle to another. She didn't move as it approached her. Her eyes adjusted to the dark and she held her breath. A fairy! The first she had ever seen! And to her surprise, it was a boy. He had blonde wavy hair, deep purple garments, and golden wings. Yet he was not girly looking at all. In fact, as he hovered right in front of her, he scowled. Then when their eyes met, he drew his sword. Sophia sat up, and her blanket fell to her waist. Hanging below her throat dangled the necklace given to her by her parents. The square setting was simple yet elegant, consisting of a large almost oval purple amethyst suspended from a chain with a smaller diamond suspended beneath it. Veronica had one just like it with a red ruby instead of the purple stone.

When the fairy saw the necklace around Sophia's neck, he lowered his sword.

Hanging from the belt around his waist was a pouch, emerging from the top of the pouch, a chain. The fairy put his sword away and began to pull the chain, first one arm's length, then another, then another and another until finally at the end of the chain a beautiful purple stone emerged from the pouch. The fairy grabbed the chain above the stone with his left hand while holding the rest of the chain looped like a lariat in his right. As he held it out toward Sophia, she reached down and saw the resemblance to her own and held it out just before the fairy. As the two stones became closer in proximity, both began to glow. A wave of what could only be described as power flowed through her. It started in her chest and rippled out to her limbs, until it tingled through her fingertips.

She jolted backward, falling against the dragon. The great beast shifted in response. The fairy darted to the back of the cave, and by the glow of both gems, Sophia strained to see what he was up to. Taking the stone in both hands, the fairy let the chain fall; he then placed the stone into the top of the Arch, just where the Alistone should go. The little Arch came to life and instead of a wall of stone, it became a shimmering, swirled-up rainbow. As the color dissolved away, Sophia could first see the black of Empty Space, then the light of other Tiers as they flashed by. Just as the Arch began to focus and form a path to its chosen Tier, the dragon stirred.

Reacting to the sound of rustling scales, the fairy shot a panicked look toward Sophia and the dragon, grabbed the chain firmly in his hands, and flew into the Arch. When he had passed beyond the threshold he turned, flew backward, and pulled on the chain. The Alistone, attached to the other end of the chain, popped from its stone cradle and disappeared into the pathway just as the Arch closed.

The dragon readjusted his position but continued to sleep. Reassured that she was not completely alone, that someone now knew where she was, Sophia was eventually able to find sleep too. As she drifted off she could not wait to tell Veronica that she had actually seen a fairy *and* a dragon.

She didn't have to wait long, she told her sister that night in a dream.

Chapter Seventeen
To Valleyridge

Veronica awoke in the morning to find food waiting for her. She ate the bread and brought the apple to Dalminyo. Zane must have been up early and was busy; all the animals in the barn had been fed and watered. Now he sat in the front doorway with a small pack and his sword at his side. His head hung down between drawn up knees. His face was hidden beneath tousled waves of dark hair.

Veronica came and sat across from him, leaning her back against the doorframe opposite him. "Thank you for your hospitality."

Zane raised only slightly. When his blue eyes met hers, he quickly lowered his head back into his hands, but not before she had seen the anguish there. "How can you thank me? I betrayed your father and now he's..."

"Now, we don't know what's become of him," Veronica said, "I do however know what's become of my sister. She has been taken by a man called Lord Leamoldae and is now being held captive by a dragon in a cave frequented by fairies. I don't know where the cave is yet, but I do know that Leamoldae left Sophia with the dragon at this Valleyridge place. That's not where they are now, but it's a place to start. Julia could find it, but she wants me to return home. I need you to tell me how to get there."

"Why are you doing this alone? Why aren't there troops with you?"

Veronica told Zane everything. She told him about her dreams, the one she had the night Sophia was taken and the one she had last night. She told him how KenKarta was preparing for war and how generals were not inclined to listen to kids, even if they were Princesses. She even told him about how her mother was trapped on Dragontier. She didn't know why, but V felt as if she could trust this boy, as if she had known him much longer than mere hours. And though he obviously blamed himself for what happened to her father, she knew it was not really Zane's fault. If he had given away her father's position, it certainly wasn't on purpose.

Zane said, "I won't tell you how to get to the Valley-ridge, but I will show you."

"No." But she could not help but be taken by the fact that he wanted to go with her.

"Fine, then you go home with Julia and I'll go by myself."

Veronica shook her head.

Zane added, "If there is one thing you should know about me, Princess, it's that I pay my debts and I am now greatly indebted to your family."

"*Now?*" Dalminyo said as he walked up to the doorway coming out of the stable. "Have you not always felt indebted to your Royal Family?"

Ignoring Dalminyo, yet feeling a little hurt by Zane's comment, Veronica said, "You feel indebted, do you? Well, I wouldn't want to stand in the way of you paying a debt. As long as you can be useful, I guess I'll let you come."

"What?" Dalminyo bellowed. "And just how do you

propose he keeps up?"

Veronica just turned and looked at her equidae with a thin smile.

"Oh no, no way! There is no way I am letting the likes of him ride on me!"

"Dalminyo," Veronica cooed as she walked up to him. Cupping her hands around his head, she looked into his striking green eyes. "Are you, a noble member of the Equidae line, not Bonded to me, and duty bound to serve me, your Royal Princess of KenKarta?"

"Don't you try and pull rank on me."

"You could always choose to let him ride with us. Besides, this would give you a chance to prove how strong you are. Then the other equidaes couldn't tease you anymore about only carrying a lightweight like me. But if you don't want to, I'll understand. There's no shame. Traveling with two is very difficult, and I would never dream of pulling rank on you."

Ears pressed against his head Dalminyo said, "I choose who rides me!"

"Of course you do, my noble, handsome steed."

Dalminyo whipped his tail from side to side, bowed his neck and pawed the ground in frustration, then announced, "For the good of the Lands I will allow it, but if he's not capable, I will not be held responsible."

Zane protested, "Not capable? I'm capable!"

Veronica said, "Of course you are, now let's get going before someone sees us."

They gathered their things and mounted Dalminyo,

Veronica in front and Zane behind.

"Hold on tight, Zane, and stay low," Veronica said.

"You don't have to worry about me. I'm a great rider."

"Perhaps, but this is different than riding a horse."

"Whatever, let's go."

Dalminyo told Veronica in a voice only she could hear to hold on and added something about 'teaching this stable boy a lesson.'

In a blink, before Veronica could stop him, the equidae lifted his rear end ever so slightly to unseat Zane, then spun around so fast that he was now facing the opposite direction.

Zane found himself sitting in the dirt. Dalminyo looked smugly down at him, and Veronica held her breath.

Wide-eyed, all Zane could exclaim through a roar of laughter was, "That was the Pinn!" He got up, brushed himself off, and then bowed to Dalminyo in exaggerated ceremony saying, "Point taken, Sir, with your permission."

With a great deal a satisfaction Dalminyo gave his head a slight bow and turned sideways so Zane could remount. As he got situated, Julia came out of the barn.

"Ready to return home then are we?" she asked.

"We're off to the Valleyridge, Julia," Veronica proclaimed, and with that they were gone.

Standing alone in front of the barn, Julia purred to herself. "Well, no one can say I didn't try."

The truth was she had resigned herself to this earlier when she had heard Veronica speaking of her dreams. The sisters had somehow formed a subconscious connection they'd never had before, one that should get stronger the closer the two girls got to one another. Yes, she was a child, but Veronica did have the best chance of finding Sophia. Making her go back would serve no useful purpose, save protect Veronica, and the price for that could be Sophia. Veronica had already decided that she was willing to risk her own safety to save her sister, but was Julia? She had already lost one of her Princesses, could she risk losing the other? At first the answer had been no, but now she saw things differently. Sophia was in, no doubt, great peril. As of right now, Veronica had the best chance of finding her. Though still a child, Veronica was Gifted and strong. Strong enough to face what lay ahead? That Julia had no way of knowing, but for better or worse they were on this quest together. She coiled her muscles and leapt forward.

Zane must be in awe, Veronica thought, remembering her first ride on an equidae. The world immediately around them was a blur. In order to get his bearings, he would have to look off in the distance. Veronica had told him to do this to keep from getting sick. Now that Dalminyo was up to speed, the ride was amazingly smooth, however they couldn't sit upright because the wind was fierce. Veronica was leaning forward, her head out over Dalminyo's neck, her forearms placed in the braces on either side. Padded and covered in soft leather, the braces that extended out from each side of the pommel were the main thing that made an equidae saddle different from that of a horse's. If you plan on riding any long distance at speed, they're needed. So were lightly tinted spectacles. Veronica was wearing some, and about now Zane surely wished he were too. Without them you couldn't look straight ahead without watering eyes. She had offered him her spare pair back at the barn, but the way he crinkled up his nose had told her that their delicate oval frames were far too girly for him, not like the ones soldiers wear. He said he'd be fine, that he didn't need them. Would he ask for them when they stopped? It was that or look like he was crying all the time. That was even less manly than the glasses, wasn't it?

Zane sat behind the saddle. Veronica had told him to place his legs against the cantle and wrap his arms around her to the pommel in front to brace himself. Then he was to lay his chest and head down on her back. The first he had done, but his arms were bowed unnaturally outward, and he was still holding his body up away from her back as to not touch her. She'd never been hugged by a boy who wasn't family, and this was a bit like a hug that would last for hours. So even she, who recognized the action's practical necessity, initially found the prospect gauche. But that was just silly! There was no other way to ride double. This was no time to be childish. Still, she couldn't blame him for not wanting to be that close to her. He must be mortified.

The minutes passed. The wind tore at them. Surely his muscles must be straining by now. How on Tier was he going to be able to hold that position all day? He must be stronger than she thought. This was ridiculous. She'd have to say something. Then in her head she heard Dalminyo: "Zane, I'm feeling a lot of drag. Are you sitting up?"

"No."

"Well, are you as close to Veronica as you can get?"

"No."

"Well, come on, stable-boy, it's bad enough I've got to carry your dead weight around. The least you can do is try to be aerodynamic. Every gap air can pass through creates drag. Drag makes me work harder. I don't want to work any harder than I have to, especially for the hired help."

"All right." Zane sighed and let his body relax ever so slightly until his chest came to rest on Veronica's back. "How's that?"

"Better," Dalminyo replied.

"I'm not squishing you, am I?" Zane said over the wind.

Twisting her head toward him to be heard Veronica said, "No, that's fine." But she miscalculated, turned too far, right into his face. It caused his lips to brush her cheek. Her mind screamed turn away, turn away! But she couldn't. Instead, frozen in embarrassment she stammered, "I'm... so sorry."

"No worries."

His soft, throaty reply lingered against her cheek and ear. For a moment her body seemed to be... melting. What was that about? Maybe it was trying to disappear so she could avoid further humiliation. The slight smile on Zane's face brightened when he turned his head aside just in time to see Julia appear. The sight was impressive. The world behind the great cat moved by in a blur, but Julia looked to be loping effortlessly, matching Dalminyo's pace. She was beautiful to behold, her fur waving and purple spots appearing brighter as rays of shine rippled off her fluid movements.

"About time you caught up," Dalminyo mocked.

"Yes well, I thought I'd stop off for a bite to eat, give you a head start," Julia teased back. "You know how hard it is for me to run this slow."

"I'm not going back!" Veronica shouted across the wind to Julia.

"I know," Julia replied as they ran on. "Where you go, I go, my Princess."

Chapter Eighteen
In the Shine of Day

When Sophia awoke she saw dayshine streaming in from the mouth of the cave. The dragon was nowhere in sight. She crept to the opening and peered out. The shine was blinding after the darkness of the cavern and it took a few moments for her eyes to adjust. When they did, her mouth dropped open.

There in the shine was Daelkay the dragon, but he looked nothing as he had in the cave. In its dim light he had seemed a dull gray and flat brown. Here in the bright, however, he looked amazing, dazzling even. His individual scales caught the rays of shine and took on a luminosity all their own. His throat, belly, and the lower half of his tail were all a kind of grayish blue, like a cloudy sky. In contrast, the top of his body was a vivid combination of purple, royal blue and a tinge of red. The further from his head, the more brilliant the colors. There in the bright of day, crouched on all fours with his wings raised and partially spread, his head held high to enjoy the warmth of the shine, Daelkay looked nothing short of magnificent.

Standing in the mouth of the cave, Sophia said, "You're beautiful."

Daelkay opened his eyes.

Sophia was still wearing a nightgown and slippers. The garment's pale color made her skin seem darkly tanned in contrast. Her hair was pulled back in two braids, one at each side of her head, but some hair had worked its way out so that loose strands hung down to frame her face.

"You are beautiful as well, Princess."

Sophia smiled then took in the view. She was standing on a large flat ledge part way up a mountain. Right in front of her only a short distance away another slightly smaller symmetrical mountain rose. Between the two peaks sprawled a large open valley. Below and to the right at the base of the mountains, a large plain stretched out as far as she could see. Close up it looked mostly brown, but in the distance it looked red, red with purple and green highlights.

"What is this place?"

"It is a place where Dragons and Fairies and other Mythical creatures once came to celebrate. But that was long ago in a far simpler and happier time." Daelkay eyed Sophia. "Are you going to try and run away from me?"

"Where would I go?" she asked, looking at the rocky, mostly barren slopes leading away from the cavern's ledge where she now stood.

"Nowhere really, but I might hurt you while scooping you up in my talons if you ran." He clicked one of his menacing-looking claws on the stone surface where he lounged.

"I don't think you would."

"And why is that?"

"'Cause I bet you're a great flyer!"

"As a matter of fact, I am. Would you like to see?"

"Would I!"

"Come then, climb up between my wings."

"Oh, no, I couldn't. I'd be way too afraid."

"Afraid of what?"

"Afraid of what it would feel like!"

"It feels like..." Daelkay stretched out his neck and turned his face to the sky. "Like freedom. Except for when you dive, then it feels a lot like the sensation of going through an Arch."

"Oh, I hate that! My mom took me through an Arch one time. It scared me half to death. My stomach got a big knot in it, then went up in my throat. Even though I held her as tight as I could, I couldn't stop shaking. I cried and cried when we had to go back home. It was awful. I'm never doing it again!"

"Overcoming one's fears is part of growing up."

"I'm sorry, but no thank you. Can I still watch you fly though?"

"As you ask." The dragon launched himself into the air, creating a wake that blew back Sophia's hair and pajamas. He rose high in the sky then began to swoop and drive back toward Virtier. He looked surprisingly graceful. Then he dropped below view on the backside of the mountain. A few moments later, Daelkay blasted back over the ridge flying hard and low. He blew right over top of where Sophia stood, then pulled up sharp and turned back to land on the ledge.

Sophia was tier struck at the display, then a bit fearful when she saw his face. His nostrils flared. The ridges above his eyes were drawn down toward his snout. The expression was fierce, even more than usual for a dragon.

"Get into the cave," he ordered.

"Why?" Sophia asked, wondering what could have changed Daelkay's mood so quickly.

"Now!" the dragon said so forcefully that a lick of flame escaped his mouth.

Screaming, Sophia ran for her life into the cave. She didn't stop until she reached the back wall where the Fairy Arch was.

Oh, how she wished that fairy would come back and take her with him. Maybe she would go through an Arch again after all, if it meant getting out of here. If the Arch would just open up. Of course without an Alistone it couldn't be opened from this side. Her necklace, what if... She took the necklace over her head and held up the purple stone to the hole at the top of the Arch. It was dark and hard to see. I need more light, she thought, and with that the crystals on the ceiling began to glow.

With a slight smile she wiped the tears from her cheeks and turned to examine the hole closer. It was square shaped with a slender notch cut into the bottom of it, a cut that might allow for the diamond that hung below the amethyst in her necklace. She slipped the stone into the hole and the

Arch emitted a soft hum. It was working! Within an array of light and color, the wall of stone within the Arch dissolved and in its place she could see the black of Empty Space. In the distance she saw a few blurred lights but they were all out of focus.

From behind her came, "Sophia."

She jumped and pulled the necklace from the Arch. Turning to face the approaching beast, she hid the necklace behind her back.

Lowering his head to see her clearer, the dragon said, "What are you doing?"

"Nothing!" she said eagerly, forcing a smile. "Just what you said, I'm in the cave; please don't be mad at me. I don't know what I did wrong."

"You did nothing wrong, I just saw something over the mountain that concerns me."

"What'd you see?"

"Nothing."

"Is it my daddy? Is he coming for me?"

"No, your father is not coming. You should not hold out hope for that."

"Why? My mommy and daddy love me. If you don't take me home they'll come for me, and they are not going to be happy."

Looking around, he said, "How did you make these crystals glow?"

"I just did!" She was still a bit scared and trying to defend herself.

"It would be best if you were quiet for a while now." The dragon's eyes were not focused on her. He seemed distracted. Just like when Sophia talked to her daddy, but he didn't hear, even though he was standing right next to her. It made her mad.

"Why, am I scaring *you?*"

Her tone caused the dragon to lose his temper just a bit, which is a dangerous thing for a dragon to do. He snorted, and fire belched from his nose. It came right at Sophia, who ducked in fear. It scorched the air but not her. She huddled against the Arch wall.

"This conversation is over," the dragon stated. He turned his back to her, once again blocking the exit with his massive frame.

Chapter Nineteen
In a Battle's Wake

It had been a long day of hide and seek across the northernmost edge of the Palousoa. They ran hour after hour with small mountains skirted by forests of pine and fir rising to their left. At the same time, the fertile rolling hills, where Veronica knew farmers grew much of KenKarta's grain supply, sprawled off into the distance on their right. Their course varied only when necessary to avoid the prying eyes of other travelers or field workers. Then as the day drew near to its end, Veronica's party came to the edge of a well-groomed forest. The trees were large but spread far enough apart that the shine still managed to reach the ground. Even so, little vegetation dotted the forest floor, and the tree branches began well above Dalminyo's head. This made it easy for them to pass, as riders and steed, but the equidae still did no more than trot once they came across the dirt road. Zane said he had seen this narrow wagon trail in Ember's vision and that following it would lead them to where the King had been attacked. Julia's anxiety grew in accordance with their proximity to the road however, so now they proceeded along its edge with ever-growing caution.

Topping a slight rise in the road, Dalminyo and Julia slowed to a walk. A clearing opened before them. Veronica didn't need Zane to tell her that this was the place Ember had shown him. The signs of a battle were everywhere. Patches of ground were scorched and debris was scattered, a broken shield here, a sword there, an overturned wagon across the way. Next to the wagon, still in its harness, lay the dead body of a camallo, the sizable beast of burden that had been pulling it. Several large carrion birds hopped away from one horse carcass and onto another.

Veronica's heart raced. Further into the meadow lay bodies of men as well. Some were members of her father's honor guard; she recognized their uniforms. But the others, the others were foreign to her. They had long white hair, incredibly pale skin (was that because they were dead?), and noses that looked more like an animal's than a man's. From this distance, V couldn't be sure they were even human. She tried to dismount, but Zane was in her way. His arms were still around her, hands resting on the saddle's pommel, even though they'd stopped.

"Veronica, wait," he said quietly, tightening his grip ever so slightly.

"You three stay there!" Julia snapped from ahead of them. "Don't come any closer. I'm going to have a look at things."

Dalminyo drifted toward the tree line, away from the battle ground.

Veronica could feel the tension in Zane's body behind her. She turned her head ever so slightly. "Don't worry, Zane, he's not here. I don't know where he is, but I know my father is not one of those men lying in that field." She closed her eyes hoping to clear her head, but instead felt a faint plea.

"Ember?" Veronica said, turning in the saddle away from the meadow to the trees.

"I felt her too, but where?" Zane asked.

"There!" Veronica said, pointing to the top of a tall tree where a splash of red appeared to be caught in the canopy of green branches.

"Veronica," Julia said as she approached them from the meadow. "Neither your father nor his sword are here."

"Thank Pinn for that," Veronica stated. "But look, Ember is hurt up in that tree. We've got to get her."

"How?" Zane asked.

"Are you afraid of heights?"

"No."

"Good, then you'll go up."

"Okay, but I can't get up there; the nearest branch is thirty feet up."

"Can you climb a rope?"

"Yeah, I climb them to the hay lofts all the time."

"I think I saw some on that supply wagon over there. Go and get it, would you?"

"Okay, but..." Zane drifted toward the wagon, scrunching up one side of his face. "Julia, why don't you just climb up there?"

Julia answered, "I will try if necessary, but I fear I am too heavy to go out on those upper branches where Ember is tangled. So I think it best to see how Veronica's plan works first."

As Zane poked around the wagon, Veronica untied her bow and quiver from Dalminyo's saddle. They had been made by a grandfather she never knew, a master bowman and bowsmith who had died before her birth. His bows were sought after across the Lands, not only for their strength and accuracy, but for their beauty as well. She stroked the smooth re-curved surface of the polished wood. The angle of the shot would be steep and the arrow's balance would be thrown off by the rope, but she could make it.

Zane returned with a long length of cord. "Wow, you

should see the size of the rats over there!"

"Rats?"

"Yeah, white ones. And they've got weird pink eyes. I've never seen any like 'um."

"Creepy. It's a good thing my dad isn't here. He hates rats more than anything on tier." Veronica studied the rope in Zane's hand. It wasn't very thick, but looked strong enough to support Zane. "Good, now tie a knot in it about every arm's length."

When that had been accomplished, Veronica tied one end to the arrow right behind the tip. As she nocked the arrow on her bowstring, Zane grabbed the bow from her hand saying, "Here, you'd better let me do this. It'll be a tough shot getting it over that branch up there, especially with this rope attached."

More than a bit annoyed, Veronica said, "You don't want to shoot it over the branch."

"Sure you do." Zane took aim and shot. The arrow flew fairly true and managed to just make it over the branch. The problem was that the rope was not long enough to reach all the way up to the branch and back down. So as the arrow fell back to the ground it brought the rope back down with it.

"No, you don't," Veronica said, snatching her bow back from Zane. She retrieved the arrow and coiled the rope neatly at her feet. Then before Zane could interfere, she once again nocked the arrow onto the string, took aim, and whispered, "Pilkraft." The black arrowhead began to glow yellow. She drew in a long breath, held it, let the arrow fly, and watched it hit the mark. It sank deep, much deeper than a normal arrow ever could, into the tree trunk right above the closest branch. The end of the cord now dangled about waist high off the ground. "There you go, Zane. Now we'll see if you can climb better than you shoot."

He sneered, and gave her a slight roll of the eyes before walking over and giving the rope a tentative tug. He pushed his hand roughly through his unruly mane. Obviously, like anyone, he didn't like to be shown up.

Oh well, too bad, so sad. He shouldn't have touched her bow. Then because she could tell what he was thinking she said, "Don't worry, it won't break. That arrow was forged in the halls of Askard by Mythicals. My uncle Rick gave it to me."

"Sure, sure, your uncle Rick. I don't suppose that's King Rick of the Askard?"

"Yes, it is. Why, do you know him?"

"Ah no, no, can't say that I do. But isn't it spectacular for us that *you* do."

Now what was his problem? Boys were baffling. Zane muttered something she couldn't understand, grabbed the rope, and began to climb.

Chapter Twenty
To Scratch an Itch

The silence had lasted the rest of the day. Daelkay had turned his back and left Sophia to occupy herself in the fairy castle, which she had done. By the time the dragon had turned his head back to see what she was up to, Sophia was feeling better. She was actually in the middle of the castle's courtyard dancing. The little crystals above were blazing, and she was hopping to and fro. When she realized Daelkay was watching, she beamed.

"Do you want to see my new dance? I just made it up." She was feeling altogether silly. Sophia had spent the better part the day cleaning, dusting, and mopping the floors using supplies bottled with fairy magic she'd found inside. Now, all clean and lit up, the room gave her comfort, even confidence.

She plopped down in front of him and asked in a small voice, "Why is your Lord 'Moldy' having you keep me?"

"Your father has something he wants," Daelkay replied.

"What?" Sophia asked.

"The Onoxmon."

"Oh, he won't give that to anybody."

"Really, so you know what it is?"

"Yes, it's a big black stone."

"Do you know what it does?"

"Yes, it fits in his sword and with it he can make the ground shake."

"Your father can make it do *this*?"

"Of course he can, he's the King."

"You've seen this?"

"Sure. One time just Mom and Veronica, Daddy and me were in this meadow and he put the tip of his sword on the ground with both hands on the hilt, and the ground giggled all over. It rattled me right onto my bottom. It was fun." She laughed, and then stopped abruptly.

"What?"

"It's just, I wasn't suppose to tell anyone that."

"Why? You would think the King would want everyone to know how powerful he is. If he can wield the Onoxmon, it proves he is the rightful King."

"Daddy said if people knew he could do that it would scare them," Sophia explained. "He says it's his job to help people feel safe."

"I did not think he had the strength or discipline to ever master it," Daelkay said almost to himself.

"What! My daddy's super strong. He's the best King ever!"

"Is that what he tells you?"

"No, I just know it. The only thing he's better at than being King is being my daddy." Then she paused, crossing her arms and cocking her head to one side. "Hey? You just said you didn't think... Do you know my daddy?"

The dragon's heavy lids slid to cover the brightness of his blue eyes. He drew in a long, slow breath then looked at Sophia. "I did once, before you were born."

"Daelkay and Dale. Your guys' names are almost the same. Once Daddy told me he almost Bonded with a Dragon whose name was like his, but then the dragon chose someone else... It wasn't you, was it?"

"Yes, it was."

She huffed. "Why wouldn't you Bond with my daddy?"

"Because I had not yet met you," Daelkay said. His gaze left hers and seemed to take him somewhere far way.

"What? He was just a kid, I wasn't even born then."

"What I mean to say is, I misjudged what kind of a man he would one day become. I chose someone, who at the time I thought was stronger, someone I thought would make a better leader."

"It made him sad."

"What did?"

"When you chose someone else, he was sad. It still makes him sad." Daelkay said nothing so Sophia went on, "Mommy says that living through the hard and sad things in our lives makes us stronger."

"Ah, your mother. It is her strength that makes your father seem strong."

"No," Sophia said with a shake of her head. "Mommy says people are wrong when they say that. She says together she and Daddy are both far stronger than they could ever be apart. She says they complement each other. Daddy says it suits him just fine if people think Mommy has greater Gifts than him. He says there are advantages to being underestimated."

"Is that what he says?"

"Yep."

"Sophia, do you know what an evil man would do with the Onoxmon?"

"He would destroy things, armies, cities, and things. If he knew how, that is, if he had the Gift to make it work. Mommy says it's a rare Gift though. That means not many people have it, even fewer can actually control it." Then her lips pulled into a thin frown while her forehead crinkled up.

"Your *Lord Moldy* doesn't have that Gift does he?"

"Yes, it appears he does."

"Is that why he wants the Onoxmon, to destroy things?"

"Yes, it is."

"Well, my father would never give it to him."

"You are correct, not even to save his own life. When he was captured he did not have it, and he would not tell where he hid it." Daelkay paused, tilting his head. His gaze probed Sophia's face. Her forehead was furrowed and she'd begun to gnaw at her lower lip. "If you knew where it was, would you tell, Sophia?"

"I don't know where it is."

"But if you did, would you tell?"

"No." Her head made the slightest movement from side to side as she blinked back the threat of tears.

"Even if it meant saving your father's Life?"

"What!"

"That is the question my Lord Leamoldae is posing to your father now. Choose the stone, or choose you, Sophia. If your father gives Lord Leamoldae the Onoxmon, then my Lord will let you go. What do you think your father will do?"

"Gi-give him the stone?" Sophia stuttered.

"I think he will too. The trouble is evil men cannot be trusted to keep their word."

She looked up at him through damp lashes. "Can dragons?"

Daelkay raised his shoulders to the roof of the cave and rubbed his scales to scratch an itch. He did not answer the small child sitting before him.

She pushed back the loose stands of hair from her face

and wiped at her eyes then sniffed. "You're not evil, Daelkay. Why do you do his bidding?"

"I gave my word."

"Didn't he give his word too? My daddy says, when it comes to Bonding and marriage, you must choose wisely." Then watching the dragon scratch his back on the ceiling she asked, "What's wrong with you, Daelkay?"

"There's something lodged beneath my scale. I find it troublesome."

"Would you like me to get it for you?"

The dragon stopped scratching and turned his head back to squarely face Sophia. "Why would you do that?"

"You're in pain. I can help, so I should."

"Is it truly that simple?"

"You'd do the same for me, wouldn't you, Daelkay?" Sophia asked as she crawled up the dragon's side. "Which one is it?" She straddled his back and slid her hands between his shoulders, careful not to bump her head on the roof, which was now just inches above. "Here? ... No? How about here?"

"Oh, that's the one." Daelkay shuddered as Sophia hit the spot.

She slipped her hand beneath the scale and felt something hard, cool, and oval shaped. It was stuck tight. She had to put her other hand under the scale too, which brought a slight wince from the great beast. She pried with her small fingers trying to get a grip. When it came loose, its weight was surprisingly heavy. With both hands she removed it, held it in her lap, and examined it in the room's shine. She was far enough away from the crystal ceiling of the fairy court that things were shadowy. Yet as she turned it in her hand, she could see light glint off an ancient symbol etched deep in the center of each side. The symbol was a spiral surrounded by ten meandering lines of varying length extending outward. It was the symbol of the Pinnacle Sun. The symbol that now represented the Kingdom of KenKarta. Beneath her, the dragon sighed with relief and Sophia froze in fear. A pulse of panic surged and shuttered through her core.

"Thank you, Sophia, that is a reprieve. What was it?"

Snapping from her trance she replied, "What?"

"What was under my scale?"

"Just some old stone," Sophia said as she tossed it away with trembling hands to the back of the cave. It rattled and chattered loudly as it struck the tiles at the back of the fairy court and skittered to a stop. What Sophia said was only partly true. Yes, it was an old stone, in fact a very old stone, but it was not just *some* old stone. Even in the low light the Princess knew exactly what it was. Sophia had just tossed aside the most powerful weapon known to her Land. The Onoxmon.

As she crawled silently down, Daelkay said, "Thank you, Sophia, I feel as if a great weight has been lifted from my old bones."

Sitting down on the floor of the fairy castle, Sophia was overcome with a sense of dread. Something very bad must have happened to her daddy because the King would never give up the Onoxmon willingly. Her voice was tentative as she asked, "Daelkay, where is my father?"

"Child, that is not something you need to know."

"Can I go to him?"

"No."

"Can you take me?"

"I will not take you to that horrid place."

"A *horrid* place! That's where he is? Why? Could you bring him to me?"

"I could."

"Will you?"

"If it is my master's wish."

"Please Daelkay, please! My daddy is a good man, he doesn't belong in a horrid place. Please, I'll do anything. Just save my daddy!"

"Anything, Sophia?" the dragon asked.

What was that look on his face? Did he know? Did he want her to give him the Onoxmon? Oh, no! Trembling she said, "Let me be your master. I would never ask you to do anything evil."

"You know not of what you speak," the dragon scoffed.

"Yes, I do. I know that if someone betrays their Bond to you, you can be free to choose another. That evil man took me; he made you help against your will. That's evil, so you don't have to be Bonded to him anymore."

"You presume that kidnapping you was against my will."

"I know it was!" Sophia began to cry. "I know you don't want to hurt me."

"Child, you presume too much."

Chapter Twenty-One
The Unucornubelluacomis

Once Veronica had secured the rope to the tree with her arrow, Zane scaled the distance with relative ease. She was impressed with his athleticism. He nimbly moved through the branches without fear. Wow, he was strong for his age. Yet, he was so gentle with Ember, tucked her in his shirt and cradled the bird protectively, all the way back to the ground. With full lips drawn and forehead creased, concern for the hawken was clear around his cerulean eyes. It touched her. And his eyes, so deep and rich in their blue, how easy it would be to get lost in them.

What a ridiculous thought!

The ache in Veronica's heart had lessened somewhat to find that her father was not among the dead in the meadow, and Ember was still alive. Yet still, she couldn't help but feel a bit disconcerted. What were those rat-men sprawled dead in the meadow beside the soldiers of KenKarta? Was *that* what held her father? She pushed those thoughts away in order to help Ember.

When he got down from the tree, Zane's jaw was set, and he wouldn't even talk to her. What was that about? It confused V, and even hurt a bit. Was *he* sulking? Just because he was a boy, must he think he'd be better with a bow than her? Oh, he was so arrogant. Perhaps he was worried about Ember. More likely, he just didn't like being around her, was regretting that he'd even come. Veronica had no time to worry about it. Why should she even care what some conceited boy thought of her? She didn't.

Her focus had rightfully been on Ember. The hawken was injured, unable to fly, and dehydrated, but thankfully, Julia felt that with rest the noble bird could recover.

The cheetatarah had led them to a lovely place to camp for the night. A short distance into the woods, it nevertheless felt like a world away from the carnage left behind in the meadow. They had covered the bodies as best they could before leaving, and Veronica vowed to make sure that all who had fallen protecting her father received a hero's burial upon their return to Karta. Their campsite was now set at the edge of an enormous lake where the approach to the water was gradual, open, and arid, with trees being sparse. Further down the shores on either side of the lake, however, the terrain became hillier and ever more covered with evergreen trees. On the far side of the tranquil water, the individual trees became a forest and off in the distance above were mountains still covered with snow at their peaks.

It had been a dusty, difficult, disheartening day, and Veronica decided to take a dip in the lake at the edge of their camp to clean up. Except for Ember, who was asleep, no one else was around. Dalminyo was off eating grass somewhere and Zane and Julia were hunting for dinner. So she stripped down to her undergarments and dove in.

The water was chilly, but clean and clear. She opened her eyes to see that the bottom dropped away much quicker than one would expect. She surfaced, drew in a deep breath, and dove down to the depths. Once she was as deep as she could go, she just let herself hang there, suspended in space and time. Her muscles relaxed as she let the silence of the water fill her head, clear her mind of the troubles her world above now held. For the first time since her mother had left she felt at peace. She wished she could linger, just hide for awhile, but her lungs were beginning to protest.

Then amid the cool blue gloom she saw a flicker of light. She squinted to investigate. There, coming toward her out of the deep appeared a canary yellow face with a pair of bulging black eyes and between them was a large white dorsal fin. And the fin was glowing! She screamed. Then she chased the rush of bubbles that escaped her lips.

She broke the surface and another scream exploded from her chest as she exhaled the last of the spent air from her lungs. She swam frantically to the water's edge, not wasting a second to turn and look behind her. As soon as her feet could touch the soft muddy bottom, she tried to run. She could feel it, whatever it was, shoving the water behind her, coming closer.

She thrust through waist-deep water. Her mind raced. 'Please, please, please don't eat me!'

"Eat you? I would never eat you, little one," came a soft gentle voice from behind her.

Veronica spun around to see not a fish with a glowing fin, but the head of a single horned creature with bright yellow skin smooth as a frog's rising from the water. She stopped and stammered, "Wha- what are you?"

The creature continued to walk up onto the shore. Not only did this beast have a long stout neck, but a body to match. It was huge. Bigger than the camallo or even the supply wagon that beast had pulled back in the meadow. Then with the water still dripping off its back, this beast raised an emerald green serpent-like tail out of the water and wrapped it back behind itself.

"I am a Unicornubelluacomis... but you may call me Bella."

"Veronica!" Zane burst through the tree line with his sword drawn in alarm. Staring up at the beast, he stopped. "What the byss?"

Veronica quickly sank down in the water so Zane would not see her without all her clothes on. Feeling her embarrassment, because unucornubelluacomis are astutely attuned to the feelings of those around them, Bella turned her head slowly to Zane and said, "I think you should wait back in the woods for a few moments, kind Squire."

Mouth gapping, Zane glanced past the giant beast to Veronica sitting in the water.

She waved for him to go. "Get out of here, Zane!"

His eyes rounded with bewilderment. His lips moved, but no words came. Instead, Zane just nodded and slowly did as he was told. Then backing up into the forest, still within earshot, he began a conversation with himself. "Girls are so weird. First she's yelling at me to come, then she's yelling at me to go. Just make up your mind already. Pinn, she's a royal pain. But what the byss is that thing by the lake?" Clearly aggravated, still gripping his sword with both hands, Zane extended his arms and yelled, "I'm not going anywhere until I get some answers." Before the last words had left his lips he swung the sword wide as he spun around in a circle to vent his frustration.

Unfortunately, Zane had miscalculated how close he was to a tree. He hit it so hard with his sword that he lost his grip and fell to the ground but not before the blade lodged deep into the tree's trunk. Disoriented, the boy warrior jumped immediately back up and looked around. Grabbing the hilt of the sword, he grunted. "That's just spectacular."

Veronica looked away and tried to suppress a giggle.

The beast on the beach was watching her, waiting.

Mere moments after Zane disappeared into the woods, Veronica was out of the water, dried and dressed. While doing so she began to feel better, better in fact than she'd felt in days. Did it have anything to do with Bella?

"It does," replied the extremely large, yet seemingly gentle giant.

"You can read my mind?" V asked because she had not been projecting her thoughts as one did when trying to talk to a Mythical creature without speaking.

"Yes, but more importantly I can read your feelings. You have a lot going on in that head of yours, little one. You're quite a jumble, a mix of emotions. I thought you could use some help, some rest, so I took the liberty of soothing you. We can discuss your concerns further, but first I must identify and relieve the pain I feel."

"You're hurt?"

"No, not I, but somewhere close by there is a being in great pain. Is one of your companions injured?"

Veronica looked over to the bush where they had made a sick bed for Ember. She appeared awake now, her fragile chest heaving with discomfort as she strained to breath. "Yes, a hawken with us has been hurt, but how did you know?"

"I am empathic. I feel the pain of others. Please bring her to me so that I can put a stop to this," Bella said, lying down with a heavy thud that shook the very ground under Veronica's feet.

The Princess moved to pick up Ember just as Zane reappeared from the forest.

"Now, do you care to tell me what's going on here, Your Highness?"

"Hi, Zane," Veronica said with an impish smile, a touch of euphoria in her voice.

Zane stopped short and just stared at her.

"In a way, you are correct, young Squire. It is a bit like she's under a spell," Bella said to Zane.

"Who are you and what are you doing in my head?" Zane snapped at the massive bright yellow creature lying on the beach with her very large, almost web-like feet tucked up close. Her green tail was scaly and wrapped around her body and over her back. The rest of her amazingly smooth skin glistened. Despite her bulk, there was something undeniably elegant about her. "How did-"

"There, there, one so young should not worry so," the unucornubelluacomis said.

"Zane, this is Bella. Isn't she wonderful? She's going to help Ember."

"Spec-" Zane managed before stopping. His gaze followed Veronica as she carried Ember over to the waiting leviathan. Then he too came to stand before the creature, hands helping V to support Ember's limp body as they offered the hawken up to Bella.

Her head was bigger than Zane's torso. Then Veronica felt the gaze of Bella's bulging liquid black eyes envelop her. V felt no fear as Bella lowered her neck and brought the horn on her forehead down on top of Ember. As in the water when Veronica first saw it, the horn began to glow. When Bella touched her horn to Ember, the red hawken was illuminated from within. A warmth and well-being radiated from her and washed outward like a wave from a stone dropped in a pond. Then, much too quickly, the light subsided, and the wave was past. Only Bella's horn glowed faintly.

"That was spectacular, completely spec," Zane said, his eyes a bit glassy.

Dreamily Veronica added, "Look, Ember is healed. Hello there, beautiful angel."

"Yes, hello beautiful angel," Zane repeated, staring not at the bird but at Veronica, whose waist-long blonde hair was now unbraided. Moments ago it had been wet, but as Ember healed, it had dried, apparently a result of the energy that had passed through them all. Now it was free to frame her face and spill over her shoulders.

"Hello, Bella," Veronica heard Julia say from the edge of the tree line, "I was hoping you might find us here." The cheetatarah had witnessed the end of the healing just as she returned to camp.

"Why Julia, it is wonderful to see you. I should have known it was you who brought these lovely children to my lake. How are you?"

"Feeling better with each passing moment, now that I'm with you. We are all in need of your company, Bella, but you might need to hold back a little. I fear your presence is a tad overwhelming for my young charges there." Julia nodded to Zane and Veronica.

The two were still standing on the beach. Veronica stared at Ember who was now upright and perched on her arm. As the bird stretched her newly mended wing, Veronica stroked the feathers as if they were the most beautiful things she'd ever seen. In turn, Zane reached out to stroke Veronica's hair. She looked at him with a tranquil smile. Then through the haze in her head Veronica heard Bella and Julia speaking again in the distance.

"Oh, perhaps I have over done it a smidge, but Julia,

both their emotions were in such a jumble. I felt real trauma."

"Yes, it's true. They've been through a lot, but our journey is not complete. So I can't have them drunk on your love, Bella."

"Very well, but at least I can bring them comfort for just one night." The giant cooed as she extinguished her horn.

V felt as if she'd awakened from a wonderful dream. She realized that Zane's hand was gently twirling a strand of her hair. When she looked at him, Zane just looked back, mouth slightly turned up, waiting. Somewhere in the distant reaches of her mind, Veronica recalled that to have a boy look at her with such open admiration should cause embarrassment. Yet right now, meeting Zane's gaze seemed very natural, comforting even. Veronica simply smiled back at him then turned her face skyward as Ember took flight to try out her newly mended wing. Nightfall was creeping across the land and with it came a peace, a sense of calm she had not felt, perhaps ever before.

Veronica sensed Dalminyo's presence as he walked out of the woods. He wanted to know why she and Zane were staring at each other as if they had Tiers in their eyes. Not now, Dalminyo... not now.

Bewildered, Dalminyo turned to Julia to ask, "Did I miss something?"

"You missed Bella." Julia purred.

Though she had toned it down, Bella was still emitting enough energy to make anyone who remained close to her start to feel really good.

"What's a *Bella*?" Dalminyo asked before turning to see the unucornubelluacomis lying on the beach, lazily whishing the end of her enormously long tail. Rearing back in alarm the equidae snorted, "What in all the Tiers is that?"

"That is a Bella." Julia sighed as she rolled onto her back, arched, then stretched her paws to the coming night sky. Seeing Dalminyo prance in place she added, "You really should go stand a little closer to her, Dalminyo. You're way too tense."

"From the looks of things, somebody around here should keep a little tension." The equidae pawed the ground nervously. Then he began to slowly back away from the monster on the beach.

"Hello, Dalminyo, don't worry. I'm just going to relax those sore muscles of yours a smidge. You've been running so far, so fast. And worried too. Here now, let me help you."

And with that Dalminyo's head lowered and began to sway slightly to and fro. He exhaled deeply, and the weight of the Tier was lifted from his back.

"Welcome to Bellafons, Dalminyo. I find this glacier-fed lake and its surroundings most relaxing. Don't you," the unucornubelluacomis said, mouth slightly upturned.

"Ah, ah huh," was all the equidae could muster before his legs gave out, and he collapsed with a plop onto the beach.

Daelkay had once again positioned himself like an impenetrable door at the mouth of the cave. Sophia had decided to make herself something to eat when rustling came from the far side of the fairy castle. She crept closer to investigate.

The noise seemed to be coming from inside the kitchen area. Then in her head she heard:

"What in all the Tiers is this? Something has been rummaging through the pantry. I leave for a few weeks, and I bet it was those nephews of mine, hooligans all of them. They have no respect I tell you."

Somewhere close by a magical creature was thinking out loud. Sophia peeked through one of the over-sized windows on the castle's first floor. The rant was coming from a little mouse. Well, that is to say, at first glance he looked a bit like a mouse. He was about the same size, yet he reminded her of something else. He had kind, large liquid brown eyes and long whiskers that twitched. Yet his face was much thicker than a mouse's, as was his tail, and his hind legs were long, thick, and powerful looking. His dark chocolate-caramel-colored fur bushed out in all directions. It made him look like a little puffball. He was small enough to sit on the palm of Sophia's hand, and she found she had to fight the urge to just scoop him up. Ah!

"You're a kangamou!" she said.

The poor little thing jumped straight up in the air and banged his head on the rafters above, only to come crashing back down into the pantry again. Food tins and small bottles went ricocheting across the counter and floor.

"Oh my, I'm sorry. I'm sorry; I didn't mean to scare you. I just wanted to meet you. Are you all right?"

The little creature nodded slowly.

Sophia continued, "Oh good, that's good, but I'm right though, aren't I? You're a kangamou?"

"I am. My name is Cordova," the little thing said,

shaking and rubbing his head in pain and bewilderment.

"Oh, do you go by Cory for short?"

"No, I do *not*."

"So, why are you here?"

"I'll have you know that I am the caretaker of Fairdra Court."

"Oh, is that what this place is called?"

"Yes, it is, and may I inquire-"

"Ya know, you really should take more pride in your work."

"I beg your *pardon*?"

"Well, when I got here there were dust and cobwebs everywhere. It didn't look like anyone had cared for this place in a very long time."

"Yes? Well I've been on holiday," he said, sitting up straight on his back legs and clasping his front paws beneath his chin. "I have been visiting friends down slope. Besides, what's the point? The fairies have stopped coming. A scout is scheduled to pass through every three cycles, but otherwise," he took a deep breath and sighed, "I fear Queen Allezell has abandoned the court for good."

"No, the fairies haven't abandoned it. I saw one just last night."

"What? You saw a fairy? Here?" The kangamou first hopped in one direction then another. "Oh dear, that is trouble. Was it a scout? The scout isn't due yet, it isn't on the schedule, and speaking of the schedule, you're not on it either. I must insist that you tell me- who are you, and what are you doing here?"

"My name is Sophia Marie, Princess of KenKarta. I have been kidnapped by an evil lord named Leo-moldy something, and I am being kept here by a dragon."

Cordova's whiskers began to twitch wildly. "That, that, that, can not be. You do not look very Princess-ee, and dragon, what dragon?" He took a half hop forward to peer out of the castle into the darkness of the cave.

"That Dragon," Sophia said, pointing at Daelkay's

back, which filled all but the very top of the chamber's entrance.

"Ooohhhh, ooohhh," Cordova sputtered, sitting back on his long haunches and hunching up his shoulders so that he looked like a shivering little ball. "This, this, this... is bad."

"Now, now, don't worry, it's all right," Sophia said. "He's asleep; he sleeps a lot."

Sophia and the kangamou spent the rest of the day visiting and getting to know each other. Cordova proved to be a great little guy to have around. Using fairy magic, he was able to make a tub with hot water so that Sophia could take a bubble bath.

"It is my job to take care of visitors. It's just been a very long time since there's been any," Cordova had informed Sophia, an air of longing for the old days in his voice.

After her bath, Cordova gave Sophia new clothes he had swirled up, ones he said were fit for a Princess. She was delighted with the soft silky green and cream gown with golden embroidery. It was so comfortable and light, not binding. Like wearing flower petals.

Cordova even brushed out her beautiful golden brown hair and placed it in a rather intricate braid that swirled around the top of her head before going down her back. Her dark-blonde highlights caught the shine as they peeked in and out of the braid's weave. It was almost as if she were wearing a crown.

"Wow, you're really magical, Cordova!" Sophia said as she looked in a mirror provided by the kangamou.

"Not really, I can't conjure things up myself. I can only

access the magic stored here by the fairies. Once I use it, it's gone. Take the defense system for instance. If I were truly magical, I could recharge it. I was hoping the scout would do it, but now I'll have to wait for three more cycles. Who knows what manner of creature will wander in here by then. I fear those hobyahs may come."

"*Hobyahs?*"

"Oh yes, everyone is talking about them down slope, 'creeping about in the dark, skipping through the tall grass.' I'm told some of my distant relatives on the northwest slope were scooped up and eaten, treated merely as a snack. The hobyahs are simply awful, dreadful creatures," Cordova said with a shiver. "The scout you saw charged the crystal sky so we'll have plenty of light, but I really wish he would have-"

"The scout didn't turn on the crystals, I did."

"You?" Cordova's eyes grew so large they filled his entire face. "*You* illuminated the crystal sky! But how? The crystals' power had been all but drained."

"I don't know. I just did. I can make them glow bright or..." She closed her eyes and thought about it being darker and the shine dimmed. "Or not at all. I like it better when it's brighter though." In her mind she ordered the crystals to glow brighter and they complied. "Don't you?"

"I do indeed, young Princess," said Cordova, "I do indeed." He brought his front paws together below his long broad chin and began thoughtfully stroking his whiskers. "In fact, may I show you something, young miss? I believe I have a problem you might be able to help me with."

Chapter Twenty-Three
Crossing the Palousoa

I know, I said I was done, and you have no idea how much self restraint it has taken for me to wait this long. But, even if you don't appreciate my insights (which by the way you'll get from no one else), you must understand, this is not really editorializing. This is vital information that Yorgide must convey. Truth be told, I might also need a small break from operating the cas. So please, just let me tell you this.

Veronica and her companions left their camp at Bellafons just before dawn of the next day. They set out early for they were guided by renewed hope. A hope that Yorgide already knows and will now graciously share with you.

With the night before had come the most tranquil sleep any of them could remember. So now, thanks to Bella, they were not only rested, but had determined the next step in their journey. Veronica had not received any guidance from Sophia in her dreams that night, probably because Bella's influence put her in such a deep slumber. However, before they slept, Bella imparted a bit of information on them that would prove very advantageous, yes indeed. The unucornubelluacomis told them that she had seen a dragon just two nights before when he had stopped to drink at her lake. She was submerged at the time, so the dragon had not noticed her. She said he wasn't very talkative. Meaning his thoughts were guarded, something dragons can do better than most, so there was little for her to pick up on. However, she did feel that he was very concerned about crossing the Great Mitigo Plains before dayshine returned.

When Julia asked if the beast had a girl with him, Bella had replied, "No girl that I could see, just a bundle that he carried in his claws. There was life within, but I could not feel what it was. If it was Sophia- which knowing what I know now, I am confident that it was- he must have put her under for the journey." By putting her under, Bella meant that the dragon must have used magic on Sophia to place her in a very deep sleep.

With this new information, the band of rescuers now knew that in order to reach Sophia, they must eventually cross the Mitigo Plains. The Mitigo Plains lay to the east, but to reach it they must first cross the Palousoa. Bellafons, the glacier and spring-fed lake where Bella lives, spills into the geologic structure known as the Valleyridge. The Valleyridge actually runs a great distance across the Palousoa, almost cutting the lush rolling green grasslands in two. This was the countryside in which the King grew up. It became part of KenKarta after he and Veronica's mother married and took the throne. Except for the city of Ken, which was far to the south of where they would now travel, the Palousoa was sparsely populated. Its landscape consists mainly of large ranches and farms.

Still, Julia was nervous about traveling out in the open, so for the first part of the day she planned for them to stay close to the ridge and small valley that gives The Valleyridge its name. That was the only thing that could provide a bit of cover as they crossed the Palousoa. Though beautiful, the tall, slender, purple-tinted trees that grew sporadically in the grasslands would do nothing to conceal her charges from harm. After the first distance however, the Valleyridge continued south until it ran into a large marsh that made travel very slow and difficult. This meant they would have to stay to the high side of the Valleyridge and at times cut across the vast open fields of the Palousoa. There they could only hope that no one took note of their passing. Look at its beauty...

The shroud of night was beginning to draw back, and a straight, broad, and brilliant line of shine crossed the horizon. At this early hour it looked bright yellow, about the same color as Bella, and was a dramatic contrast to the deep green grass beneath it and dark blue sky stretching out beyond. Above the light line, the heavens faded from blue up to black. Where it was still dark enough, she could see the spiral shine of a few tiers over head. While V watched, the thin spear-shaped trees turned from black to deep purple as the shine began to illuminate them. Absentmindedly, she wound her long golden mane into a single braid. Today they would cross the Palousoa. Night would be coming by the time they reached the other side and the tip of the Pringer Forest. V was familiar with it because her dad's friend Cletus lived at the heart of this vast and ancient stand of evergreens.

Veronica turned to where Zane stood a short distance away. As he pushed a stray lock of black hair back from his face and turned his angled jaw skyward, she admired his profile. A shiver ran to her heart and caused it to skip a beat.

Get a grip, V! What is *wrong* with you? Yeah okay, there's no denying he's attractive- gorgeous really. But still, like Dad says, boys are nothing but trouble. Not interested. Don't want them, don't need them. Besides, he doesn't even like me. Last night was all Bella's doing. Like he'd really think I'm a 'beautiful angel.' I mean, come on! Now, he won't even look at me.

Veronica tore her gaze away from Zane and instead searched to see what he looked at in the sky. There, the hawken glided overhead, in and out of shadow. Ember swooped down and lit gently on Zane's extended arm. Veronica busied her hands with the task of finishing her braid. She turned her gaze back to the sky, but could still hear them speaking. Warm tingling waves of contentment washed over her as she listened to him use his new Gift.

"Can you hear me, Zane?"

"Yes, I can, Ember."

"It is nice that you have found your ears."

"I'm sorry I couldn't understand you before."

"All things come in their own time. I knew you would learn your Gifts. I want to thank you and the others for saving me."

"Did I see what happened to you? I mean, is what I saw really what happened?"

"Yes. You were the closest person I could think of to try and connect with."

"I thought it was a dream."

"At first, yes, but you put the pieces together. Otherwise we wouldn't be here now. That was a chance I had to take. I had to make sure someone knew what really happened to the King."

"Is he...?"

"He was alive when they took him. I am going to fly ahead and keep an eye out. I'll let you know if I see anything."

Veronica clenched her jaw and stared out across the

endless sea of rolling green fields she must navigate. She flipped the finished braid over her shoulder with self loathing. How could she even think about such a trivial thing as boys? Her father and sister were missing. Her focus must be on what she could do to help. Right now, the only thing that mattered was finding Sophia.

Chapter Twenty-Four
The Fairy Princess

When she woke up, Sophia discovered that Daelkay was gone. Where his massive body had been was now an empty opening, a clear path to the mouth of the cave.

Sophia quickly redressed in the clothes Cordova had given her and took the opportunity to retrieve the Onoxmon unobserved by the sapphire eyes of the often sleepy, yet ever-wary dragon. She had worried it might have been damaged when she threw it to the back of the cave, yet now in her hands it seemed unscathed.

"What's that you have there, Young Miss?" Cordova asked as he emerged from his quarters at the back of the fairy castle, right where the Onoxmon had rested unnoticed near the Arch.

"Nothing!" Sophia squeaked. She jumped up and put her hands behind her back.

The kangamou's forehead and nose wrinkled and his eyes narrowed as he studied her for a moment. Then one side of his brow arched higher than the other as he said, "Very well. What can I be getting you for breakfast then? I fear there's no reason for you to hurry. No chance of escaping this morning, if that was in your head. That dragon is right outside having a breakfast of his own."

"Really, what's he eating?" the Princess asked curiously, while at the same time afraid the answer might be gross.

"A zadeer, poor thing, dragons love them, so do most any Mythical creatures with a taste for meat. The Mitigo Plains below are full of them. The beast must have snuck out while we were sleeping for an early hunt. I'm sorry I didn't realize earlier, so we could have planned some kind of escape, but by the time I awoke and went to see if the coast was clear, he was already back. I think he used some magic on you, I do, to make your slumber deep, and me being close by, and small in stature, it beguiled me as well. Don't you worry though, young thing, Cordova's looking after you now. You are a guest of Fairdra Court. How'd you like the bed I swirled up for you last night? It appears you slept sound, maybe too sound, huh?" The tiny kangamou chuckled slightly and swayed his head back and forth, clearly amused by his own banter.

"It was very nice, thank you, much softer than Daelkay's leg." Sophia smiled.

"It is the least I could do after you recharged the castle's shield crystal for me. The shield cannot keep the likes of a dragon at bay, but it can certainly slow down others who might come. I still can't believe you were able to do it, Miss, though I am sorry that it drained you so. I should not have asked so much of one so young. I think you fell asleep before your head even hit the pillow. I feared you'd drained your very essence complying with my request."

"Don't worry about it, Cordova, I feel great now. Say, are there any good hiding places in this cave?"

"You mean for someone your size? No, young one, I'm afraid not."

"No, I was thinking about something more along your size."

"My size, well there's my tunnels."

"Really, maybe after breakfast you could show me?" Sophia asked, slipping the Onoxmon into the pocket of her garment undetected.

Light flared at the back of the cave. Sophia spun to face it and jumped away all in one motion. Colors swirled within the Arch's frame then shrunk to occupy just a small space at its center, while the rest faded to reveal the black of Empty Space. There was a disruption in the colored area, then a tiny blur erupted into the cave from the center of the arch.

Sophia stood stone still, but Cordova hopped into action. The little kangamou hustled to the center of the little castle's courtyard and bowed deeply. The blur flicked across the room and hovered slightly in front and above him.

Still looking down, Cordova said, "Greetings, Princess Parisia, this is indeed an unexpected honor... Does your mother travel with you?"

"She does not, Cordova, as far as she knows I'm in the forest collecting samples for one of my never-ending lessons. I trust nothing will alter her perception."

"Oh, Your Highness, my legendary discreetness is always at your service. I can hardly remember the last time I saw you, and have you grown?"

She smiled at him. "Cordova, you old flatterer you, as a matter of fact I have, a whole feather's depth. Now where's my hug?" The petite fairy dropped down to Cordova at ground level and wrapped her delicate arms around him. Then her translucent wings fluttered furiously, to the point of being nothing but a golden blur, and she lifted the little dark-brown kangamou right up off the ground.

Hanging, his full body length above the tiled court-yard, Cordova squeaked, "I cannot tell you how wondrous it is to have you here, Princess, but truly you shouldn't be here. It isn't safe."

She lowered Cordova with a slight oomph back to the

floor. "Safe, shmafe. So where is she? The rumors are flying all around the Tier. Did the scout really see a human girl here?"

Cordova turned his face away from the fairy, toward Sophia. She was in the shadows at the end of the fairy castle's right side and still hadn't moved a muscle. She looked from Cordova to where the fairy was. She was gone. In a blink she had flown across the courtyard. She now hovered at eye level in front of Sophia. Her violet eyes sparkled, and a broad smile covered her narrow face. Her hair was a slightly deeper shade of brown than Sophia's, and her long bangs were tucked behind each of her delicately pointed ears. She was perfect. Everything Sophia had imagined a fairy should be.

Without looking away from Sophia the Princess asked, "Where's that dragon the scout spoke of? Is he really holding her hostage?"

Cordova replied, "He's outside eating, and yes, she really is his hostage."

Parisia's nose wrinkled as she placed her hands on her

hips. "Does she speak?"

Cordova hopped over near Sophia's feet, and while the fairy executed a mid-air curtsy, he said, "Your Highness, allow me to present her Royal Highness, Princess Sophia Marie of KenKarta."

"A Princess? Oh that's even better. I'm a Princess too! Princess Parisia, daughter of Queen Allezell."

"Yes, I heard," Sophia whispered. Then with a curtsy of her own added, "Nice to make your acquaintance." That was it. She could contain her excitement no longer. "I have been begging my parents to meet you for such a very long time. You're even more beautiful than in my dreams!"

The fairy flitted from one side of Sophia to the other. "Oh you're a keeper. Isn't she a keeper, Cordova? I love her already. That settles it. You are coming home with me right now."

Cordova timidly asked, "My Princess, it is true that Sophia is in dire need of assistance, but your mother-"

"Ah, what's she going to do, ground me? Everybody's already grounded. You do want to go with me don't you, Phee? So tell me, Phee- is it all right that I call you Phee?"

"Yes and yes, of course, See- it is all right if I call you See, isn't it?"

"Oh, I like the sounds of that, Phee and See, the best of friends. Oh, the adventures we two will have."

Sophia bit her lower lip. "It's just that... how are we going to get there, to your home I mean?"

The tiny Princess's nose wrinkled up again. "Through the Arch of course. What's wrong, don't you like tier-jumping?"

"I hate it! It's way too scary for words. Isn't there

another way?"

Giggling, Parisia said, "Another way to Fairytier? Not even if you sprouted wings and tried to fly."

Cordova drew himself up to his full stature. "Forgive me for interrupting, Princesses, but Princess Parisia, you are not a trained guide, and even if she were willing, Princess Sophia is far too young to be tier-jumping without assistance. The consequences could be catastrophic."

Parisia waved a dismissive hand at Cordova. "Oh, we'd be all right. She's very powerful, I can sense it. I'm sure she could do it."

Sophia brought her hands up and clenched the hair at her temples. "No. I can't. I can't do it."

Wagging a tiny finger in admonishment and placing her lips in a pout, Parisia flew higher so Sophia had to look up at her. "Well, certainly not with that attitude, you can't. We are really going to have to work on your self confidence, Phee."

A terrible gnashing came from the mouth of the cave. The sound of bone being crushed by teeth.

Parisia twirled around to face the entrance. "By the light of the moon, what in all the Tiers was that?"

Cordova had hopped up to one of the castle's balconies, so now he was close to Sophia's waist. "The dragon. I told you, he's eating a zadeer right out there on the ledge."

Parisia darted to the mouth of the cave and peered out. In two blinks she was back before Sophia. "Are you sure you'd rather stay here with that nasty dragon than come with me?"

"No! But I can't-" Sophia slumped to the floor and burst into tears.

"There, there, Young Miss." Cordova was now perched right next to Sophia's head. He reached out to stroke her hair with his petite paw. "Princess Parisia, I must insist, it is far too dangerous for Sophia to go through the Arch."

Parisia flailed her arms about and flew in a slow circle as if performing in an overly dramatic stage play. "All right, all right! Geez, don't cry, Phee, I didn't mean to make you cry. It's just, I mean, there's got to be something we can do."

After a moment of reflection, Cordova said, "Maybe you could appeal to your mother? Perhaps with your insistence she'd at least get word to Sophia's family concerning her whereabouts."

"Fat chance she'll help!" Parisia scoffed. "That would be interfering with the *wretched* humans, don't you know. But, I might be able to finagle it, even without her help."

Wiping her eyes and cheeks, Sophia sniffed. "Thank you. And, there is one more thing-"

"Just name it."

"I have something, something I need you to hide for me."

Chapter Twenty-Five
Cascade in the Glen

All day they had raced across the rolling hills of the Palousoa, slowing only to hide from the occasional farmer, rancher, or passing traveler. Now at the bottom tip of the Pringer Forest, Veronica looked around at the glade Julia had chosen to camp in for the night. The far side of the grassy meadow sloped away and was surrounded by tall evergreens. Their trunks were thick and their bark had a yellowish tint to them. In striking contrast, their needles were bluish-green. Just beyond those trees lay the great Mitigo Plains. Bella told them that the dragon had taken Sophia across it, but to where exactly they did not know. Sophia was in a mountain cave, but there were lots of mountains on the far side of the great plain. And Pinn only knew how many caves could be found in them. Hopefully tonight she could dream speak with Sophia again and learn more about where to find her sister.

They camped on a level area at the top of a gentle rise in the glade. A high ledge arched into a slight semi-circle to enclose the backside. Vines grew down lazily from above partially covering the stone, stone that in the center looked remarkably smooth and shiny. At the base of the ledge, a small pool of water and a little stream meandered to the center of the semi-circle. Set back from the water's edge sat a stone that somewhat resembled a large chair. It all looked vaguely familiar, almost like the cascade room at home. Veronica stepped around to the other side of the stone and sat down. In her exhaustion, her thoughts strayed to home. She closed her eyes and wished she were sitting in front of a cas screen with a bowl of popped corn (her favorite snack), surrounded by family. There they would watch a ge-im together, one of her favorite pastimes.

Ge-ims were geodes, or sphere-shaped rocks, filled with crystals that could be used by truly Gifted cascaders to capture stories so that they could be projected onto cascade screens again and again. The Royal Family could enjoy this favorite form of entertainment without intrusion. All one had to do was set the selected ge-im and a charged piece of silver into the basin where a cascader would place his hand when transmitting a live cas. The charged Piece in the basin provided energy to power the ge-im, energy that would otherwise be provided by the cascader. The story inside the ge-im, which was captured within the crystals inside the stone, was then channeled onto the cas screen.

Right now as she sat alone on the cold stone chair, even more than wanting to watch a ge-im, V wished she could reach out and put her hand into warm slick cas liquid and talk to her mom. Almost involuntarily while she daydreamed she had put her hand out to the side and rested it where a basin would be in a real cas chair. Her eyes shot open when her fingers dipped into cold water. Was this a basin? It was filled with water. She scanned the top of the glade. The stream actually went from one edge of the pond to this basin then back into the pond! Holy Pinnacle! Could it be? She took a small geode from the set of Pieces tied to her belt and placed it into the basin. She put her hand on top of it and focused her thoughts.

Slowly a shimmer of light emerged from the geode and crept across the channeled water toward the pond. There the light's low glow faltered, then was gone. Despite the failure, Veronica was encouraged. This was a cas. She just needed a whole lot of energy to activate it. Good thing she brought the unused set of Imperium Pieces she had taken from her mother's closet. She searched in the bag until she found a Piece of silver and clenched it in her fist. Usually this would cause a charged Imperium Piece to begin emitting energy, but the Piece of silver in Veronica's hand did nothing.

"Oh, come on! How can you be dead? Who would give a Queen uncharged Pieces?" She frowned for a minute, thinking, then smiled and called out to Zane and the others.

When they were all gathered, Veronica explained to Zane, Julia, and Dalminyo that she needed their help to try and charge the Piece of silver.

Dalminyo asked, "That's a refined Piece, Veronica. Isn't it already charged?"

"Yeah, well I thought it was, but the charge seems depleted, and I really need it."

Zane's face crinkled up as he shrugged. "Why?"

"I'm going to try and call my mom on that cas." She pointed over her shoulder to the rustic stone chair and screen beyond.

"What? That's not a cas," Zane said.

Julia said, "Actually it is, Zane, or at least it once was. Though to make it function now would take a great deal of energy."

Veronica said, "That's why I need your help to charge this Piece. I can't do it by myself."

"We can't do it at all," Zane said. "Can we? I mean, I know I can't, but can you guys?"

The hair along Julia's neck and back rose slightly. "Not if we have the same defeatist attitude as you, we can't. Veronica is young and inexperienced, but she has managed to give a slight charge to various refined Pieces in her lessons."

"That's right, I can't capture all the energy I focus on the Piece yet, but that's why I'll need your help. If all four of us focus our Gifts on the Piece, then I should be able to direct enough energy into it to charge it. All we have to do is charge it enough to create a pathway. Once the path is open the Piece will keep drawing in energy on its own. At least for a while, it should be enough to operate the cas."

Veronica held the Piece in her right hand while she held the other up to the side of Dalminyo's head. At the same time she had Zane place his right hand on Julia's head and his left on top of her right. This was something Zane had never done before and skepticism shown in his deep blue eyes, but she was sure that he could help.

Zane let out an exasperated sigh and withdrew his hand from Julia's head. "This is a waste of time. I'm not going to be any help here. I'm going to go cook dinner."

"It is not a waste of time, and we need your help *right here*," Veronica said, grabbing Zane's hand and firmly replacing it on Julia's cheek. "Just try and focus. Think about drawing energy in from Julia, like a deep breath, then channel it toward my hand and the Piece, like you're exhaling it."

"Why don't we all just hold the stone and transfer the energy directly to it?" Zane asked. "Why do we have to draw energy from Julia and Dalminyo? Won't that weaken them?"

Julia replied, "Dalminyo and I are very good at drawing energy from the environment around us, which is the power we will be passing on to you, not our own essence. Besides, it is much easier to receive and transfer energy to and from something that is living, someone who is a willing conduit. Now please, Veronica can do this. She just needs all the extra

154

power we can muster. Zane, just make sure you are letting the energy pass through you. Don't pass along your own essence or it will weaken you."

Dryly Dalminyo added, "Pass on enough, and it will kill you."

"What?" Zane exclaimed jerking back his hand as if Julia had threatened to bite him.

Julia moved her head under Zane's hand and tilted it gently until his palm rested once again on her cheek. "Don't worry. With all four of us using our Gifts to contribute, Veronica should be able to charge the piece long before that happens."

After a bit more reassurance, they finally proceeded. They focused all the energy they could into the Piece, stopping only when Zane's grip slipped and he almost crumpled to the ground.

Julia asked, "Are you all right, Zane?"

"Yeah, yeah, I must have locked my legs or something, 'cause I got a little light headed, but I'm fine, really."

"You didn't lock your legs, *stable boy*. You were passing on your *own* essence," Dalminyo snapped. "That's a big novice no-no. Didn't you listen, or are you just too feeble minded to prevent it?"

Without waiting for a reply, Dalminyo turned and pranced arrogantly down to the meadow, tail held high. Veronica sighed and opened her mind to just him. 'Yes, yes, Dalminyo, we all know you are superior. You don't have to be such a show pony to prove it.' Dalminyo stopped. Slowly he turned his neck back toward Veronica, eye lids partially lowered. She felt his mocked disdain and smiled broadly at him, barely able to suppress a laugh. The white and black spotted equidae simultaneously tossed his head high and away from her while whipping his tail around. Veronica laughed.

Julia purred with reassurance, "Do not pay any attention to him, Zane. You did very well for your first time. The energy you were receiving from me will counteract the effects in a few minutes. Just sit and rest a spell."

Veronica put the newly charged Piece in the basin and tried to activate the cas. She focused all her thoughts on reaching out to her mother. Nothing happened. Julia, and then even Zane drifted off to make their camp ready for the night, but determined, Veronica kept trying. Then, remarkably, a faint image of her mother trickled down the water that flowed over the rock in front of her.

The Queen seemed in the midst of giving a battle briefing:

"Sir Mark and the Hunters have retaken control of the Arch at Bedforda from a band of hobyahs. They found ge-ims that held images of the false reports we had been given about the summit meeting. Thankfully the activity at this Arch has been limited and mostly outbound. That is not the case with the Arch at Moldea however; the dragons tell me that over the past cycle there have been disturbingly high levels of activity there. Activity that abruptly ended the day that Sophia was taken. It seems that whatever is coming, is coming from Moldea.

"Sir Mark, Kirk, and Kameron are racing through Pringer Forest on equidaes, gathering forces as they go, and are heading to the Mitigo Plains by way of Yolnegue. Sir Keith, with the help of my nephew, Eric, has gathered what will be our main fighting force. It's comprised of volunteers from the cities of Medius and Ken plus the outlying areas all the way into the Palousoa. They are now on the move toward the Mitigo Plains as well. As in the past, Brython has sent word that they will stand with us, while Sparthena waits to see what is to come."

Zane asked, "Who are these people that she speaks of?" The sound of the Queen's voice had drifted across the meadow, and all of Veronica's travel companions had once again gathered behind her.

"They are my family," whispered Veronica as her mother paused to listen to people they could not see. "Sir Mark is my uncle and Kirk and Kameron are my cousins, they are Hunters like their dad-"

"Hunters?" Zane asked. "That's a pretty elite entourage, and what they hunt can be dangerous, aren't they a bit young?"

"Shhh, Sir Keith is also my uncle, he lives in Medius with my aunt Leanne and is normally in charge of all of KenKarta's supply trains. Eric is my cousin as well, son of my aunt Vicky. He is in Ken going to school while his mom is an ambassador to the Upper Tiers. All of my cousins on my mom's side of the family are much older than me, including Kara and Justin, who lived with us while they attended University in Karta. Now Justin is a member of Konakua's Island Council and Kara is an ambassador in training-"

"You've got a lot of family," Zane said.

"Yes, but unfortunately, I don't get to see them much. I really miss them."

"Well, at least it sounds like they're there when you need them," Zane said, then paused as the Queen began to speak once more.

"Lady Karol has put our forces at Kief on full alert. In case we are wrong, and the aggression is not originating in Moldea, she is keeping a watchful eye to the west for any sign of attack from the Chinjana. I have sent word to King Rick in the hopes that he would move his forces up from Askard in the Southeast. If we are right and the attack comes from Moldea, then my brother could be able to flank their army as it leaves the Inculta Moldea. However, I have not heard from him, and I have no way of knowing if he will come.

"Our troops posted in KenKarta are ordered to stay in reserve with you and Lady Leanne, General Fooney. Lady Leanne and her girls should be arriving from Medius at any time. In addition, I have sent word to warn my sister, Lady Sheryl, and her husband, Sir Robert, plus Justin and my parents who are all currently on the island of Konakua. I have spoken with the King's brother, Sir Rod and his wife Lady LeAnne, in Seatella as well, and they tell me that Dale's parents are currently safe with them there. None of them have seen anything out of the ordinary in the west, which only reinforces our information that the attack on KenKarta is originating in the east. Our family in Konakua and Seatella are all too far away to help us in this immediate fight, but if we somehow fail, it will be up to them and theirs to carry on, to come to your aid. So be sure you keep them apprised of what's happening.

"Lady Vicky and Lady Kara are on special envoys trying to ensure cooperation amongst our allies in the Upper Tiers. As soon as the Arch here on Dragontier is repaired I will come and join the fight. I just pray it will not be too late."

Here the Queen again paused as she listened to a question from someone Veronica could not see or hear, but she assumed it was from General Fooney. Then the Queen continued.

"No. Regrettably the Dragons say this is a fight of our own making, thus they will not come."

"But that's not true!" Veronica yelled at the cas screen. While she and her companions had been listening intently to the cas, the shroud of night had drawn across the land. Now in the darkness it was easier to see, and while she watched her mother, out of habit Veronica had reached into the basin and placed her fingers on the geode submerged there. Her contact with the Piece completed the connection and had actually allowed her voice to be passed on. Her mother's speech faltered. The Queen closed her eyes and cocked her head to the side slightly as if she were listening for something in the back of her mind.

Veronica continued, "Mom, you've got to tell them that it was a dragon that took Sophia."

The Queen's breath caught and her eyes shot open. "Veronica? Veronica, is that you?" To the cascaders helping her communicate, the Queen ordered, "Break off the other paths and focus in on her." Then searching for her child she asked, "Veronica, are you all right?"

"Yes, but Mom-"

"Where are you?"

"Some old ruins in the woods next to the Mitigo Plains."

"Casglen?"

"I guess... so."

"She's at Casglen, focus all your energy there," the Queen said off screen to the cascaders. If they knew where V was then they would have a better chance of retaining contact. That done she turned her attention back to the cas. "A bit more, there, now I can see her. Hello, baby."

"Hi, Mom." Veronica's voice cracked.

"Oh, when you get home you are in such trouble." Despite the harsh words the Queen's tone was soft.

"I know," Veronica replied with a crooked little smile.

The Queen began slowly, "Okay, okay. You're okay?"

"Yes."

"How much did you hear?"

"A lot, but-"

"How, who's helping you operate the cas?"

"Zane, he's a friend, Mom, and Julia and Dalminyo, they all helped me charge the Piece."

"Zane? Zane Slayer, Scott Slayer's son?"

"I'm not sure?" She looked over her shoulder at Zane, and he nodded. "Yes."

"All right, sweetie, as much as I want to know how that came to be, you'll have to explain later. We must speak quickly. If you were able to hear, others might be listening too." Then off screen she directed, "Protect this path, fortify it. Don't let anyone eavesdrop." Then looking back again at Veronica the

Queen asked, "Are you sure you're okay, honey?"

"Yes. Mom, I've had another dream talk with Sophia."

"Is she all right?" the Queen's voice betrayed her a bit here, revealing the anguish and concern she carried for her youngest daughter.

"Yes, it was a dragon that took her, Mom, a dragon and a man. The man is gone, but the dragon still guards her. He's taken her to some big mountain across the Mitigo Plains, and she's in a cave. She says it looks like an old fairy hall."

The Queen looked down and her hands came up, indicating that Veronica should pause. She began lightly rubbing, almost tapping the thumb nail of her left hand against her lower lip. Veronica had seen this before and knew her mom was scanning her memory for something. "Fairdra?"

"What?"

"Mount Fairdra..."

"She's still okay, Mom. Sophia says Daelkay hasn't hurt her-"

"Daelkay? Did you say Daelkay?"

"Yes, but Mom, did you say Mount Fairdra? Isn't that one of the two big peaks you can see across the plains?"

"Yes, Mount Fairdra." Then as much to whoever was in the room with her as to V she said, "Daelkay has taken Sophia to Mount Fairdra."

"Mom, do you know this dragon?"

"Yes, he is Bonded to Cort Leamoldae of Moldea."

"Wait, is he the traitor you and Daddy had banished to the Lower Tiers?"

"Yes."

"That's not good," Zane murmured, from a few yards behind the cas chair where Veronica sat.

The Queen was looking down again, finger to her temple. "No, it's not good." She raised her chin and sighed. "It means they've opened an Arch out of the Lower Tiers."

Veronica said, "But Arches on the Lower Tiers only work one way!"

The Queen's eyes, now a hard steely blue, locked with her daughter's. "Veronica, you need to go home right now."

"But Mom, on Dalminyo I'm only a day way from Fairdra!"

"It is not safe!"

"Mom, if what you just said is true, soon nowhere on Virtier will be safe. I can help."

A loud screech rang out from the darkness. It came from just beyond the light of the fire that illuminated the center of their camp behind them.

Julia growled and leapt into action.

Running to grab his sword, Zane yelled, "Veronica! Hobyahs!"

Veronica looked one last time at the screen to her mother's faint image. She touched the first two fingers of her left hand to her lips, kissed them, then stretched them out toward her Queen and whispered, "I'll get her." Then she removed her right hand from the cas basin to grab the hilt of her sword.

The connection quickly dimmed and was broken.

Chapter Twenty-Six
Trapped on Dragontier

Alison, still trapped on Dragontier, lunged at the liquid wall and cried out to her daughter's fading image. As both her fists lodged against the stone cascade and its oil began to flow over them, she bowed her head. She took several deep breaths, trying to subdue the emotions that now threatened to completely overwhelm her. Right now her oldest daughter was in a fight for her life, and there was nothing she could do. Her youngest child had been kidnapped by a madman, and her husband, she dared not even think what his fate might be. She wanted nothing more than to scream, cry, and lash out, to release the oppressive anxiety that now smothered her. Yet a small part of her knew that such a display would only hurt her cause, her quest to save them all. She could not lose face with those currently in the room with her. They had long thought that humans were too self absorbed, emotional only about their own plight. She must make them see that this was something much more than her own personal tragedy.

Long moments of silence passed. Then the Queen turned. She opened her hands, palms up, slightly stretched away from her waist. As the oil dripped from them, she addressed the members of the Dragon Council who had been listening in the giant cascade room. "You have misjudged this crisis. It is not of our own making. One of your own has brought this ruin upon us all."

Chapter Twenty-Seven
Tiers in the Sky

After Parisia left, Sophia spent most of the day with Cordova. A funny little creature, he had lots of information about fairies and was an entertaining playmate. He freely used the stored fairy magic to pamper his young guest, even giving her a pedicure, and was much cheerier than Daelkay. The dragon had spent the day outside on the ledge watching the opposing horizons, apparently deep in thought. Darkness had crept across the sky before his scales scraped and claws clicked the stone floor inside the cave.

Hearing the great beast approach, Cordova dropped the brush he was using to paint Sophia's toenails. He then hopped for the safety of his tunnel, which Sophia had learned, ran all the way to the outside slope of the mountain. It was the castle's backdoor so to speak, unfortunately, only large enough for a fairy or kangamou to utilize.

"Come outside with me, Sophia, I think you could use some fresh air," Daelkay said.

Sophia finished applying paint to her last toe, then complied. The night was cloudless, and she could clearly see the spiral shine of tiers dotting the sky.

"Why does the shine from the Tiers spiral like that?" Sophia asked as she sat down on Daelkay's front leg like a bench and peered up at the night sky.

"Because they turn on an axis, and only one side reflects the shine of the Pinnacle."

"Virtier doesn't spin around."

"No, it remains stationary. And the answer to your next

question is no, the Pinn does not turn away when it is night. The Pinnacle is always there. During the day you call its Shine the sun. When the shroud of night is pulled in front of the Pinn, so that man can rest, you call it the moon. Yet no matter by what name you address it, it is always there. Too many fail to realize there is so much more to the Pinnacle than its light. Deus's grace is always ready to help those with true faith and conviction."

"How did you know I was going to ask about the Pinn?"

"Because all children of men are the same."

They both sat quietly for a time taking in the view, but finally Sophia broke the silence. "Why do most Mythical creatures live on the Upper Tiers instead of here with us?"

"Deus gave Virtier to men," the dragon replied, beginning a tale that had been told countless times. "Yet in the beginning this land was occupied as much by the Mythicals as by man. At first men adhered closely to the laws of the Pinn, and with that closeness came the realization of their many Gifts. With their Gifts, men became more powerful, but as their power grew, so came greed. Soon, instead of sharing how to use their Gifts with others, men began to horde their knowledge. Then they fought amongst themselves in the hopes of obtaining more. To the victors went the knowledge of Gifts and with that knowledge the power to control. Men grew arrogant and turned away from Deus, and their chance to unite with him in the Pinn. They were strong and felt they no longer needed the infinite wisdom found in its shine. Yet the further they wandered from the shine, the more corrupt their power became. Eventually most men lost use of their Gifts, their spirits too broken to tap into them. The knowledge of the Gifts was almost completely lost, and man was left to toil in hardship."

Sophia blurted, "The Gifts weren't lost completely because dragons safeguarded them, became the keepers of secrets and lore."

"Yes, it was they who formed the Mythical Council, but you skip ahead. If you know this story maybe I should stop."

"No, no, please continue." Sophia sat quietly, then lightly ran her fingers across her lips to indicate that she would not interrupt again.

"Others, too proud to acknowledge their mistakes, chose to be corrupted by the power of the Abyss. It is their descendants that now occupy the Lower Tiers and answer to Abaddon. But before they were banished, they wreaked terror across the Lands, dominating and destroying all good they could find. It was then that most Mythical creatures began to lose faith in man. They could no longer bear to watch him destroy himself, so they asked Deus for help. Those who held favor were given a Tier of their own to retreat to. Most chose to leave, but some hoped to help mankind find its way back to the shine, so they stayed. Eventually, with the help of their Mythical allies, good men did manage to banish most evil to the Lower Tiers and so began the long struggle back to the shine of the Pinn. It has been an arduous journey thus far, and few think mankind will ever fully complete it. That is why they leave; they leave when they have given up on man. They retreat to the Upper Tiers when they realize the one thing that will keep man from reaching the Pinnacle and uniting with Deus."

"What is that?"

"Freewill," the dragon replied. "Most creatures were given just a taste of it, but man was granted its full measure. I used to be jealous of that fact, that man could choose to be good or evil, choose to follow the laws of Deus or not. Now I have grown to realize it is your kinds' greatest burden."

Chapter Twenty-Eight
The Battle at Casglen

Hobyahs! V gasped. Julia bared her teeth and sprang right into the middle of the largest group that was flanking them on the right. Dalminyo reared, kicked, and tramped at three of the beasts dashing up from the tree line. Zane ran toward Veronica, sword already in hand. His blue eyes focused on a point above and behind V's head. He stepped between her and the cas screen. A hobyah leapt from the ledge at the top of the screen directly above them. Zane pushed Veronica to the side. The creature collided only with him. They hit the ground. It shrieked, then fell silent as Zane rolled from beneath it and withdrew his sword from its chest.

Zane nodded upward, a half-smile slipped across his lips. "Now'd be a good time to get in the fight, Princess."

Veronica turned, sword in hand. The ugliest face she'd ever laid eyes on swooped down. Its skin looked like a gray membrane had been pulled over its frame then had all the air sucked out. Each bone threatened to poke through. Something slimy dripped off its hooked nose. It bared its jagged teeth and made some sort of clucking sound with its tongue and cheeks.

Veronica's blood ran icy. With sickle in claw, the hobyah rushed her. She raised her left forearm. "Scutuma!" The bracelet on her wrist glowed then burst forth a shallow umbrella of bluish-black energy. The oval shield took shape just in time to deflect the hobyah's blow. The sickle crashed into the arm of the cas chair and shattered the basin that held the Imperium Pieces. Veronica jumped in. With a guard, parry, riposte, that hobyah was down and the Princess ran to the next.

168

The four companions fought hard and well. Though sorely outnumbered, they managed to hold their ground. As they tired, they positioned their backs to the cas screen, since no creatures had come over it for some time. Veronica had managed to retrieve her bow. The damage she inflicted helped push their attackers back, out of its considerable range. The hobyahs' withdrawal brought a lull in the fighting. They tried to catch their breath.

Their enemy regrouped at the far edge of the glen. A knot of about ten remained. One, not quite as ugly as the rest, a bit feminine, had taken charge. The female carried herself more erect and moved with confidence among the others. Two began to fight amongst themselves. She back-handed one and kicked the other to the ground. They scurried away from her. Boney hands on her hips, she stared across the meadow toward Veronica and her tired companions. A sneer crept across her deep purple lips, and she spun away. She was enjoying this. Veronica nocked her last arrow. If she could just reach the female, that might end this.

Zane said, "Don't waste it, Veronica. They're out of range."

Veronica gave Zane a slight sideways smile and drew. "Pilkraft." The arrowhead came to life. She took aim at the female's back. Released. The arrow flew true. Just before impact the creature spun to the side, long hair lagging behind. The arrow sliced through its dark mane then struck the male hobyah standing behind. It fell dead.

The female glared across the meadow directly at Veronica and screamed. Her hatred filled the air and the other hobyahs responded in kind. She motioned her perverse followers forward for a full-on frontal assault.

"This is it, little ones," Julia snarled. "The final stand."

"The final *stand*?" Dalminyo whinnied.

Julia said, "After this charge it will be either us or them still standing."

"Oh, *that* final stand," Dalminyo said.

Zane straightened his shoulders and lifted his sword. "Get behind me, Veronica."

"I'm not getting behind you! You get behind me if you're scared." Veronica spoke with a bit more bravado than she truly felt.

"I'm not scared!" Zane yelled. "You know, Princess, you are unbelievable."

"*I'm* unbelievable!"

Pawing the ground Dalminyo said, "I hate to interrupt your *little spat*, but can we please focus on the ensuing battle at hoof?"

"Here they come," Julia snarled. "Stay close together, you two. Guard each other's backs. Dalminyo and I will meet the charge out front."

"Spectacular," Zane spat.

"Yes, quite," Dalminyo added. "Is that our only option?"

"Yes," Julia growled.

From behind and above came a commotion. It sounded like hoof beats, and... barking?

"What is that?" Zane asked.

A white dappled equidae vaulted over them with apparent ease and landed right in the midst of the advancing hobyahs.

"Gallantae!" Dalminyo snorted.

In the saddle bag on his back was a small wheaten-colored ball of fur. It barked incessantly, causing the hobyahs to cover their pointed ears in pain. Hobyahs as it turned out were very sensitive to certain pitches, and the barking coming from the saddlebag hit one of those pitches on a regular basis. The racket caused them so much discomfort that some of the final nine even dropped their weapons.

"What the byss?" Zane swore.

"Scoobee!" Veronica proclaimed.

The dog leapt from the equidae's back, right on top of the closest hobyah. Scoobee went straight for the creature's neck. The other bewildered hobyahs scattered and became easy prey for Scoobee's companions. The tide had turned. The battle was soon won.

In the aftermath, they determined that only the female-like hobyah appeared to have escaped their wrath. Julia oversaw the disposal of twenty dead hobyahs, but the female's body was nowhere to be found.

While they worked, Scoobee explained to Veronica that he and Gallantae had started out as soon as the equidae had given a report to General Fooney concerning what the Princess had done. Of course the General was furious, but then relieved when he learned that Julia and Gallantae intended on handling the situation. Finding them hadn't been easy. The dog and equidae had lost Veronica's trail several times. Scoobee assured her that a lesser pair would have failed. However he, her loyal confidant, was determined to sniff her out.

When the carnage was cleared, Veronica sat in silence by the fire. Zane soon came to join her. He tended to a rabbit on a spit over the coals. He had caught it before the battle, and it was now going to be their supper. Zane's pants were cut, the jagged edge wet, blotched with something a bit like blood, but the wrong color.

"What's that? Are you hurt?"

"What?" Zane asked, looking up from the rabbit.

"That there." Veronica pointed to the spot.

"Oh that, that's nothing," Zane said as he wiped at the spot. "Just some blood that got on me when I stabbed that she-hobyah thing. It's weird though, this blood isn't black like that of the others." Looking a bit closer, getting his face right up to it, he added, "It looks almost yellow. Ya know, I've always heard that Abyss shape-shifters have yellow blood. You don't suppose that thing that got away was one of those, do ya? A she-byss? I guess I could have used a shield like you, that thing's the Pinn! I've never seen one used by anyone so young."

"I'm still getting the hang of it. I can't keep it intact very long."

"Maybe sometime you can show me. See if I can activate it?"

"Sure." Veronica shook her head and stared into the fire. How could boys be so brutal? She gripped the cloth she used to clean her blade.

"What's wrong?"

"Nothing, it's just..."

After waiting a short time, Zane prodded, "What?"

"It's just that I've never taken a life before." She looked up from the flames, biting her lip.

"Really? Not even for supper?" Zane stood, wagging his head.

"No."

"How's that possible? Don't you eat meat?"

"Yes, I eat *meat*."

"Oh, that's right, I forgot- you're a *Princess*, so someone else does your dirty work," Zane joked.

Veronica glanced up at him. Hot tears welled up in her eyes. She averted her gaze to the tiers in the night sky.

His voice softened. "Well, don't worry about it, Princess. You still haven't taken a life."

"What do you mean?" Veronica asked as she looked down to the blackened blood-stained cloth she had used to clean her sword.

"I mean, don't feel bad about killing these creatures. I feel more remorse for the animals I butcher for travelers back at the Crossroads, or that rabbit there, than for those soulless sods." Zane motioned toward the part of the forest they had drug the hobyahs to.

"He's right, you know, V," Scoobee chimed as he plopped down by the fire and began gnawing on a bone. "They really are soulless."

"Thanks for the support, my fierce little friend," Zane said.

"Wait, you can hear him?" Veronica asked Zane.

"Yeah, my Gift seems to be letting me hear all magical creatures now," Zane said.

Veronica kept her gaze fixed on her dog, "I knew it! You can talk to whoever you want, can't you, Scoobee?"

"Hmmm...." Scoobee growled while busily removing the meat from his dinner bone. The noise was grating.

"What's that?" Dalminyo asked from where he stood just behind Veronica a mouth full of grass.

174

"What's what?" Scoobee replied.

"What's that you're chewing on there?" Dalminyo said, bobbing his head at Scoobee.

"Oh, this! I'm just enjoying the fruits of our labor. Biting the hand that feeds me if you will." Scoobee chuckled.

Zane asked, "You're eating one of the hobyah's hands?"

"Yeah-"

"Oh, Scoobee." Veronica groaned. "That's so gross!"

Dalminyo and even Zane moaned, although Zane did it through a smile.

"What? It tastes like mole," Scoobee said while working on a knucklebone with his molars. "A bit stringier, not as tasty as morning dove, but it will do in a pinch."

More groans erupted from around the fire. Then Zane added, "That's quite a royal dog there, Princess. I had no idea mole and hobyah were on the menu at KenKarta Castle."

"What? Everyone else is eating." Scoobee turned to Julia who was just approaching the fire. "Hey, Julia, tell them."

"Scoobee, you know I never eat and tell." Julia purred as she lay down next to the fire and began cleaning her paws. "You really must learn to have more discretion, Little Man."

Everyone laughed and relaxed a bit. Finally, Gallantae came closer to the fire and said, "I'll take first watch, so you should all get some sleep. We're going to have a long run tomorrow."

"Gallantae," V began, "I'm grateful that you and Scoobee followed our trail. And I'm really glad you found us when you did, but I'm not going back without Sophia. Now that I know where she is, I'm going to go get her."

"Julia was filling me in earlier, Veronica. I know about your dreams and what your mother told you." Gallantae paused.

"And..." Veronica stood.

"And, I serve at the pleasure of my Princess. Where you go, I go." Then checking his pride, Gallantae added, "If the boy rides me, we can reach Mount Fairdra in a day."

"Thank you, Gallantae," Veronica said as she wrapped her arms around his massive neck. "Thank you."

"Yes, well, agreed then," Gallantae responded.

"Agreed then," Scoobee yipped, "anyone care to join me for seconds? I'll give you a hand-"

A collective "Ah" rose above the campfire from those surrounding it, and Scoobee just rolled onto his back and crowed, "Rrow, Rrow, Rrowww..."

Chapter Twenty-Nine
The Dragon and the Fairy Queen

In the darkness, he heard a small lyrical voice say with true authority, "Unless you wish to become a statue of stone, be mindful of your movements."

He knew she was there before she had spoken. So before he even raised his great heavy eye-lids, in a low purr he simply said, "Hello, Allezell."

She hovered directly in front of him flanked by four of her guards. With two below on either side, it could not be lost on him that they were positioned just like the five points of an Arch, especially since the little Arch at the back of the room was directly behind them and open. An Alistone with a long delicate chain hanging beneath was now seated at its top. In addition, each of the fairies held a staff topped by a large jewel. Each glowed dimly in the cave's darkness, and if activated together, the Queen could indeed carry out her threat, meaning she really could turn the dragon to stone. This display of power showed she was not here on a social call.

Allezell, Queen of the Fairies inquired, "Why are you here, Daelkay?"

"Can't a dragon rest his head in a place that brings back memories of better days?" Daelkay replied.

"Those days are gone, gone in no small part because of you."

"I see. It is I who am to blame."

"Do you claim innocence?" the fairy asked.

"I claim to have done what I am *bound* to do," Daelkay replied almost ceremonially.

"Ah, isn't that convenient? It's never the dragon's fault, is it? No, it's always those weak evil humans you're Bonded to that lead you astray." The Fairy Queen pointed her bejeweled staff at his snout.

"You know the law."

"Yes, I do. Once the Bond is made the dragon cannot break it, but it is the dragon who makes it. If you come looking for pity you will not find it here. For all your ills flow from a choice you made, Daelkay. A choice you were advised against." She broke contact with his gaze to look at the child who slept in a bed nestled against his foreleg. "And now you bring *this* to my threshold." Her sour tone hung in the cave's still air.

"What, this urchin I found wandering alone in the dark?"

"Your sarcasm will buy you nothing here, beast," Allezell snapped. "My Tier is closed to these wretched beings, but it does not prevent their tales of woe from cascading across Empty Space to poison the harmony of my Land." Turning her full attention back to him she said, "I know what you have done, Daelkay. I want to know why you are *here*."

"Sweet Queen, what is it that you would have me say? That you were right, and I was wrong?" Daelkay closed his eyes and took a long slow breath. Then exhaling said, "You were right. I was wrong."

These six words left the Fairy Queen's mouth hanging slightly agape. Daelkay knew she had not expected such an admission.

"More than twenty annuals ago, my arrogance led me to make a poor decision, not the first or last time mind you, but it is the one that will cause all the Tiers to suffer."

"What is it that has come over you, Daelkay? You've

never known such humility."

"Perhaps my pride has been tempered by my time below."

"A Lower Tier, that's where you've been? But why, why did you go? You could have just stayed on Dragontier. It had all been arranged. The council had pardoned you. You were free."

"Free, I was not free! Unlike you, I do not relish spending the ages with only my own kind. Ten annuals surrounded by none but dragons passed slower than the hundred before." Daelkay snorted. "Besides, he called to me. From the edge of the Abyss he beckoned me, Allezell. Across Empty Space, I could see into his heart, as never before. His thoughts were now beyond ambitious; they were growing more and more dark and twisted. Leamoldae was going mad and taking me with him. I had to go. Do you know that the hobyahs do his bidding? And he now rules the pallamales. He even manages to control the cavevils."

"With a dragon at his side it is no wonder-"

"No! He did this without my help. He allied himself with a shape shifter, a she-byss of formidable power. Through their unholy union has their reign been achieved. It was well underway before I arrived on the Tier. I thought if I were there I could sway him. I was wrong. The Bond with the shape shifter strengthened him, but warped him at the same time. She gave him an heir and in return he spared her life. It wasn't out of kindness or love mind you. As long as they remain Bonded he can draw from her power as he does from my own. I, like her, am nothing more than a slave to him now. When I saw I held no sway over him, I sought to contain him. And for a time I did, but now he brings the pallamales, cavevils, and hobyahs to Virtier, a soulless army at his command. And this is just the beginning. If he gains the Onoxmon, nothing will stop him and I am to blame. It was I who provided him passage out of the Lower Tiers."

"How?"

"I brought an Alistone from Dragontier. The Council thought it was destroyed when I sabotaged the secondary Arch right before I left. However, the truth is I took the stone to Exiltier. I didn't reveal that I had it at first, but-"

"You're an irresponsible fool, Daelkay," Allezell scoffed, "but what should I care if Leamoldae conquers the human realm? People are stupid. They are selfish and cruel and refuse to see the good for goodness sake. They only wish to exploit it."

"If for no other reason you should care because Leamoldae won't stop with Virtier. He craves the power the Upper Tiers could bring. He works for Abaddon now, Allezell. He has no hopes of redemption. You say humans refuse to see goodness for goodness sake, are you sure the same can't be said of you?" Daelkay nodded toward Sophia. "It has been a generation since I have seen such power in such an innocent form. Honestly, I don't know if I ever have. It has been apparent that she is truly Gifted from the first night we were here. In her fear and panic, she actually charged an unrefined crystal."

"Really? Impressive, but not unheard of," sniffed the Fairy Queen as she crossed her arms around her staff.

"True, but there is more. I'd introduce you, but she's speaking with her sister now."

"You lie."

"No, though I have never met Veronica, she too must be remarkable. For I know that at barely eleven annuals, she

181

is currently on a quest to save her sister Sophia here. And it seems-" he said, closing his eyes and drawing in a long slow breath as he tapped deeper into Sophia's dream, "that she and her young friends fought a dangerous battle tonight against some hobyahs. They were largely outnumbered, but still managed to prevail. And ah, very clever, Veronica has learned this place is called Mount Fairdra. Even now she tells Sophia not to worry for she is coming for her." Daelkay opened his eyes and looked at the Fairy Queen. "Very sweet, but I fear it will be too late. You see, Leamoldae is also on his way here, that too I can see."

Allezell motioned toward Sophia and said, "I'm told she wears a Star of Grace."

"Does she? Well, that would explain, at least in part, how she opened your Arch."

"You're saying it was this *child* who opened the Arch, not you?" Allezell's eyes narrowed as she fluttered backward, putting more distance between her and the dragon.

"It was, and yes, I too was shocked. She couldn't focus a pathway to an exit Arch, but the entryway was quite steady. It would be best if she had a guide to help her find and stay on a path, but I'm beginning to think that if an Arch were left open with a bridge to this one, she might just be able to make it on her own."

"That's preposterous! She'd end up floating through Empty Space, and you know it. Are you trying to get her killed so you don't have to do your own evil deeds? Even with a fairy guide the chance of her drifting off the path would be too great a risk." The Queen's voice became increasingly louder and sterner. "In addition, humans are not allowed on Fairytier!"

"Ah yes, a law you yourself instated, Allezell, so you could hide on your Tier and avoid the rest. Very enlightened approach, Your Highness."

"I had to protect my kin, people were taking advantage at every turn, and we were going to be enslaved all over again."

"Tell yourself what you will, Allezell, but time is running out. Hobyahs are on their way and when they get here I will be forced to go to him, and she will be left alone with them." Daelkay softened his voice before adding, "You were right, Allezell, her line is strong, even without my influence on her father."

"It will have to be strong without my help as well." Re-crossing her arms as if bracing for the answer she then asked, "Do you take him the Onoxmon?"

Daelkay looked down his snout at the fairy and replied, "I do not have it to take."

Allezell glanced back over at Sophia. The child's eyes were now open.

"Greetings, Your Highness," Sophia said formally with a bit of excitement. "I have long hoped to be privileged enough to make your acquaintance."

"What could you possibly know of me, child?" shot the Queen. "Such frivolousness as purple is the favorite color of fairy folk and that they like to throw parties?"

"I know that you are Allezell, Queen of all the Fairies. You fear the appearance of the First Tier at night because if it is seen alone, that means bad things are going to happen. You love to see the moon full because it was the first thing you saw when fairies were set free from slavery, and you are even more beautiful than the painting I have of you in my room at home."

Allezell stared at Sophia unblinking with her violet eyes. Her lips were pulled into a thin straight line. Her chin was raised so she had to look down her nose to command the child below her, "Show me what you wear around your neck."

Sophia pulled up the chain that lay at her throat to reveal the rather large purple stone in her necklace. It began to glow as she held it out toward the Fairy Queen and Sophia said, "My mother gave it to me and she told me that it was given to her by a fairy... she said that you gave it to her?"

"A moment of weakness, I assure you." Allezell sniffed. "Guards, we are leaving."

"Can I please come with you? I would very much love to see your Tier," Sophia pleaded softly.

"Before I can help you, child, you must first learn to help yourself." For a moment the tiny Queen's deep purple eyes softened ever so slightly beneath the dark brown curly locks that framed her face. The Fairy Queen's hair was long but pulled up high in a bun. A few spiral ringlets fell loose about her neck and face and Daelkay waited as Sophia admired her openly.

"I thank you for the hospitality your court has extended to me. Your servant Cordova has been a kind and gracious host."

Allezell and the other fairies darted through the Arch. The Alistone was pulled through after them by the chain and the Archway abruptly closed. Where moments before there had been a splash of colored lights surrounded by Empty Space, now stood only the drab slab of the cave's cold stone wall.

Chapter Thirty
The Mitigo Plains

Veronica stepped to the edge of the trees and looked out into the open. She saw Zane astride Gallantae's back. Before them lay the great Mitigo Plains, the no man's land of Virtier. She focused on Gallantae and found his mind unguarded, ready to be read like an open book. Currently, Gallantae was listening to Zane's thoughts, and since his mind was unguarded, Veronica could listen in as well.

Zane had always dreamt of coming here, the place no man could claim and only the animals could call their own. This was the place where his father, his birth-father, had fought at the King's side and died. Zane did not know the details. His mother didn't speak of it. His stepfather frowned on any mention of what their life was like before he came into it, but Zane did know that somewhere out on this vast plain was where his father, Scott Slayer, had died.

His mind drifted back to the Crossroads stables, and Veronica went with him, to the night the King had offered to sponsor his admittance to the Mythscola:

Zane's stepfather, Harold Plow, was furious. He was a good man, but a simple man. He did not believe in Gifts; he believed in hard work. He thought studying anything but the physical cause and effect of things was a waste of time. That night at the risk of banishment, Harold Plow spoke out openly against the King of KenKarta. In no uncertain terms he told the King that his adopted son would not be allowed to leave the Crossroads; Harold said Zane's place was there with him and his mother.

In his sorrow, Zane bolted, and hid in the stable loft. Lying in the loose hay, he pounded his fists against the floorboards and wondered how Harold could be so mean. He must really hate Zane to take an opportunity like this away from him. Then below him in the stable alleyway Zane heard voices. It was his mother and the King; they were unaware of his presence.

The King said, "Mira, I meant no disrespect to Harold. I only want what is best for Zane."

"Your Highness, I know you mean well, but Harold is my husband now. His ways are not your ways. He is not Gifted, nor does he want to be."

"That may be. And if you feel you must turn your back on your own Gifts to live with him that is your choice, Mira, but Zane is Gifted, just like his father and you. I know it, and you know it. In his heart, Harold knows it too; that's what scares him."

"What scares me is the thought of losing my son!" Mira snapped. The harsh tone his mother was using with the King shocked Zane as he listened from above. "Without a second thought Scott left his infant son and me and followed you to the Mitigo Plains, Dale. There he fought for your right to remain King, and there he died for you! Is it not enough that I was forced to sacrifice my husband for KenKarta? Now you want my son as well?"

After a slight pause wherein the King's tightly drawn expression suggested he was leaving many things unsaid, he replied in a calm even tone, "Like Scott, Zane will grow restless here, Mira. He will not be content as a stable hand for much longer; neither you nor Harold will be able to change that. Thankfully, the boy has more of your temperament than Scott's. He is not nearly as reckless, but nonetheless, he is Scott's son. If his newly developing Gifts go untrained, they will become a burden rather than an asset to him."

Peeking through the floor boards, Zane watched his mother's eyes fill with tears and a fear he did not understand. "Not yet," she pleaded her voice now low and soft. "I'm not ready, please, not yet."

"He's not ready either, Mira, but when the time comes just remember, the offer remains open. Zane can study at the Mythscola. Looking out for him there is the least I can do."

"I cannot go against my husband."

"Then you will lose your son, and it will not be to me."

A slight breeze whispered against Zane and Veronica's faces. It carried an unfamiliar, yet comforting scent. It was not sweet. A bit musky, but lighter, somehow fresher. They drew in a deep breath through their noses. The breath pulled Zane's thoughts back to the present, and Veronica continued to follow. Curiosity continued to win over manners. While listening in on others people's thoughts was considered poor etiquette, it certainly was enlightening.

Zane's gaze settled on the source of the soothing fragrance emanating from the flowers before him on the Mitigo Plains. The elongated royal-red pellets, surrounding large purple centers, held upright on thick bright green stems, were a vivid contrast to the brown virtier from which they sprang. Firedancers. Literally thousands of blossoms spread out before him. Alone each looked as if it had a head of fire dancing atop outstretched green arms. Together they created a carpet of red that flowed across the vast chocolate and caramel-colored plain.

High above the flowers and virtier, the deep azure-blue sky was streaked with wisps of white. Beneath its striking blue, yet above the vibrant red below, hung three large fluffy but somewhat ominous-looking purple clouds. The bottom sides of these clouds were so dark they appeared almost black, while the sides closest to the shine held hints of lilac tipped with white.

Throughout all of Virtier, here on the Mitigo Plains was the only place these kinds of clouds were seen. They were called Violaqum. From them a light misting of rain fell almost continuously as they drifted endlessly back and forth across the plains. These clouds provided the wellspring of life on the Mitigo. In their wake, the firedancer flowers constantly bloomed. The blooms were not only beautiful, they were life sustaining. Great herds followed the blooms while in turn other animals followed the herds.

A short distance off, Zane could see a herd of zadeer. Veronica could sense that this was the first time he had actually seen any of these graceful creatures other than in ge-ims. Their caramel-colored coats were painted with red strips, the same shade of red as the petals of the firedancers. As expected, most appeared to be does, for they had no antlers. However, scattered amongst the delicate heads that held only large yet graceful ears were the tangled racks of the antlered males. It was a blissful setting. Or at least, it should have been.

Instead, Zane's mind was racing. This was where his father died, where Scott Slayer gave his life for the King. Now here he was traveling with the daughter of that same King on a dangerous quest of their own. Sitting atop the Queen's own equidae, Zane found himself wondering if he could make the same sacrifice as his father.

Gallantae closed his mind, and Veronica was abruptly shut out of Zane's thoughts. She now saw the Mitigo Plains through her own eyes again. Poor Zane. How horrible it must be to lose a parent. Her mind filled with fear for her father. No! She wouldn't think of it. She wasn't one of those kids who wished to be rid of her mom and dad. She loved them, loved to be with them. She could never even imagine what life would be like without her parents!

Veronica walked up to the field of flowers just a short distance to the left of Zane and Gallantae. The Crown Princess breathed in the ever-present but delicate smell of the flowers. She compared her own senses with the way Zane had smelled them. They didn't smell quite as musky to her. She felt the boy's gaze and turned to see him look at her from Gallantae's back. Veronica gave Zane a crooked little smile. A bit of shame washed over her. She shouldn't have eavesdropped on his thoughts. She could no longer hear them, but felt as if she knew his mind merely by the way he looked at her. Yes, like his father, Zane would give his life to protect the royal line of KenKarta. It was a matter of honor. But he needn't worry, she would never ask such a sacrifice of him.

Zane fidgeted with the spare pair of riding glasses he'd finally agreed to wear. Did her eyes reveal too much? Did he know she had heard his inner dialogue? Of course he didn't know, but before Zane had a chance to become too self conscious, Veronica put her fingers to her lips and broke the silence with a loud high-pitched whistle. The lazily grazing herd of zadeer lifted their heads in unison, and all eyes and ears focused on the source of the unfamiliar noise. In rhythm with the breeze, the firedancers swayed gently to and fro making it look as if Veronica were waiting on the shoreline of a red ocean. Then from beneath a small rise off to the left, Dalminyo's head emerged. He chewed a mouthful of firedancers as he trotted toward his girl. It was a scene right out of her dreams.

Scoobee and Julia appeared next to Gallantae. In order to see over the flowers, Scoobee reared up. For balance, he placed one of his front paws on Julia's shoulder then asked, "Which one is it, the one on the left or the one on the right?"

Julia answered, "The one on the left is Mount Fairdra, the other is Drafair. In times before man, dragons and fairies would hold gatherings for all the Mythicals there."

Across the plain on the far horizon, Veronica could make out two mountain peaks; from this distance they looked small.

"You've been here before, Julia?" Zane asked.

"I grew up on the Plains, Master Zane," the royal cheetatarah replied.

"Are you ready to ride, Scoobee?" Veronica asked as she and Dalminyo walked up to the eclectic band of travelers.

Scoobee said, "As much as I look forward to accompanying you, V, I do not look forward to being rattled to bits by your young steed."

"Watch it, stubby, or you'll be finding your own way through this posy patch," Dalminyo replied. "Which could prove difficult since even the flowers are taller than you are."

Scoobee's hair bristled, and his tail stood at attention. But before he could respond, Julia intervened. "All right, boys, it's going to be a long day, so why don't you two try to be on your best behavior?"

Veronica picked up Scoobee and slid him into the saddlebag that she had transferred from Gallantae's saddle to Dalminyo's.

Then as the Princess mounted, Scoobee quipped, "Hey Julia, if I promise to be on my best behavior will you catch me a zadeer for dinner? I'm drooling just looking at those tasty morsels walking around over there."

The great cat gave the dog a sideways glance then purred, "Time for paws and hooves to fly, boys. Stay close... if you can."

Julia uncoiled onto the plain, and the firedancers parted in her wake. And with that, first Dalminyo with Veronica and Scoobee on board, then Gallantae who carried Zane, set out after the cheetatarah across the Mitigo Plains. With shared purpose they rode toward Mount Fairdra to rescue Princess Sophia.

Chapter Thirty-One
Moldea

Before I continue, Yorgide must inform you of what has been happening in Moldea since before our story began. Again, this is not for editorial purposes, though Yorgide's opinions are of course valid and the wise do heed them. This is simply information you must be made aware of, yes indeed.

The Land of Moldea lies on the far side of Mount Fairdra. A large portion of it is arid wasteland. Only a few inhabitants try to scratch out a livelihood in the Inculta Moldea. It is harsh, yet holds a beauty all its own, not completely unlike some of your deserts on earth, actually. However, as the land moves up the slopes into the foothills of The Raknorock, the Inculta gives way to an oasis.

As I mentioned in passing earlier, The Raknorock are the high mountains that encircle all of Virtier. These peaks are so high they cannot be summited by humans, for air is so scarce up there. They are quite literally the end of the world. Beyond them is Empty Space.

In the Land of Moldea, at the base of The Raknorock, sits the city of Moldea, a jewel in the desert. Or at least it once was. It is here that Cort Leamoldae was born, and from here that he plotted his first attempt to usurp power, first from his own and then the adjoining Lands. It is here too that he, as Lord Leamoldae, returned from banishment.

For reasons beyond Yorgide's comprehension, his kin welcomed him, as if a prodigal son had returned. As if his once wicked ways were all in the past. But then, as he brought more and more creatures through the city's Arch from the Lower Tiers, his cousin, the King, tried to withdraw his hospitality. It was too late.

True to his character, Lord Leamoldae killed the King and made the rest of his kin swear their allegiance to him. The few who would not joined immediately in their late King's fate. I mean really, could they not see this coming?

When Lord Leamoldae left with Daelkay for KenKarta, where they stole away Sophia, the Dark Lord had left strict instructions for his banmen (or men who have been banished) and pallamales to continue bringing his army up from the edge of the Abyss. He expected the task to be all but complete when he returned. This way, once he forced King Dale to reveal the location of the Onoxmon, by offering Sophia's safety in return, the Dark Lord's army could sweep across the Lands of the Center Tier like a plague. In truth, Yorgide knows all too well, if Leamoldae leads an army from the Lower Tiers with the Onoxmon in hand, nothing on Virtier will stop him.

Leamoldae is a lot of things, but dumb is not one of them. He knew something was wrong as soon as he tried to use the Arch at Bedforda, only to find that KenKarta's Hunters had retaken it. Immediately, Leamoldae sent one of his most trusted servants to find Daelkay. By his own command the dragon's mind was closed to his calls for five days, but now this must change. The trusted servant was to leave some troops to guard the girl and bring the dragon back to him.

In the meantime, since he could not travel by Arch from Bedforda to reach and torture King Dale as planned, Leamoldae rode his poor tormented equidae nonstop, day and night, toward Moldea. He sustained Hellantae's pace through powers of the Abyss, and he did it with little regard for the long-term effects such exposure might have on his steed.

Yes, Hellantae truly is Gallantae's twin brother, whom everyone thought was dead. Poor thing. As a colt, he was swept through an Arch by accident, and from there he drifted through Empty Space for a great time until one day by sheer happenstance he was pulled onto a path leading to an Arch on a Lower Tier. The annuals of exile in Empty Space had damaged Hellantae's young mind and made him susceptible to dark influences. In such a diminished state, it was not hard for Leamoldae, after his banishment to Exiltier, to press the equidae into his service.

Though their flight was swift, Leamoldae's mood was foul. The extended overland journey cost him time he could not spare. So when he arrived in Moldea only to find that passage through the Arch below was no longer possible, he was enraged. Right after he and Daelkay left, the Arch on the Lower Tier failed. Meaning, no additional troops had been brought up to Virtier. Meaning, his army was incomplete.

Thinking it must be sabotage, Leamoldae sent most of his kin through the Arch to Exiltier. One after the next he dragged them before the Arch. He opened it. Surrounded by the black of Empty Space, he let them see the unwelcoming orange glow of Exiltier flickering at its center. He observed as terror twisted and contorted each face, as he read between the lines, watching for the answer. When he saw none, he pushed them through and started again with the next. One of them must know why the Arch no longer operated in both directions. One of them would surely offer a solution to repair it, rather than remain trapped on a Lower Tier. Yet, thus far, the evil Lord's efforts proved fruitless.

In Yorgide's opinion, the only thing Leamoldae managed to accomplish by banishing his kin was to ruin the quality of dinner conversation in Moldea's castle. No one came back through the Arch, thus there was really no one left from the royal court to talk to. Now Leamoldae ate his meals alone and boiled with rage.

Leamoldae bit into the leg of the roasted entrée before him.

He seethed, but clung to a thin strand of hope as well. If anyone could get the Arch up and running again it was Daelkay. After all, he was the one who had brought the Alistone from Dragontier to make the Arch operate in both directions to begin with. But where was the beast? If Leamoldae's servant could not find him, then the dragon would not try to contact its master until at least the fifth day.

The Dark Lord could not wait for that. Surprise was no longer on his side. His army, while large, was not at full strength, and he did not have the Onoxmon. His mood was foul indeed.

The Dark Lord pushed away from the table and stepped from the shadows onto the balcony into the shine. He lifted his lean chiseled face to the sky to drink in its rays; he had always loved the feel of shine on his skin. Yorgide must tell you that they do not call him dark because of his appearance; there is nothing dark about it. Nothing about his shine-kissed hair and fine features look menacing on their own. No, his appearance is both handsome and deceptively wholesome. The darkness comes from somewhere deep within him.

Leamoldae slammed his fist down on the railing of the balcony. The white-haired pallamale standing at attention behind him in the shadows flinched and blinked his large pink eyes as the Dark Lord yelled, "W h e r e is my dragon?"

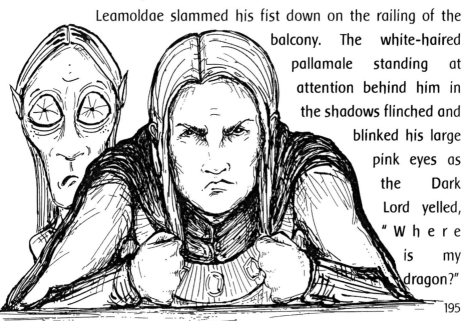

The pallamale's long angled face remained blank. Leamol-dae's bellowed question was rhetorical, and he knew better than to try and answer it. Below, Lord Leamoldae could see his army of miscreants. In the shine of day they were truly hideous, revolting even. Pale skin marred with scars, and twisted, damaged forms were the norm. It's hard to believe, but the worst of them were still trapped on the tiers below.

Though endlessly annoying, Leamoldae had sent the hobyahs through the Arch in large numbers first. Tenacious pawns, they made great scouts and could live off of anything. However, a heavy hand was imperative to manage them, otherwise it was like herding monkeys. Lucky for Leamoldae, like his heart, his hands were stone. He found fear to be a wonderful and, in fact, a preferred motivational tool.

By Leamoldae's estimate, pallamales made more than tolerable soldiers. With frames and dexterity not unlike humans, they were good archers and shields-men and adequate swords-men when properly enticed. They were industrious and, most importantly to Leamoldae, they were obedient. Unlike the smaller, more ruthless and obstinate hobyahs, pallamale's rarely questioned orders. The Dark Lord brought up their numbers next.

The original plan sought to bring most of the cavevils up last because while they would wreak the most havoc, they were the hardest to control. The smallest of the cavevils stood more than a story high, and their shoulders were as broad as a horse from nose to tail. Their muscular forms were covered with heavy dark gray fur. They walked upright on two legs like a man, but their arms were long so when they ran they dropped and loped along on all fours. They were fast, strong, and mean. All their facial features were flat, as if they'd run into something, except for their teeth, which were fangs. Time and again, they'd proven unable to go any significant period without shredding something or someone apart. Leamoldae had just started to bring up their numbers when the Arch below failed.

The Dark Lord also brought up other humans, banmen, who

had been sent through the Arch to the Lower Tier as banishment for crimes against their former Lands. He used these murderers and traitors to keep the cavevils in line because the pallamales were too terrified of them. Truth was, even the nastiest banman could only keep a cavevil in line for so long.

The time to act had come. If he sat here much longer the army that KenKarta was surely raising would be able to trap him with his back against The Raknorock. Not to mention that if he didn't get this army on the move, it would begin to tear itself apart, literally.

Daelkay would show, but Cort Leamoldae could not wait until then. It was time to move. "Ready the troops. We march at once," the Dark Lord said without turning away from the balcony.

The pallamale blinked and twitched his nose. It turned and walked silently from the room.

So there you have it. That is what waits beyond the Mitigo Plains and Inculta Moldea. And it saddens Yorgide to tell you that that is what our band of rescuers runs recklessly towards. I guess ignorance is bliss, for them not you of course. For now you have insight into a far darker picture than what our would-be heroes can currently see. Let me show you...

Chapter Thirty-Two
Crossing the Mitigo

Their journey across the robust plains proved beautiful. Strange and wonderful creatures popped up everywhere. Veronica's favorite so far had been the camallo. She marveled at their long shaggy cream coats waving in the breeze over their thick powerful legs. It wasn't that she hadn't seen them before, for camallo were used as beasts of burden across most of the Lands. Despite their great size and strength, they were gentle, friendly creatures even if a bit smelly. She had seen them in service plenty, had even seen one dead back in the meadow just yesterday, but this was the first time she had seen them roaming free. Their heavy heads swayed slightly from side to side atop their strong necks as they lumbered lazily across the plains. All creatures on the Mitigo Plains were free. It was theirs, not man's. No man was allowed to live here. People could only pass through. The people of the Yolnegue ventured onto it daily from their Lands to the north, but they could not stay to settle it. The Mitigo Plains were long ago set aside as a haven for Mythical and non-mythical creatures alike.

Veronica, Zane, Dalminyo, and Scoobee had never seen anything like it. They all expressed a desire to linger, to examine every creature they passed up close and in detail, but since they could not stop, the countless wonders were usually gone as quickly as they appeared.

Yet, despite their desire to do so, the distance was too great for the equidaes and cheetatarah to run full speed the entire way across the Mitigo Plains. This meant they had to slow to a trot from time to time. On one of these occasions the group came upon a pair of the largest animals Veronica and Zane had ever seen. Kaboukaba were in fact the largest animals to walk Virtier. Their bodies were about twice the size of a dragon, even bigger than Bella's. Their necks were much longer than hers as well and their tails stretched out rather stiffly in an equal distance behind them. Known for their incredible eyesight, kaboukaba could see great distances across the plains when they lifted their heads.

As the group of travelers got closer, they could feel the

ground tremble under the kaboukabas' plodding steps. Julia's tail twitched from side to side to keep her balance as she approached closer to offer them a greeting. A high-pitched whine burst from one of the great beasts. The kids covered their ears, Dalminyo flinched, and Scoobee ducked his head down into the saddlebag in pain.

Gallantae simply said, "That is their way of saying hello."

"That could make a guy's ears bleed," Zane said. "In fact I think yours are, Dalminyo."

"Your wit is transparent, *stable boy*, and mine is too sharp to be fooled so easily," the equidae replied. Then he closed his thoughts to Zane and asked Scoobee, "Seriously, Little Man, my ears aren't bleeding, right?"

Distracted, Scoobee replied, "What?"

Dalminyo twitched his ears and turned his head from side to side as if to catch a glimpse of them. "I mean you'd tell me if they were, right?"

"Who knew you were such a hypochondriac, Dalminyo. Be quiet, head case. I'm trying to hear."

"Well yes, of course, I am too. No need for name calling just because I take pride in my appearance. Unlike a certain flea bitten, wolf-want-ta-be I happen to know."

They were too far away to hear the rest of the non-verbal exchange between Julia and the kaboukaba, but Veronica thought she would never forget the image of two massive beasts with short burnt-orange-and-yellow-stripped coats bowing their necks down to the ground to converse with a large purple-spotted cat that somehow still looked small next to their broad elongated heads. Dalminyo wanted to stop, but Gallantae insisted that they keep going. So while the conversation ensued, the equidaes continued to trot on, slowly passing by the odd trio.

Dalminyo asked, "Have you ever seen anything so big in your entire life?"

"Nope," Scoobee replied.

"It's a good thing they're friendly. I can't imagine how you'd go about fighting something like that," Dalminyo said, turning his head to face Scoobee and watch the trio that was now behind them.

"Ahhh, don't be such a foal, Dalminyo," Scoobee said with a growl deep in this throat and just his head and front paws poking out of the saddleback. "We could take em!"

Dalminyo began, "Well of course we could-"

Virtier shook. The two giant kaboukaba turned away from Julia and headed off in opposite directions. A high-pitched wail split the air. Dalminyo jumped sideways, almost unseating Veronica while Scoobee ducked his head down once again into the saddlebag.

Zane laughed. "That's spec! Look at the mighty warriors jump and hide."

Veronica's laughter mixed with Zane's as the kaboukabas moved further away. They covered ground quickly, and the virtier shuddered less with each passing step. Veronica's thoughts drifted and she wished, as she often had over the past days, that Sophia was with her. Her little sister would think the kaboukabas were the Pinn.

A moment later, Julia appeared just ahead of the equidaes, stopping them short. "A dark army is on the move in Moldea. It's headed right for Fairdra." She turned to face the mountain that loomed ahead of them now, and then over her shoulder added, "There's no more time to waste. We've got to reach Sophia before that army does."

Veronica's heart raced as remorse pumped into her veins. This was all her fault. If she hadn't chased Sophia from her room that night the little twerp never would have left the protection of the castle. Sure, Sophia frustrated her, drove her crazy sometimes, but Veronica loved her sister. She could not bear the thought of something bad happening to Phia. Guilt squeezed her lungs until she could hardly breathe. Dalminyo felt her distress and reared up slightly on his back legs. She leaned out over his neck, his front hooves hit virtier, and they were off like lightening uncorked from a bottle.

Sophia thought she heard a child's voice outside the cave, so she snuck to its opening. She peered around the rocky lip and saw the back of a girl with long black hair talking to Daelkay.

"Crystal, your current form suits you. You're growing up so fast."

"Pet names and flattery will get you whatever you want, Daelkay," the girl said sweetly with the slightest hint of a lisp. "Why have you eluded me so? I passed this way just days ago and saw nothing. It's as if you didn't want to be found."

"I hide only from my enemies."

"Your little bird in a cage has been chirping to her sister. I think they dream speak."

"Not to worry, Your Highness, we'll be gone soon. I trust that is why you are here."

"Our master summons you, that is true, but the plan has changed. The Arch on the Lower Tier is broken. He is beyond furious." She tipped her head as if to listen to something and then continued, "We go, but the girl is to stay here. My men will stay to guard her." She spun around.

When the girl turned, Sophia had to hold in a scream. This wasn't a girl at all, but a hobyah! Sophia thrust her body back flat against the stone wall. Her stomach knotted. Her chest heaved. She was breathing, but no air reached her lungs. Tears filled her eyes to the brim. Then a beautifully masked red bird came to rest on the antlers of a zadeer the dragon had snacked on earlier. From its gruesome perch it looked directly at her.

"Ember?"

"Sit tight, Sophia, help is on the way," Ember said with her mind. A rock struck the carcass, just missing the hawken.

She took flight and was gone. A second hobyah ran up to the carcass. Sophia pressed her back even harder to the wall. Her vision blurred and went dark. Then an image appeared. She was looking down the slope of a mountain, it was Mount Fairdra. At the base of the mountain she saw movement amid a grove of small squatty trees. The image focused in, and she could see Julia and Veronica. Crouched down, they crept up the mountain's slope.

Much too abruptly, Sophia's own vision returned. She screamed. Instead of the magnificent sight of her loved ones, a horrible monster was right up in her face. The hobyah snarled at her, spattering spit all about.

Still screaming, Sophia turned and ran toward the back of the cave.

Behind her, Daelkay's voice boomed, "Stop."

The hobyah might have complied but Sophia kept running toward the fairy castle courtyard.

Zane said, "I see her, Veronica! I think I see Sophia! Ember has found her."

"Is she all right?" Veronica asked.

"Yes." Then Zane's breath caught, and the blood drained from his face as his vision focused through Ember's eyes to see high up the mountain's slope. "There are hobyahs, and there's the dragon."

"We've got to get to her!" Veronica said as she began to scramble recklessly over boulders toward the open slopes of Mount Fairdra.

Julia leapt in front of her to block her path.

"Veronica, stop!" Gallantae whinnied.

"We've got to get to her!"

Julia moved in until her shoulder was against Veronica's waist. "We will, but we are no match for a dragon, Veronica. We must think this through. If we don't, you'll get us all killed."

Sophia huddled behind the back edge of the castle against the cold polished stone of the cave wall, her gaze glued to the entrance. At any moment the hobyah would surely burst through and attack her. Time crept by.

Cordova slinked to the edge of the castle, peered out, and squeaked, "What's happening, Miss?"

Tear-lines streaked Sophia's cheek. Her voice tore at her throat. "Hobyahs, they're real, they're after me."

"If they come in, you must use the shield, do you remember how?"

Sophia was too afraid to answer.

"Young Miss, do you hear me?"

Something rustled at the front of the cave. Sophia let out a whimper as she clutched the wall. Cordova shrunk down as small as he could get and pulled in his limbs until he resembled nothing more than a fur ball with eyes. Sophia feared she would scream. Something was coming. Near the top of the wall that blocked the entrance from her view she glimpsed a bluish-purple snout with flared nostrils. Daelkay's head appeared around the corner. Cordova scrambled for cover.

Sophia sobbed with relief and ran toward the dragon as he continued to enter the cave. "Oh Daelkay, please don't let them get me!"

"Do not worry, Young Princess. They will not harm you. They are here to guard you in my absence, nothing more. I must leave now, but if you stay inside the castle's courtyard the hobyahs will not be able to reach you, even if they wanted to."

"No, Daelkay, you can't leave me!"

"I must."

"Why?"

"My master sends me on a mission."

"A mission, what mission? Daelkay, please, you already have a mission."

"What do you think my mission is, child?"

"To bring me my daddy!"

Daelkay's eyes narrowed, and he lowered his head level with Sophia's. "A dragon must follow the wishes of the one he is Bonded to. It is doubtful I will ever return to this cave, so-"

"Please Daelkay, please!"

"You are too young to understand."

"I'm not too young!" Sophia screamed, more frustrated than angry but balling her hands into fists all the same. "*Please*, I'll do anything!"

"Anything, Sophia?"

"*Yes*!" she wailed. "What if I could give you something, something you need?"

The Dragon paused for a long moment, and then in a low voice rumbled, "You have nothing to offer that I need, child."

"I do-"

Daelkay raised his voice enough to scare her. "Stay within the castle's defense system. It will protect you now that you have helped the kangamou charge the crystal."

"But how did you know?" Sophia said, wiping away tears.

"There is much I know that you do not, little one. For

instance, I know that I must now say farewell, Sophia Marie, Royal Princess of KenKarta." He bowed his giant head. Traditionally the gesture and use of her full name was a sign of respect and courtly manners dictated that she now do the same.

"Fine! Who needs you anyway?" Sophia crossed her arms in defiance and stomped back onto the tile of the courtyard. In a further attempt to prove that she didn't need his help, she focused her thoughts. The castle's shield flashed from floor to ceiling, showing its activation at her command. "Go on your mission, you old beast, you, you, false keeper of secrets and lore."

Without breaking form and without showing the slightest anger over her display of disrespect he nodded and said, "As you ask, young mistress."

Daelkay the dragon turned and exited the cave while Sophia the Princess crumpled to the floor and cried.

Chapter Thirty-Five
The Rescue

The band of rescuers had just snuck up the western slopes of Mount Fairdra. All froze when the form of a dragon took to the sky. Was someone on its back? Veronica tried to be sure, but the creature banked hard to the east and north and was quickly out of sight.

"All right, now is our chance." Julia purred. "We have no way of knowing how long it will be before he returns."

Zane said, "Ember sees only four hobyahs. They appear to be guarding the cave that I saw Sophia go into earlier."

Veronica said, "Yeah I see them, but there might be more inside with her."

Gallantae said, "We should fan out and take the four outside quietly."

"Leave the far one, the closest to the entrance, to me. I'll take him first," Julia said, her claws extended and lip drawn slightly to bare her teeth. "He'll never see me coming, but I will be the last thing the others ever see. When they turn on me, you can take them from behind."

Sophia sat on the tiles of the fairy castle's court with her arms tightly wound around her knees, pulling them up to her chest. She slowly rocked back and forth. Her sobs had quieted, but she still hid her face in the skirt of her dress. What was that sound? She was too afraid to look up. She didn't want to see that face again. Even if the hobyah would not be able to get to her, she didn't want to see its deformed spindly form ever again.

The cave was quiet. But in her head the Princess heard her name: "Sophia?"

That voice? "Julia!" Sophia exclaimed as she looked up to see the large cat with purple spots padding toward her around a slight bend that led from the cave entrance to the chamber she was in.

Sophia jumped up and ran to Julia. Just before she reached the threshold of the court, the place where the defense system would have been activated, Cordova rushed to remove a crystal from a pedestal within a small room in the castle. His action disengaged the defense system, and Sophia ran straight through. She wrapped her arms tight around the cheetatarah's neck and buried her face in Julia's fur.

Arms still firmly locked around Julia's neck, Sophia saw Veronica slowly round the corner, sword drawn, alert and wary. Their eyes met. Veronica dropped her sword and ran to her. Sophia stood up and gave her sister the biggest hug ever.

"Oh, Sophia, we've been so worried. I'm so sorry."

"Why are you sorry? I knew you would find me, Veronica. I just knew it." Her sister's embrace had never felt better. She was safe!

After a few moments Sophia noticed a boy watching from the chamber's threshold. He started forward only after Gallantae assured him he would keep a look out for more hobyahs.

As he approached, Veronica said, "Sophia, I would like you to meet Zane, he's... he's a friend."

Sophia began, "It's nice to meet-"

Scoobee came running into the cave. Skidding, his paws flew frantically to make the turn. "Oh, there's my pretty

Princess. Make way! Let me at her!" He zipped right between Veronica and Zane and jumped up on Sophia. She knelt down to receive his wet little kisses all over her face.

Sophia laughed. "Oh Scoobee, hello there, Little Man."

The dog's muscles tensed. His ears and tail spiked. Scoobee's attention abruptly turned to the fairy castle. He left Sophia and began sniffing intently, sticking his head into one room then another.

Veronica asked, "What is it, Scoobee, what's wrong?"

Scoobee emitted a high-pitched cry. Started to move one way, snuffed, then darted back to where he'd just been. The hair on his back went up and his tail quivered.

"Oh, no! No, Scoobee, No!" Sophia yelled, running to grab him by the collar. "Veronica help, he's going to eat Cordova!"

Against his protests, which included a few growls, Veronica picked up Scoobee. In full-on hunt mode now, there was no reasoning with him. Meanwhile, Sophia reached inside the room Scoobee had been trying to enter and scooped up the cuddly little kangamou. He did not look pleased.

Veronica cooed, "Ah, what a sweetie. Is that a kanga-mou?"

"Yes," Sophia said, "and he is our host."

"I am so sorry about my dog, sir," Veronica said to the kangamou. She frowned at Scoobee, whose body was still stiff but no longer straining against Veronica's grip. "He has obviously lost his furry little mind! But I assure you, he meant no disrespect."

"Oh *no*, I'm *sure* he was going to eat me with the utmost respect," Cordova replied.

"Veronica, this is Cordova," Sophia said as she lifted

him up for them all to see.

Veronica said, "Hello there, Cordova, it's nice to meet you. Mind if I call you Cory?"

"As a matter of fact I do," the kangamou said, fluffing out his fur here and there, then licking his paw and drawing a whisker through it.

"Oh, okay. Then Cory it is!" Zane teased. "You can call me Zane."

Upon taking flight, the dragon headed northeast, directly toward Moldea. He plummeted, a mere wingspan above the slopes of Mount Fairdra, until he reached the wide mouth of the valley that would rise up to meet the Inculta Moldea, where the fertile ground turned porous and the ridges became limestone cliffs. Their swift descent caused his passenger to let out a shrill squeal. It sounded terrified, but the dragon knew this noise was really a sound of delight. He also knew that for the moment the young creature's mind was on nothing else, just the thrill of flight.

He continued up the valley, steadily gaining altitude. From his vantage point high in the dimming sky, Daelkay could now see Leamoldae's army moving through a narrow valley within the Inculta Moldea. A disruption had broken out amongst the ranks at the head of the column, and progress had stopped. The dragon flew to the rear of the army where Leamoldae could normally be found, for he was not the sort of commander to lead by example.

As the dragon's talons touched virtier, the female hobyah dropped to the ground. She scanned the area. Then barked orders at creatures that dwarfed her physically. Nonetheless, they hurried to comply. "There is no time to waste, Daelkay. You need to go to Exiltier, torture that false King, and bring back the Onoxmon. I will tell our master that there is no army between us and the Mitigo Plains."

"As sound as your plan may be, you forget one thing, young Crystal... you are not my master."

"That is true, at least for now, fair dragon," the hobyah hissed through a sneer. Several of the Dark Lord's banmen were paying close attention to their conversation. "You know as well as any the special place I hold in the master's heart. I will take responsibility. His fury will be great if you wait only to be told to do what we already know to be his wish."

"As you ask then," Daelkay replied with a slight nod.

He sensed that the watching banmen were adequately impressed with the smaller being's ability to command the dragon. She turned and stalked away with her head held high. The dragon pushed off with his powerful legs and took to the ever-darkening sky. As amusing as he found her to be now, Daelkay knew the day would come when Crystal would have to be dealt with. This day however, he must do his master's bidding.

Chapter Thirty-Seven
From Joy to War

Once Sophia assured her rescuers that the dragon would not be coming back, Gallantae and Julia determined that the cave would be the easiest place to defend the Princesses until morning. Veronica agreed. So despite the youngsters' jokes about his name and with numerous reassurances that Scoobee would no longer try to devour him, Cordova was a gracious host. Using fairy magic, the little kangamou swirled them all up a wonderful feast. The brightly colored food covered a low platform like a sculpture and pillows were strewn around all sides. Spires twirled upward with what looked like delicate leaves, vines, and flowers spinning off. It was like nothing they'd ever seen. It looked more like art than food. It was too gorgeous to eat, so instead they just sat on the pillows and stared.

"Don't be shy," Cordova told them. "Dig in, Fairy Feasts are legendary."

Sophia asked, "But how? And what parts?"

"Oh, with your fingers of course, this is not a formal banquet. This is but a small sampling of what a real Fairy Feast is like, but I thought a celebration was in order, nonetheless. Everything you see there is edible," Cordova said, motioning toward his handiwork.

Veronica eyed the small kangamou cautiously, "But what does it taste like?"

"It's delicious. However, if you don't like the initial flavor, just think about how you want it to be, and it will taste like whatever you wish."

"No way!" Zane said before they all broke off a taste.

For a few brief hours the woes of the Lands were pushed back and Veronica, Sophia, and Zane, even Dalminyo, were able to act more like the youngsters they really were. This all occurred under the watchful eyes of Julia of course, while Gallantae and a sulking Scoobee stood sentry outside.

Their bliss was short lived however. Just as the last shine was being shrouded for the night, Scoobee trotted in to announce that they all needed to come outside.

There, from their vantage point high on Fairdra, under a tiery sky, the companions could see what those at ground level could not. Though still some distances off, on the plains beneath them, were the shadowy movements of three armies. They were on a collision course.

Now it is time for Yorgide to let you in on a little secret. Unbeknownst to most, King Rick had indeed gotten the message from his little sister, the Queen of KenKarta. He had raised his troops and left Askard immediately. He rarely sees his youngest sister, for he left Karta many annuals before she became a Queen, to conquer the wilds of Virtier's southeast and carve out a Kingdom of his own. His Land is remote and secluded, a haven for magical and Mythical creatures really. Many of this ilk seek out his realm because he and his wife Nancy are known to doctor them back to health when they are ill and protect them from unwanted human attention. Rick and Nancy love their Land and rarely leave it. However, Alison is family and when family needs your help, you help. So when Rick received word of his sister's latest troubles, he marched his army north without hesitation.

Now with the fading shine he is positioned just southeast of Mount Drafair, the sister mountain to the south of Mount Fairdra. The small mountains that rim the Inculta Moldea block his view to the north where Leamoldae approaches with an army of his own.

Lord Leamoldae has been driving his forces at a relentless pace down from the north across the Inculta Moldea. At the rate he is traveling, Leamoldae's minions will arrive at the foot of Mount Fairdra by morning.

To the west out on the Mitigo plains is yet another throng still shielded from view of the other armies. KenKarta's and Brython's forces joined at the edge of the Mitigo and are pushing hard as well. They are headed right at the gap between the two mountains of Fairdra and Drafair. Only our young heroes on the slopes of Mount Fairdra had a clear view.

And now they had a decision to make…

Based on Gallantae's and Julia's assessments, they decided that Gallantae would head off to meet the forces from KenKarta. He would warn them of Leamoldae's approach so they could time their arrival accordingly. If the sight of KenKarta's army in a seemly unprepared position could entice Leamoldae into venturing out onto the enclosed plain between Mount Fairdra and Mount Drafair, then they would have a chance to box him in.

In addition, Julia must race to meet the girls' uncle Rick and slow him down. Otherwise he would arrive at what would soon surely be a battlefield before Leamoldae's forces did. If he instead held up his advance and hid until the Dark Lord finished crossing the Inculta Moldea, then the King of

Askard would be in a position to flank the evil horde.

By the time the equidae and cheetatarah were off on their ways, the shroud of darkness had drawn completely. It was clear to Veronica that all needed rest. Calling once more upon the fairy magic stored within the little castle, Cordova made beds for the three children. They would sleep within the castle's protective shield. Dalminyo volunteered to stand watch at the cave's entrance and Scoobee would provide a secondary line of defense inside.

Not until the three children were all lying down did Sophia, who insisted on sleeping with her sister, whisper into Veronica's ear, "I have the Onoxmon."

Veronica listened intently as Sophia told about her stay with the dragon and how she found the stone lodged under his scales.

Zane offered that the King must have hidden it there as he was being captured. From what he had viewed through Ember's eyes, he'd seen it was possible.

Veronica asked, "Where is it, Sophia?"

"I hid it somewhere where no one bad could get it," Sophia said with a grin.

Shaking her head, Veronica asked, "And where might that be?"

Sophia's eyes gleamed. "On Fairytier!"

Zane said, "On Fairytier? How? Why in Lands would you put it there? We've got to get it back!"

"No." Veronica was not sure what to make of the development. She wished more than ever that her father were there so she could just give it to him. Unafraid, he would know what to do. Fear clawed under skin. What had become of her dad? What would become of her Land? Only one thing was certain. It was good that Leamoldae had not acquired the Onoxmon. And Veronica intended to keep it that way.

Chapter Thirty-Eight
To Face Your Fears

Veronica had good cause to worry about her father, yes indeed. He was in a fearful place, a place most could not endure. A place Yorgide does not wish to show you, but fears you must at least learn about. We all have fears, it is only natural, nothing to be ashamed of really. How your worth is determined, what you are measured by, is what you do when you must face those fears. That is what really counts. And perhaps that is what you have come here to learn.

Just as Ember had shown Zane, Lord Leamoldae had ambushed and captured the King in the meadow at the Valley-ridge. Leamoldae had always enjoyed causing others pain, but since his banishment, this was a practice at which he now excelled. He tortured King Dale until death crept fearfully close, and consciousness left him. Then the King of KenKarta was taken to a horrid place, Exiltier, a Lower Tier, a place from which those sentenced did not escape. I will show you only the shadows of this place, for that is all either you or I can bear.

In the center of a circular domed chamber, he was bound to the top of a large stone tablet by his wrists and ankles. The walls, dark and smooth, were carved out of solid obsidian. In truth, they had then been fired by dragon's breath. Yes indeed, the reflective qualities of the stone made it almost impossible to draw any natural power from the surroundings. It was no accident the King was here; this was a chamber made to imprison those with great Gifts.

Dale's blue eyes fluttered opened. He tried to pull his arms down and tugged against the restraints around his bare ankles.

222

He shook his head and squinted to see in the darkness. Then high above him in the gloom he saw the faint glow of a crystal. With his encouragement, the crystal began to shine. And you should know, in his weakened condition, with no environmental power to draw from, this normally simple feat was far more difficult than most could manage. By the crystal's dim and discolored orange glow, Dale took in his surroundings.

There was movement. Startled by the increased light, a darkly hooded and cloaked human shape hurried to escape. As the figure tried to open the door, the King reached out with his thoughts to probe the mind before him. 'What is this place?' he questioned. In response he read confusion and fear. Panicked by Dale's intrusion into its mind, the creature spun around to reveal his pale almost translucent skin and bulbous pink eyes. The pallamale's broad nose twitched and its thin lips quivered as its mind hissed, 'No speak, Leamoldae kill if speak, don't think of plan, don't let false King know plan.'

Pallamales are from the Lower Tier of Pallatier, so its presence on Exiltier was distracting, to say the least. It indicated that Leamoldae could travel between Lower Tiers. But how? But I digress. That's a question for a later time.

"What plan must the pallamale not speak of?" Dale asked out loud since it was clear the creature had been warned of his ability to read and influence those with weak minds. And let Yorgide assure you, pallamales are not known for possessing sparkling intellect. But would the King's question have the desired effect?

Yorgide knows that the shocked pallamale shut its eyes and thought, 'Think not of the invasion, my lord says think only of rats, false King hates rats, call the rats. Rats!' Mind still racing, the pallamale made a shrill whistle-like squeal, turned, and fled the room through the heavy giant door.

"Nooooooo!" the King roared in frustration, pulling against his bonds as the huge, dragon-sized door clunked shut with a loud but dull thud. He tried to reach through the door of this crypt with his mind, but as expected, he could not. As designed, the reflective surface of the door and walls, as well as his weakened condition, prevented it. Then out of the darkness came scratching, snuffing, and squeaking. Dale looked down to the far edge of the chamber and there, through a series of small openings, came white haired, pink-eyed, rats. He shuddered, then dropping his chin to his shoulder the King said, "Of all the creatures on all the Tiers, of course, he puts me with rats."

Did you know that long ago the King and Cort Leamoldae had gone to school together? Of course you didn't, but it's true. Their history is deep. Back then they knew each other well, too well. It was from those school days that Leamoldae knew of Dale's severe rodent phobia. The young would-be King hated the sight of mice and rats even then. He knew it was illogical, but the fear was paralyzing all the same. As a parent he taught his children that they must overcome their fears, yet here was one he himself had never been able to beat. A bit 'do as I say, not as a do,' don't you think?

Out of fury and frustration, King Dale called out to whoever might be listening: "Where's your evil lord now? Are you afraid to do your own dirty work, Leamoldae? When you spoke of your countless minions, I should have known you were speaking merely of rats. Rodents are the only things that would ever follow you."

The King drifted in and out of consciousness. Time passed without measure. Each instance he opened his eyes he felt weaker than the last. He waited for someone, something to come. Surely there would be more torture. Leamoldae had waited annuals

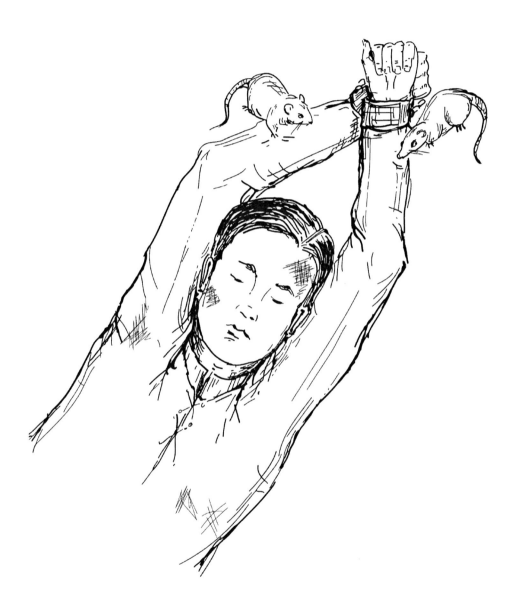

for this; he would savor it. Time slid by, but there was nothing, nothing but the rats. At first they scratched and sniffed about the chamber's edge, but now they grew bolder. They moved ever closer. It was torture. But torture enough to satisfy Leamoldae's blood lust? Doubtful. Where was he? The pallamale spoke of an invasion.

Though it repulsed him, Dale came to the conclusion that he must let the rats touch him. The walls surrounding him were sealed by dragon's breath, so the powers of no natural elements were at his disposal. This meant he had to rely solely on the power of his own mind. Yet, despite his weakened condition, he did manage to control a few of the rodents' feeble brains and force them to gnaw at the straps that bound him. Their scaly tails and whiskers brushed up against his bare hands and feet. His stomach turned. His skin crawled. And on more than one occasion, unable to control his reflexes, his jerks knocked a few of them off onto the floor. Snippets from youthful nightmares featuring encounters with rodents on his father's farm flashed before him. He winced, but he had to do this. There was no other way.

When the last bond broke free, Dale jumped to his feet atop the stone slab where he had been tied. The creatures in closest proximity to him scattered. Then and only then, across the room, across a sea of white rodents, he saw his sword and boots on a rock shelf. The only way to get to them was to walk barefoot through the throng of rats milling about on the floor. He hung his head in only somewhat mock defeat and sarcastically muttered, "Ah, come on, you're killin' me!"

Chapter Thirty-Nine
No, Not Yet

Zane ran in to the cave. "Veronica, you should see this!"

He turned and headed back outside, then returned again when no one followed him. V and Sophia sat on one of the low feather mattresses they'd slept on. They were putting on their shoes, but Veronica remained aware of Zane. He was hovering, picking impatiently at the edge of a stone protruding from the cave wall. They stood. Sophia adjusted her dress, and Veronica arranged her weapons. Veronica glanced over and caught Zane rolling his head and eyes, his thought quite clear: How long were they going to take? Veronica giggled. Zane locked his gaze on her. Lips pursed and eyebrows raised, he held up his hands to Veronica and motioned for her to come.

Veronica smiled. "All right, all right." Then teasing, she turned back to pick up her sword, "Oh wait, I almost forgot-"

Her body jerked slightly and spun. Zane had her by the wrist and was pulling her out onto the ledge. She should be mad. You don't just drag a Princess around like a pet on a leash. He would get in big trouble for doing something like this back at the castle. She should pull away and make a point of berating him. Instead she followed willingly, smiling up at him. Her amusement turned to concern however, when the first rays of morning shine highlighted his deep blue eyes, flashing with excitement but narrowed in anxiety.

The approaching armies were almost upon each other.

227

The shine was dim in this early-morning hour, but growing brighter in the east behind Leamoldae's forces. The pale-skinned pallamales marched forward as if fleeing its light. Behind them plodded the monstrous cavevils. Hobyahs scurried like ants amongst them all. While men, scarred and twisted by time below, intermingled and shouted orders.

Sophia asked, "What are we going to do?"

"We are going to stay right here," Veronica said.

"We can't just *sit* here!" Zane exclaimed. His hands clenched at his sides as he glanced from Veronica to the armies below.

"Yes, we can, and we will. We've done what we can by getting word of Leamoldae's advance to our forces. Our duty now is to stay here and keep Sophia and ourselves safe."

Zane began to pace. "But Veronica, what about the Onoxmon? Shouldn't we get it to our soldiers? Sophia, how do we get it-"

"No," Veronica said. "Without my father it's useless. No one else down there- except for, if what Daelkay says is true, Leamoldae- has the Gift to use it. What if we take it down there, and we lose it? Well, then he gets what he's wanted all along."

Veronica braced herself, prepared to defend her position. Zane glared at her, disbelief flashing in his blue eyes. She flipped her braid out of her way, squared her shoulders to him, and set her jaw. She would make him see that this was the best course. Order him if she had to. It was only natural that he would want to fight, but she would not risk losing Sophia, the Onoxmon, or him for no reason. His gaze flicked away from her then back again. His chin and eyebrows rose. He drew in a quick breath, and his lips parted as if to speak.

She waited, but instead he just exhaled and stepped back. His chin dropped and shoulders slumped ever so slightly in defeat. Ouch, how bruised was his ego? No time to worry about it now.

The bulk of KenKarta's forces were concentrated below her entourage on the northern part of the plain, at the far edge between the two mountains. She could just make out her uncles Keith and Mark plus the rest of the Hunters mounted on equidaes at its rear. Brython's forces, moving in slowly from the south, were behind, and as a result Veronica knew the line there was weak. From his vantage point at the high side of the valley, Leamoldae must have seen this too. His troops maneuvered to make an end run south to capitalize on it. All the troops on KenKarta's front line were armed with shields similar to Veronica's.

With the order to invoke them came a flash so bright it halted the enemy's advance. But only momentarily. Several rows of troops interlocked the shields to form a bluish-black shimmering wall that began at the ground and curved up over their heads. To most it would prove impenetrable, but if merely half the stories about them were true, and clearly their descriptions were not exaggerated, the cavevils were not like most. So long ago had been their banishment that none present had faced their likes before. Their reputation was fearsome.

To the rear of Leamoldae's main forces, a large group of pallamales had formed ranks and extended in a line across the leading edge of the Inculta Moldea. From the ledge, V had difficulty at first seeing exactly what they were doing. But there was no escaping the high shrill whistle. When it sounded, a swath of orange light appeared above the pallamales. In response, KenKarta's archers invoked the tips of their own arrows. A line of yellow light spread across their side of the battlefield.

The arrows flew in volleys from the rear ranks. Veronica glanced over at her sister. Sophia closed her eyes, covered her ears, and ducked to hide behind a boulder at the edge of the ledge. At least there, her little sister could not see the orange and yellow light from the arrows' glowing tips streak up and across the dark blue sky. But V worried that Sophia could still feel the ground shudder as navitas-telum, or arrow-like shafts of magical energy conjured by the Truly Gifted on both sides, began to bombard the opposing armies. Navitas' hue is dictated by what kind of Imperium Piece is used to generate them, so now the air filled with an explosion of color. Streaks of red, green, blue, and purple mixed with the yellow and orange from the arrows. As the colors met and then crossed, their arched pathways formed a rainbow of destruction overhead.

The armies clashed troop to troop. The roar rose off the battlefield to reach them at their vantage point above. While Sophia hid, the others stared through cracks in the boulders that shielded their position to witness the butchery below. Veronica was sure that none of their young eyes had ever seen anything so brutal or mesmerizing, but awe turned to horror when the first cavevils smashed their way through the southern edge of KenKarta's line.

Veronica glanced again to check on Sophia. Her eyes were now open and fixed upward. Veronica tensed and looked to the sky. There, with her back turned from the battle, she saw the silhouettes of five dragons coming over the peak of Mount Fairdra. The lead dragon was white and had a passenger on its back.

Next to her Sophia said, "Mommy?"

Astride the lead dragon, the Queen looked down at the edge of the Inculta Moldea and caught a glimpse of her enemy. Leamoldae was still at the rear of his forces and had not yet engaged in the fight. As the dragons passed overhead, the Dark Lord lay one hand on his jewel-inlaid armored chest and pointed the other at the white dragon leading the rest. Though they looked decorative, the jewels were really Imperium Pieces and he knew all too well how to utilize their power. The Queen flinched, expecting navitas-telum to fly her way.

Instead, Leamoldae abruptly lowered his hand and strode forward. He roughly knocked several pallamales from his path and knelt out of view. The Queen craned off the dragon's side to see what Leamoldae did. There! An enormous mortar pointed up, right at her dragon. Unlike the smaller shafts of navitas-telum that Leamoldae would be able to generate himself, this mortar could create a larger, deadlier, stream of navitas.

Leamoldae hunched at its pedestal, no doubt giving the large but volatile Piece housed there an extra charge. Please, just blow up in his face! He stood and motioned the surrounding Pallamales forward. More afraid of their Lord than the possible explosion, they lay their hands on the cylinder to stimulate it. The green navitas-fluo that spat forth from the mortar was as malignant and full of malice as the evil lord's own heart. Alison had no time to warn Saphina. The great dragon did not see it coming. The navitas-fluo struck the white giant from beneath and behind. Her wings crumpled. She plummeted to Virtier.

The impact knocked the Queen from the dragon's back. She freefell with her face to the sky. Her mind raced, but the overwhelming thought that filled her consciousness was 'I have failed, failed them all; the girls, Dale, my people.' Then the wind in her ears filled with the screams of her daughters. The anguish in their voices was agony. With her arms outstretched to the Pinnacle above she quietly begged, "Please, not yet, don't take me yet. I'm not finished here."

She focused on suspending her fall, on making herself buoyant. Her plummet slowed ever so slightly. There was hope, then a jolt. It was shocking, coming sooner than expected. With a thud she felt a pulse of pain and her vision went dark. Her descent had ended.

Focus dead, her thoughts drifted. She imagined herself in her husband's embrace. She gave into it, clung to it, but her mind slipped. She was rising again, rising to the Pinn. That's it then— it's over. Though it remained unwelcome, death had come.

From their ledge, Sophia gripped her sister's hand like a vice as they watched in disbelief. Veronica knew the navitas blast had delivered a deathblow to the giant white dragon on which the Queen rode. She heard the shrieks of horror explode forth, as both the dragon and their mother tumbled toward the ground. Yet, somehow she was only vaguely aware that not all the piercing cries came from Sophia, some originated within her own chest.

A deafening boom of impact drowned out their wails of pain. The concussion wave caused by the creature's great weight colliding with Virtier amidst KenKarta's rear reserves coursed outward. It sucked up the air and ended the screams in an abrupt and shocked silence. Dust and debris flew in all directions, as if a meteor had struck. The roar faded to a distant rumble. Then, for a moment, an eerie quiet hung in the airborne rubble drifting above the battlefield.

The first word spoken was Sophia's; it was simply, "Daelkay..."

Right before the white dragon hit the ground something had streaked across the sky at a steep downward angle. Now the rising dust made it impossible to see clearly. Veronica could have sworn she saw a dragon with a rider pass under her mother mere moments before she hit the ground.

"That was Daelkay, Veronica, Daelkay just saved Mommy!" Sophia said.

"And Daddy, Sophia, Dad was on that dragon," Veronica added.

A victorious roar spread and rose above the troops of KenKarta as they too realized what had just happened. Their King and Queen were about to join the fight.

The world rushed back in on Alison as she heard the King say, "Sorry I'm late."

With a gasp she opened her eyes and found she had not been imagining her husband's embrace. She had no idea how, but there he was, looking at her with those mischievous blue eyes. Both of them on the back of an enormous purple dragon, climbing high in the sky, a dragon she knew but had not seen in annuals. A dragon who had stolen her child! She drew the King's sword. "Where is Sophia, you beast?"

"She is safe, my Queen."

"Your Queen— -"

Dale asked, "What *about* Sophia?"

Daelkay turned his neck as he flew so that the Queen could look deeply into his vivid sapphire eye. "My word as a dragon. Focus your efforts elsewhere for now."

She sensed the truth in his words. Yet, none of it made any sense as she heard herself say, "This is so like you, Dale, never around when I want you, but always there when I really need you!" She kissed him with relief then added, "What kept you?"

"Rats! Lots of them, big ones, the biggest of which it appears awaits us below. So, is there a plan?"

"The plan was for the dragons to form a giant traveling Archway, through which we'd send them all back to the Abyss. Get me to Saphina. She carried the Alistone, without it the Arch cannot be achieved."

"Alison, we don't just need the stone, we need the

dragon. A traveling Arch is not something that can be formed by humans."

"Says you."

"Says everyone."

"Well, it's a good thing you've brought us another then, isn't it?" She waved her hand over the dragon beneath them. "Daelkay, are you up to the task?"

"I will need your assistance, my lady."

"Good enough, first thing we've got to do is get the Alistone."

"Well, let's go then. I'm tired of waiting," the King said, using one of his favorite sarcastic sayings to tease and irritate his wife.

As they swooped out of the clouds, the Queen could see the chaotic battle scene below. She looked to her husband. He stared down. His brow deeply furrowed.

The line was holding on the north, but Leamoldae's cavevils ripped holes in the front line that KenKarta's forces had established across the plain between Mount Fairdra and Drafair on the south. One section had collapsed at the base of Drafair, and Leamoldae's troops crashed into it. Like waves on a beach the incoming tide of cavevils eroded KenKarta's forces like sand.

Brython's commander, who was in charge of the reserve forces, sent his troops to reinforce and prevent KenKarta's forces from being completely flanked. However, he set his line back at the opposite edge of Drafair. A pocket was forming, and Leamoldae's horde rushed in to fill it. KenKarta's reserves moved to form a new line as the old one began to slowly swing open like a gate to prevent them from being flanked. From the air it was clear that Brython's line still had room to move forward. Yet it did not. Brython's King, Norman, was a seasoned battle leader and a trusted friend.

The King exclaimed, "Why doesn't Norman advance? They're going to flank us!"

"Don't despair yet. Look." The Queen gestured toward the other side of Drafair where a valley led away to the southeast.

There, hidden from Leamoldae's view on the ground, stood a contingent of men and Mythicals. Judging strictly by numbers it was smaller than KenKarta's or Leamoldae's armies, so looked less formidable from this height. But the Queen knew better, for she knew its origin. This was an army used to being outnumbered and used to winning at all cost. The King glanced back at his Queen. He arched his shoulders and head away from her slightly to get a better view of her face. His eyes narrowed, searching for a clue as to who it was.

With a slight smile she simply stated, "Rick."

"You got Rick to leave Askard?"

"Well, you know, I promised him a fight, glory, all the usual. He waits to close in from behind."

He curled the left side of his lip into a half smile, and the playful lilt returned to his voice. "You know I love you when you're devious."

Matching his tenor she said, "I know." Then changing her tone to better suit the severity of the situation she said, "It won't do any good unless we get the Traveling Arch formed with the dragons and you drive the evil spawn through it."

"You don't ask for much do you?"

"I fear this time you'll have to unveil your ability to wield..." she raised the sword in her hand and saw a hole where the Onoxmon should be. "Where is it?"

The King said, "Apparently, lost."

The Queen groaned. "We can't do anything the easy way, can we?"

"Apparently, not," Dale said, and took his sword back from his Queen.

Daelkay landed next to the broken mass of the white dragon. As Dale and Alison's captains gathered around for instruction and to protect them, Daelkay rolled it over to reveal the Alistone hanging from an elaborate and ornate collar around its neck. The force of the crash had cracked the gem in two.

Stating what they all knew to be true, Alison said, "Without the stone we cannot achieve the Arch." Then to Dale she said, "As things stand we're seriously outmatched. Only the fastest of our forces could get here."

"Wait... We have another Alistone," Dale said. "Daelkay, can we achieve an Arch with the stone you carry?"

"Yes." The dragon growled, using the claws on his front leg to raise some scales on his chest to reveal the Alistone he had taken from the Secondary Arch on Dragontier two annuals before.

Alison was surprised, but she quickly put the pieces together and understood. "Are you ready to try and gain redemption for your many past misdeeds, dragon?"

Daelkay simply crouched, making his back accessible for the Queen to mount.

To those gathered, the King said, "Hear me. Continue to let Leamoldae gain ground in front of Drafair. Get word to have King Rick close in behind him and hold him there. The Queen and dragons will form the Arch against the mountain's slopes and we will drive Leamoldae's horde straight through."

238

Above the fray, Alison heard a distant cry... of her children? She snapped her head up and saw Veronica and Sophia on a ledge high above the plain. They waved frantically to her. Her heart raced. They were alive! Her relief was short lived though, for beneath them she saw a band of hobyahs making their way up the slopes toward her girls.

As she stepped toward them, Daelkay's giant head lowered to block her path. "If you go to them now, all will be lost."

"Get out of my way."

"My good Queen, you may save your children, but in doing so your Tier will be lost. You must complete your mission."

"Alison," the King said, grabbing his wife's arm. "We'll get them. You go with Daelkay."

"Dale?"

"Look, the boys are already on their way. They'll get our girls." He nodded toward the base of Fairdra where Kirk, Kameron, and Eric, the girls' cousins, already fought their way up the slopes toward the ledge.

Arrows fell like neon-rain across the battlefield. Shields large and small flashed on and off. Bolts of navitas streamed from side to side, some missing, others finding their marks, all shuddering virtier. Numerous large lumbering beasts, Mythical and non, collided with thunderous results. The clash of blade against blade rang out across the plain, and the cries of the wounded and dying hung in the air.

The King's eyes were not as steady as his voice when he said, "You must go now; it's our only chance to save them..." His gaze swept around the scene then returned to her. "All of them."

"Alison, your children will survive." Daelkay's voice rumbled low in his throat. "But only if you come with me now."

Chapter Forty-One
Back on the Ledge

Sophia held Veronica's hand as they watched Daelkay take to the sky with their mother on his back.

"We've got to get the Onoxmon to Dad," Veronica said. "Sophia, you said you opened the Arch. Can you do it again?"

"Maybe, but Veronica, I can't go through."

"Don't worry, Soph. I'll go," Veronica said. "Zane, you stay here with Sophia; Dalminyo, you let Dad know that we're coming with it."

An errant bolt of navitas from the enemy struck beneath the ledge. Veronica, Sophia, and Scoobee rolled across the ledge back toward the entrance of the cave. Rocks and small boulders skidded across the ledge. As the girls regained their feet, a hobyah dropped down from above and landed between them, Zane, and Dalminyo.

Veronica reached for her sword. She yelled to Zane, "Change of plans. Let my dad know we'll bring help."

"Veronica!" Zane hesitated.

"I've got this. You two get word to my father. Dalminyo! No matter what." Zane looked at them frozen with indecision. "Go!"

Zane vaulted onto Dalminyo's back as the hobyah sprang at Veronica. He made one last glance back to make sure that she had the upper hand. Dalminyo turned and was half way down the slope before the hobyahs there even realized it.

Daelkay landed high on the slope of Drafair and let the Queen slip to the ground.

"Daelkay, as soon as the others land we must..."

On the mountain ridge across the plain, her nephews were still only midway up the slope engaged in a fierce battle with a large swarm of hobyahs. She tracked upward until she found the outcrop where she had seen the girls. Her children were in danger of being completely overtaken by a group of hobyahs located just below the ledge.

"Alison, here is the Alistone," Daelkay said, blocking her view with his chest, pulling back the scales that had been covering it. The blue stone shone deep at its center. "Take it."

"Take it? No, you must do this. I need to help my children."

"You cannot help them now, Queen. It is those below who you must help. I will help your girls. I can still reach them in time."

"You could, but we need you to form the Arch. Have you deceived us yet again, Daelkay?"

"No, Queen. It is time that you follow your own lessons, face your own fears, and fully embrace your Gifts. You do not need me here to lean on. You can do this on your own."

"No human can do this alone-"

"True. If you are to survive this you are going to have to use not only what is inside of you but also what's beyond. Ask for help, Alison, but not from one as unworthy as me." Daelkay placed the Alistone into the Queen's hands. "May Deus be with you," he said and took flight.

Sophia watched over her sister's shoulder. Veronica fought bravely. She had dispatched the first hobyah with little trouble and moved toward the entrance to the cave. Then two more of

the gray beasts had jumped down to block their passage.

Engaging her shield, she had said, "Sophia, stay behind me!"

Amazed at her sister's skill and horrified by the danger, Sophia complied. Sophia had seen Veronica spar before, but it did not compare to this. With Veronica's intensity, the hobyahs' rage, and Scoobee's distracting yips and nips, death loomed real and imminent. Sophia winced as Veronica struck down both hobyahs only to be assaulted from behind. Now they were pushed back just over the cave's threshold. Scoobee barked loudly, making the pointed-ear creatures flinch and slow their advance. There were too many. If they turned and ran, they'd be overrun for sure.

Then in her mind Sophia heard Daelkay say, "Go deep into the cave, Sophia, clear back to the Arch. It is time for you to help yourself. I will do what I can here."

"Veronica, we have to go," Sophia said as she pulled her sister back into the cave. "Veronica, please, we have to go now! Look." Sophia pointed to the sky. Daelkay flew straight at them.

The winged giant swooped down and laid a trail of dragon's breath across the entrance to the cave. The girls ran deeper into the stone. The agonized screams of hobyahs caught in the superheated flames followed them. When they reached the back wall, Veronica turned and prepared to fight. The air carried the stench of scorched meat. Just up the tunnel, at the corner blocking the entrance, several pairs of eyes glowed in the smoky gloom. They started to slink forward and Scoobee broke into a relentless chorus of barking. It echoed off the stone surfaces of the cave and for the moment halted the hobyahs' advance.

Sophia called to Cordova, but then remembered that before the battle started he warned her that kangamous are not known for their courage. He planned on hiding deep in his tunnels until the fighting was done. So she wasted no time. She reset the crystal on its pedestal, activating the fairy castle's defenses herself.

Chapter Forty-Two
Achieving the Arch

The four dragons, who had been circling well out of fighting range over the battlefield, took their places below the Queen. With two at the base and two more midway up the mountain, the five points of the Arch were in place. Queen Alison raised the massive Alistone before her with both hands. The dragons raised their bejeweled chests and looked to the sky, each doing their part to try and connect the stones. In unison all of the dragons' Arch Stones began to glow. The stone in Alison's hands flashed briefly but then quickly dimmed.

Below on the battlefield, Lord Leamoldae's twisted but Gifted banmen drew upon their leader's unholy alliance with the Angel of the Abyss. Bolstered by Abaddon's dark power, they relentlessly pounded what remained of the KenKarta front line with menacing blasts of navitas-fluo. The shields of the Queen's forces failed fast now.

Julia's muscles quivered as she sat with King Rick atop a mêlée platform strapped to two armored camallo. Currently they were watching the battle unfold through Ember's eyes. The hawken had flown up the valley over Lord Leamoldae's troops and located the Dark Lord himself. He was still positioned deep enough in the Inculta valley that its small rounded mountains blocked his view to the south. The Dark Lord's troops possessed great brute strength, but cooperation and communications amongst the ranks was lacking. As a result, Leamoldae clearly had no idea the forces from Askard were lying in wait.

King Rick chuckled with disdain. Leamoldae, already so confident he would soon know victory, now lounged under the cover of a fabric awning. He barely even watched the current battle. No doubt, too busy plotting who on Virtier he would go after next.

When he shot the white dragon, the wretch had not even watched her fall. Julia had seen him smile with satisfaction when the concussion wave hit his back as her body impacted the ground. He had faced his army to bask in their cheers of praise. Julia's fur stood on end just thinking about it. Though distasteful, his act of disrespect did turn out to serve them well, for it kept the Dark Lord from seeing Daelkay. The arrogant fool actually believed the Queen was dead and the King was locked away somewhere. Why else would he be so confident that the battle was already his?

An intense flash of colorful light caught the lounging leader's eye, and he reengaged in the situation around him. He scanned Mount Drafair's slopes. His jaw locked as he jumped to his feet. He'd finally seen the dragons! With the loss of their leader, they had initially retreated. And because Lord Leamoldae knew better than most just how reluctant dragons were to involve themselves in the affairs of men, he had apparently concluded their part in the battle had been successfully deterred. He now seemed to be reevaluating that conclusion.

Two of the dragons crouched about a hundred yards apart at the base of the mountain. Two more perched directly above each of them about a hundred yards up the mountain's face. This alignment filled four of the five positions necessary to form a traveling arch, a feat only achievable by dragons, or on a much smaller scale, fairies.

Leamoldae glanced across the battlefield to see that the body of the great white dragon still lay where it had fallen from the sky. A slight smile crept across his fine features. It faded quickly though. It must have dawned on him that the four remaining dragons could still combine the strength of their Arch Stones to make a powerful weapon and use it against his forces.

The Dark Lord mounted Hellantae, skirted the battle-line, and fought his way to the middle of his horde that now gathered in front of Mount Drafair.

Alison looked at the giant gem in her hand. How could she channel enough energy to power the Alistone? No one, not even her husband, believed the feat to be humanly possible. A thunderous yet strident roar reverberated through her. From below on the mountain's slope, a dragon cried out in pain. Bursts of navitas-telum spat forth from Leamoldae's hand. Sitting there trying to form the Arch, the four great and noble creatures were virtually defenseless and would remain so until she completed the connection. Only then would the power of the Archway protect them.

There in the center of the chaos, the root of this evil sat alone above the fray, straddling a black equidae. His fair hair and features seemed grossly out of place amongst the vile-looking monsters that surrounded him. That was always his strength though, wasn't it? Making everyone believe he was what he appeared to be. He looked angelic, but in reality was just as vile as any of those now around him. She could not let him succeed.

Alison focused her inner strength and energy as before. But this time when she closed her eyes, she also prayed.

Julia remained impatiently perched next to Askard's King watching the battle, though now through her own eyes instead of the hawken's.

Leamoldae's attack on the dragons was short lived. Once he was positioned in the middle of the battlefield, a blaring bass-pitched call pierced the air. King Rick's battle cry! A commotion to the north followed. Three kaboukaba clambered into view from behind Mount Fairdra. Their size and presence caused most of Leamoldae's reserves to rush down the valley away from the Inculta Moldea, their only true line of escape. Those who stayed behind faced the crushing weight of the kaboukabas' feet and swaying tails.

Then the King of Askard gave the order for his main force to move in from their hidden position in the valley just east of Drafair. Hearing the advance, the cavevils on the southern line turned toward their new foe. But another kaboukaba led the Askard charge. It lumbered down the valley to the edge of the plain, then stopped. As the cavevils closed in, teeth bared and snarling, the kaboukaba turned sideways and swung his massive tail just above Virtier's surface. The impact sent the beasts airborne and cleared a path for the rest of Askard's advancing troops.

Julia looked up at the King. He flashed a broad smile at her. He laughed knowingly and waved his hand forward. "Your duty here is done, noble cheetatarah. Good Hunting to you!"

Finally! She catapulted from the platform and streaked down the valley.

Chapter Forty-Three

Empty Space

The entranceway of the cave filled with hobyahs. Sophia watched them slink along the walls. Closer and closer they drew to the girls' position. When they attacked there would be too many.

The first wave that had tried to rush them met with quite a shock. Earlier, under Cordova's instruction, Sophia had been able to charge the fairy court's defense system. She rearmed it as soon as they ran inside away from Daelkay's dragon breath. So when the first group of hobyahs tried to cross the threshold of the castle's courtyard, the pulse of energy and light blew them backward through the air toward the cave entrance where they now remained crumpled and smoldering. Sophia had beamed when Veronica said she was impressed.

Unfortunately they had no time to recharge the system, more hobyahs were already on their way. Scoobee's bark was growing hoarse, and things didn't look good. In fact, they looked pretty dire.

Veronica faced the front of the cave keeping her shield between them and the enemy. "Sophia, can you do this?"

"Stop yelling at me, Veronica." Burning tears filled her eyes and Sophia heard her voice echo off the stone walls. It sounded shrill.

"Soph, I'm not yelling, but we don't have time for a tantrum. Now's the time to remember what Mom says. Don't cry. Try!"

Sophia looked at the tiny Arch against the back wall of

the cave. She wiped a tear from her cheek, reached under her shirt, and pulled out the necklace her parents had given her, the one with the large purple amethyst, a Star of Grace. A Star of Grace was a Piece refined by fairies. Though relatively small in size the power it held was legendary.

Sophia tore off a long piece of her skirt and tied one end to the necklace's chain and the other to her wrist. Then she held the Piece up to the hole where the Alistone belonged, and as she had done before, slipped it in.

The Star of Grace began to glow. The Arch hummed to life. A swirl of color dissolved the stone center of the Arch. There some distance back was the glow of another open Arch. Fairytier, she was sure of it! Daelkay had asked Queen Allezell to leave the Arch open, and it appeared as if she had.

"Veronica..." Sophia said, as her sister turned to see the open Arch.

"You did it, Sophia! That's fantastic. All right, we've got to go right now."

"Wait, you said *I* didn't have to!"

"Look over there." Veronica motioned to the advancing hobyahs. "I can't leave you here."

"But I can't. I can't jump! I'm too scared."

"I'm scared too," Veronica said, looking into her sister's eyes, "but Sophia, I- *we* can do this; together we can do this."

Behind them, Scoobee growled and barked, but the hobyahs closed in. V dug into the pouch of Imperium Pieces tied to her belt. She pulled out the silver-pink piece of yttrium and handed it to Sophia. "Hold this. It'll help." Then Veronica put an arm around her sister's waist and called, "Scoobee!"

The dog leapt into Veronica's chest. She turned, dragging Sophia with her, and ducked into the open Arch.

Sophia gasped and held her breath. The cloth cord tied to her necklace grew taut in her hand. Their forward motion stalled. There in the darkness of the Arch they were suspended between Tiers, floating almost adrift, exactly what you don't want to have happen. Her heart raced. And then she felt the pop. Her necklace broke free from the Alistone in the cave. There was no turning back now, yet their forward momentum had stopped.

Before them in the distance beamed a small but brilliant Archway of light and color. If they could not reach it, if they drifted off the path, they would be forever lost in Empty Space.

Two young girls trapped in the never-ending darkness of Empty Space. I know, it's nerve racking! However, you must know that the Princesses' message about the Onoxmon had indeed reached the King. But let Yorgide tell you, that was the easy part. Now the King must prepare his allies for what was to come. He knew this would change everything. You see, having the power to wield the Onoxmon and using it were two very different things entirely. No matter the outcome of this battle, the balance of power on Virtier was about to change. In the wake of victory all would be unsettled. Alliances would be tested. Opponents would likely be more combative. Troubling to be sure, but not nearly as troubling as the thought of letting Leamoldae win.

"Stop the advance. You have to keep them all back," Dale told Cletus, the Commander of Pringer's forces.

Cletus was a good friend of the King's, who had all but convinced the tribes of the Pringer Forest to merge with KenKarta's Kingdom. It was a union Clet hoped would help his rather nomadic people to prosper, so he'd been pushing for it, even while other tribal leaders hesitated. If this came to pass, Clet, a leader in his own right, would give up his own chance at a crown. Such selflessness is rare in men, yes indeed.

"Don't let anyone advance beyond our current lines. Just contain them," the King repeated.

"Are you *insane*?" Cletus yelled to be heard over the sounds of battle that surrounded them.

"That makes no sense, Dale," Norman, the King of Brython said, pushing by guards to join them. "We have them boxed in now, but they won't stay that way for long. We've got to close and try to finish this. Their only way out is over the top of us and that's a course they won't mind taking."

"Alison is taking care of that." The King motioned toward Mount Drafair where the dragons prepared to activate the Traveling Arch.

The Traveling Arch was a feat all present had heard of but few had ever seen. Dragons did not interact with men the way they once did. Yet now, four of the large creatures, two red, one orange, and one green, shone like beacons of hope on the slopes.

"Do you see?" the King asked.

"I see," Clet said. His tribes of Pringer had historically suffered much at the hands of Leamoldae and his kin. There was little good will to find between the two peoples in the best of times. "And I know that if the Dragon Arch is formed, Leamoldae will not go through it voluntarily. We are going to have to push him through. An effort to which most here will likely be asked to give their lives, but if we fail, all our Lands will be lost. There is no other way."

"There is one," the King of KenKarta stated soberly.

Dale gripped his sword by the blade and lifted it hilt first between himself and his colleagues. The leaders gathered around Dale eyed the hole in the sword suspiciously.

Like all on Virtier, these men knew the legend of the Onoxmon's power, but none of them had ever witnessed it. Five generations had passed since anyone could actually wield the power of the Onoxmon. So rare was this Gift that in the past simply

255

being able to make the Onoxmon glow had been enough to propel young boys toward a bid for the crown. Dale and Cort Leamoldae had both been such boys. They had been plucked from their homelands and brought to the Mythscola in the hopes that with training, one day a true King able to fully wield the Onoxmon's power would once again unite the lands of Ken and Karta, and even beyond. The fact that two boys within the same generation had exhibited the potential excited the countryside, but it had also begun a rivalry that would almost tear Virtier apart. Ah, Yorgide remembers, those were wild times indeed.

Up until this point, King Dale had only proven he held the potential to tap what lore said was held inside the Onoxmon. The man they now faced across the battlefield had shown similar ability at a young age. Yet as far as any of these leaders knew, this was one Gift neither had ever been able to master.

King Norman looked at the empty hilt and asked, "What is it you propose?"

"That I use the Onoxmon."

"Where is it?"

"Coming," Dale said, and you can believe Yorgide when he tells you that silently the King prayed his word was true. "And when I place the Onoxmon in this hilt, I put forth… that I should use it to fling Leamoldae and his throng through the Dragon Arch into the Abyss."

Truly they would be going to a Lower Tier, which would be more accurately described as the edge of the Abyss, but still.

The King of Brython asked, his cadence slow and measured, "There is truth to its power?"

"There is," Dale replied.

Wagging his head slowing, Cletus asked, "And you have harnessed it?"

"I have."

Being an astute man, the King recognized the clenched jaw and squint that flashed ever so briefly across his friend Cletus's face. Of course Clet felt betrayed. If such a feat were possible surely he'd have been told. The King knew he would have to make Clet understand why the information had been withheld, but later.

"When the Arch is formed I will not have much time, I cannot guarantee my accuracy that quickly on this large a scale. Anything between the Arch and me is going to go through it. When the Arch is opened, we must pull back to insure our troops get out of harm's way."

The King of Brython locked gazes with Dale for a long moment, then said, "The word will be passed." Norman reached for his peer's hand, his eyes wary, but chin set in resolve. "May the Pinn guide you."

"May Deus guide us all," Dale replied. Then as Brython's commander left, he turned to Clet.

The King's old friend clasp his shoulder and leaned close. "When this is over… we will talk?"

"At length," Dale said, firmly squeezing his friend's shoulder in reassurance.

Cletus pulled himself back to his full stature and said, "Then, where you go, I go. I'll ready the troops on the southern line."

So now the King had warned his allies, but Yorgide must point out, that was a good thing only if the Onoxmon was retrieved and the King was able to use it. Otherwise he had just made a promise to other leaders he wouldn't be able to keep. The political fallout would be disastrous. Of course, that only mattered if any of them made it out of this clash alive. Not a foregone conclusion. The King of KenKarta knew time was short. Onoxmon or not, he had to lead. He had to fight.

Chapter Forty-Five
Don't Cry, Try

The girls and Scoobee were suspended in the darkness of Empty Space. They must go forward, but there was nothing to push off of, nothing to pull on. Panic threatened to seize Sophia as she thought of what to do. Her stomach hurt. She tried to ignore the knot forming there. Her mother always told her the power to travel, to propel oneself through an Arch and Empty Space, came from within and from the Pinn.

Veronica had her sword and Scoobee in one arm and the other around Sophia's waist. Veronica concentrated on a point of light beyond Sophia. The Archway. The knot in Sophia's stomach tightened. She wanted to cry, but instead she too focused on the Arch of light. That was Fairytier, and Sophia willed with all her heart that they were there instead of adrift in this darkness.

The hair on her neck stood up. Energy rushed down her limbs. Then they sped off toward the pool of light as if they had stepped off a cliff. They plunged into it. Like water, it abruptly slowed their speed, but didn't hurt. Sophia lost her balance and rolled away from Veronica, who struggled to right herself. Behind them, a loud crack emanated from the Arch. A high-pitched squeal burst from the lungs of a twisted form as it tumbled by them through the air and onto the moss-covered ground in front.

A hobyah had ridden their wake through the Arch. Disoriented, it stood to face them. Scoobee leapt from Veronica's arms and hit the ugly gray midget full force in the chest. His blow knocked the beast backward into the undergrowth of the forest that surrounded the Arch. Both Scoobee and the hobyah rolled. Righting himself, Scoobee launched after his prey. It hissed and ran for its life through the forest, Scoobee barking his pursuit.

Veronica thought about joining in, but after watching him fight the past couple of days she was confident that Scoobee would get the job done on his own. She smiled; the amazement of what they had just done starting to sink in. Sophia was sitting, knees tucked beneath her, on the ground before Veronica. She was not smiling. Her eyes were wide and fixed on a point just over Veronica's shoulder. Another hobyah? It must stand right behind her, preparing to attack.

Veronica didn't turn. She knew the hobyah would be upon her before she could spin and raise her sword. So instead she switched her grip. Now instead of her thumb and index finger being next to the blade they grasp the end of the hilt. She capped her right hand with her left on the sword's hilt, raised the tip so that it pointed behind her, and stepped back. She felt the blade penetrate its target and drove it deep into the creature behind her. Only then did she withdraw the steel and turn to face her attacker, sword ready to finish what she had started.

Veronica hardened herself. She fully expected to see the twisted form of a hobyah snarling at her. She did not. There was no hobyah, wounded or otherwise. Another stood in its place. With both hands grasping the wound above his hip, the wound she had administered, stood Zane.

Veronica's breath caught, her arms collapsed to her sides, and as her sword dropped from her hand she died a thousand deaths of despair. "What have I done?" she said in a hoarse whisper, unable to breathe.

Zane looked up from his wound with dark eyes. "Why?"

"No, Zane, I thought-"

Sophia stepped between them and grabbed her sister's arm. "Veronica. No! Don't!"

In shock, Veronica didn't really hear her sister. All she could hear was the wailing of her heart. How could she have stabbed Zane, this boy who had risked his life to save her and hers? This boy, whom though she'd only known him for days, she cared so deeply for. How?

"Veronica," Sophia shook her sister's arm, "that is no boy!"

"What?" Veronica asked, still in a daze.

"That is no boy; look at its eyes!"

"Well, you are the observant one aren't you, Sophia," Zane said. As he stared at Veronica his dark almost black eyes, with just a glint of yellow, turned back to the blue she knew.

Then before either of the girls could react, he stepped forward, pushed Veronica to the ground, and grabbed Sophia by the neck.

When she hit the forest floor, Veronica jolted from her haze. She reached for her sword, which lay on the ground beside her.

"Ah, ah, ah..." Zane warned, tightening his grip on Sophia's throat. The younger Princess coughed, unable to breath.

Veronica drew her hand back from the sword and placed it instead at her own throat, clutching her shirt. "Don't you hurt her!" Veronica snarled.

"Well now, that is up to the two of you," Zane said. Then in Sophia's ear he hissed, "Give me the Onoxmon."

Sophia choked. "I don't know where it is."

"Now that's a real pity," Zane said with a cough. A bit of yellow spittle emerged on his lower lip. "Next best thing then. You sit right there, Princess Veronica, while we go through the Arch, and I'll let her live."

"Why?" Veronica stammered.

"You stupid girl, if I go back empty handed now there will be real byss to pay." He winced with pain from his wound. "She'll make a nice gift for my father."

"Your father, I thought he was dead?"

Laughing, Zane said, "You think my father's going to die in battle? Guess again, *Blondie*. He's got too much to live for, like plotting his revenge against your father."

He stepped back toward the Arch behind them. It was still open, but showed no clear destination. Flashes of different Tiers appeared in the distance only to return to the darkness of Empty Space. Veronica glanced at the wound in Zane's side. The blood seeping thru his fingers wasn't red, it was a very deep brackish yellow. He wasn't human at all. What then, what had yellow blood? The answer came to her like a thunderclap. Legend said that demonic shape shifters had yellow blood. He had told her that himself, hadn't he? The night they fought the hobyahs in Casglen. *That* was what had Sophia? A chill passed up her spine. Her throat went dry.

"You tricked me. For how long?" she croaked, already fearing the answer.

"From the start, my Princess," the shape shifter responded. "It's been fun, but now we really must jump."

Tears filled Sophia's eyes, and she struggled for each

breath. Her fingers, clutching at the inhumanly strong hand around her throat, were white. Veronica was still on the ground, hand at her own throat. She was too far away to reach them in one lunge, not even in two, but by Deus she would not let this monster take her sister. Her fist closed around her shirt in frustration. She felt the necklace her parents had given her. It held a Star of Grace just like Sophia's, but instead of an amethyst hers was a ruby. Now the red stone was hot to the touch. Her fingers began to tingle. Could she...? She looked into her sister's eyes.

Glancing over its shoulder into the Arch the he-byss said, "I don't suppose you'd like to lay out a path for me, Princess? I mean, you wouldn't want your sister drifting around forever in Empty Space, now would you?"

"No," Veronica replied, "but I won't cry when you drift away!" She shifted her gaze to the he-byss's wound, willing Sophia to understand. Even if she did, it might be futile, but they had to try, didn't they?

"Sophia, don't cry, try!" Veronica said.

Sophia let go of the hand around her throat and drove her elbow into the he-byss's side, right where Veronica's blade had entered. The shape shifter howled in pain and lost its grip. Sophia sunk to the ground. The creature's complexion turned ashen. Its nose began to hook. Its teeth darkened and drew to points. It looked more like a hobyah than a boy now. Its eyes were dark again and flashed with hate. Gaze locked on Veronica, it began to reach down for Sophia.

The odd tingle in Veronica's fingers grew and spread. She thrust one hand out at the he-byss's chest and pressed the other into the ruby at her throat. Heat gathered at her core. It seared a path to her shoulder and scorched down her arm. A cry of pained determination escaped her lips as a long pulse of red navitas passed from her palm through the air and into the creature's torso. The shape shifter catapulted backward into the Arch. Its form reverted to Zane.

Reaching out to her, he said, "Veronica, what have you done?"

Given that a path was not laid out to any one particular tier, he drifted back into the darkness. As he did, his form again shifted shapes, rapidly now. Zane morphed into a cheetatarah, then a small horse or deer. The distance made it hard to tell. As it drifted from Veronica's view, the creature turned its face away toward the vast blackness of Empty Space. Again its shape shifted. It changed into... a girl? A girl with long black hair?

The Archway closed. In the place of Empty Space now stood the bark of a very large tree. Sophia lay still on the ground, looking up toward the forest canopy above. Her breathing was raspy. Red impressions of fingers still dotted her throat.

Veronica crawled to her sister's side. She was surprised at how weak she felt, dizzy even. "Sophie, are you all right?"

With a raspy voice and cloudy eyes Sophia replied, "Veronica, I see fairies."

Veronica rolled to her back with a slight smile, then blinked, trying to clear her vision. "Wow, magical battle really does a number on your head," Veronica said woozily, "cause I see fairies too." She tried to focus on the flittering shimmer above her, but her mind tugged her inward. She fought to resist. Fought to push back the blackness creeping in to envelop her. But her head hurt. Oh, so tired. Sophia was safe. Surely it'd be okay to rest, just for a moment... drift away from the pain... Wait! The blackness paused its advanced. Veronica reached back out through the pain and clasped her sister's hand. "Sophia, get the Onoxmon to Dad."

Then the Tier went dark.

Sophia's stomach knotted as tight as a fist. Her arms flew out for balance. Her eyes blinked to focus. She was back in the cave. Parisia hovered before her, a staff topped with a large lavender jewel in her hands. Sophia had conquered it twice now, but tier-jumping was still scary. She hated to leave Veronica on Fairytier, but Parisia had sent for her mother whom she swore would help. And Veronica had said, "Get the Onoxmon to Dad."

From the shadows at the front of the courtyard came a snarl! Parisia aimed her staff and said, "Silex!"

Purple navitas flew forward and struck the snarl's source. A hobyah turned to stone where it crouched. Its features, twisted and frozen in place, reminded Sophia of the gargoyles around one of the old churches in Karta.

Glancing between it and Sophia, Parisia said, "Wow, did you see that, Phee! I've always wanted to do that."

"That was tremendous."

"It was, wasn't it," the fairy Princess said as she darted around the room. "All clear. Now, let's get you to your father."

Sophia followed Parisia to the mouth of the cave. Beyond the ledge the battle raged. Booms and cracks filled the air. Colorful navitas streaked across the sky.

Dalminyo reared up over the ledge, galloped the distance between them, and skidded to a stop before Sophia. "Where's Veronica?" he asked.

Sophia felt the knot in her stomach tighten again. "Still

on Fairytier."

Dalminyo's ears went back. "What's wrong? What's happened?"

Parisia chimed in, "She's a hero if you want to know the truth. She used seriously advanced magic to save her sister here from a nasty shape-shifting he-byss."

Dalminyo brought his head down to Sophia's height. "Is she hurt?"

"Yes, really bad." Sophia swallowed, pushing the knot back to her stomach.

Dalminyo snorted. "Take me to her."

"Don't get your tail in a twist there, big fella. My mother will take care of her."

Dalminyo swiped his tail at the fairy flitting about him like an annoying oversized fly. "Who are you?"

"I'm Parisia, daughter of Allezell, Queen of all the fairies. Maybe you've heard stories. No? Well, by Deus above, you can believe me when I say Veronica is in the best hands to help her. You'd never fit through the Arch in there, and besides, there's a mission your Bonded one wants you to complete."

Sophia placed her hand inside the pocket of her gown. She withdrew a hard oval shape and held it out for Dalminyo to see. A point deep within the black stone had begun to glow, so now the etched symbol of the pinnacle sun resonated dark blue. "Veronica said to get it to Dad."

Dalminyo slid one of his front legs straight out before him and lifted the other, curling it back. His bow was so deep that Sophia could easily reach his back. She slipped the Onoxmon back in her pocket and climbed onto his saddle.

"I'll wait for you here, Phee," Parisia said. "If I let any

other humans see me, my mother will lose her ever-lovin' mind. I'll guard the Arch and take you back to Veronica when you're done."

"Thank you, See-"

"'Tis noth'n." The young fairy smiled. "Now, go save the Tier."

Dalminyo turned to the edge of the ledge. Below on the slope of Mount Fairdra, Sophia's cousins were fighting hobyahs from the backs of three equidae. Sophia heard Dalminyo call to them, then to her he said, "Hold on, Sophia."

The knot in her stomach squeezed tighter. She gripped his black mane in both hands and shut her eyes. Her body lurched forward, and she could hear Dalminyo's hooves beat out a cadence on the virtier beneath them. Beyond, she heard the sounds of war. Navitas boomed. Swords clanked. Enemies howled. It was awful. She listened instead for just Dalminyo's hoof beats. Then his were joined by more.

She opened her eyes. Squinted against the wind to see. In front and on each side were equidaes, astride them her cousins. Kameron was in front, leaning low so his sword reached below his steed's neck to slash through hobyahs there. Eric was on her right doing the same.

On her left was Kirk. He smiled at her and said, "Don't worry, Sophia, we've got ya." A hobyah leapt at him. He twisted and deflected it with a thud as they ran by.

Chapter Forty-Seven
The Onoxmon

The valley below swirled with the colors and sounds of war. There. Just in front of KenKarta's newly forming line, Sophia saw him. With sword in hand, her father walked purposely forward. A few pallamales made the mistake of trying to close on him. The ones nearest to him were swiftly cut down by his blade. Those blocking his path out of steel's reach were struck and hurled backward by a wave of transparent black navitas light that emanated from the King's left hand. To do this, her father merely needed to slide his right hand up the sword's hilt and touch a black-diamond Imperium Piece mounted there. She had seen him conjure navitas before, but never directed at anything living.

A short distance in front of the King, swarmed Leamoldae's army. Pale faces with giant pink eyes, hobyahs with scythes, massive gray beasts breaking men like sticks. It was horrific. And she was running right at it. Though thankfully, most of the deformed hordes were engaged in battle with KenKarta's forces on the right and left and not with the troops directly before her.

Sophia realized her father would have to be careful when she got him the Onoxmon. The lines were all mixed up. If he misdirected or made the power too intense, he could wipe out not only the enemy but also his own men, or worse, Sophia's mom who now stood directly opposite them high on the slopes of Drafair.

The sky grew notably lighter above Drafair. The stone in the Queen's hands radiated a brilliant blue shine. An explosion of light and color flashed from her to the other four stones held by the dragons. The slopes of the mountain disappeared in a sheet of light. Then as panic froze Leamoldae's ranks, the Archway turned black with only a small window of light visible at its very center. The light was orange and uninviting.

Dalminyo's hind-end sunk as he slid to a stop. They had reached the back of KenKarta's reserve line. He couldn't get through. Her father turned. Did he see her?

She had to get to him. She was close enough to hear him now.

"Give the order to pull back! Everyone behind me!" the King yelled as he strode out further in front of his troops.

Sophia slid down Dalminyo's leg. She rushed forward with Dalminyo neighing after her to wait. But she couldn't wait. She had to get to her dad! Her small size allowed her to slip beneath most of the throng. She pushed low through the last of KenKarta's reserves. He saw her too! She ran straight for her father. "Daddy!"

His gaze darted to the side. Then his eyes widened with anguish. His lips mouthed "no" as he raised his hand. Sophia turned to see what he saw. A banman!

A sneer crossed the banman's blood-splattered face when his murderous stare locked onto her. Pinnacle, no! Sophia was almost within his reach. His grimy fingertips grasped at her face. She opened her mouth to scream. A purplish-brown streak flew over her. It struck the banman like a navitas blot. It and the banman tumbled backward across the ground. When he came to rest, the banman lay dead. Julia released her bite on his throat, pounced up, and was back at Sophia's side by the time the King reached her.

Shaking, Sophia handed her father the Onoxmon. "Veronica said to get this to you."

Inhaling, his lips parted, but no words came. Instead he took the stone and placed her hand on the small of his waist as he turned back toward the plain. She clung to the back of his leg and peeked around. Part of her wanted to look away, but she couldn't. Their fate was literally in her daddy's hands now. He placed the Onoxmon into the sword. Magic locked it in place.

Word to fall back had passed quickly, though not nearly fast enough, and the enemy was not completely cooperative. Pockets of their and other allied troops remained entangled with Leamoldae's horde. Nevertheless, Sophia realized the King was going to act now while the majority of the beasts were awestruck and the Arch steady. Who knew how long her mom and the dragons could keep a pathway open? Oh no! Those who had not already disengaged would be lost. Dizzying movement and noise swirled around her. She gripped tighter to her father's leg and felt Julia's fur brush against her arm in support.

Inhaling, Dad closed his eyes. Her own body began to tingle. His jaw hardened to stone. The tingle intensified. He raised his lids. The lively blue eyes Sophia knew to be his had grown dark. He stared out into the fray with sightless determination. The tingle became a vibration. It rattled Sophia's teeth.

Then some of the blue returned to her daddy's eyes and the vibration vacillated. The King's gaze now focused upon something straight ahead. His mouth slackened in despair. Sophia scanned the battlefield. There, struggling to keep a cavevil at bay was her father's good friend Cletus. Sophia felt her dad's weight shift forward. She felt his instinct will him to go to his friend and help. But then Clet saw Dale. The warrior saw his childhood friend's resolve falter. Knowing it would seal his fate, Clet yelled to his King, "Do it! Do it *now*!"

Her father shut his eyes and clenched his jaw. The tingle became a vibration again. It threatened to rattle her very bones. The King took the hilt of his sword in both hands and pointed the tip down toward virtier. Dropping to his knee, he planted the blade firmly in the soil. Sucking away the very air she breathed, the vibration peeked and pulsed and sped past Sophia's quivering body.

It was as if the King had reached down, grabbed the ground, and snapped it like a rug. A wave of virtier rose and grew in size and speed. Its crest curled higher than the kaboukabas' heads, and it traveled toward the Arch as fast as a cheetatarah. Ear-splitting thunder peeled as stone grated against tier. Those at its edges stared in awe. Those in its path stared at death.

Chapter Forty-Eight
The Dark Lord's Descent

Flying high above the battlefield, the dragon listened in on the Dark Lord's thoughts but had yet to reveal his presence. Unseemly as it was, Daelkay realized he enjoyed Leamoldae's confusion when the Arch formed on the slopes of Drafair. The evil master looked at the peak to identify the dragon that must have arrived to help establish it. When he saw Alison he bellowed, "Impossible!"

Even as a child, there had always been arrogance, Daelkay thought, but was the malice always there? And if so, how could he have been so blind to it? Leamoldae never underestimated his own Gifts, but was prone to underestimating others. He just couldn't believe that anyone could possibly be as Gifted as he. Nor could he understand self sacrifice. Would such arrogance be Leamoldae's ruin?

Daelkay felt the Dark Lord's fury as he took aim and fired at the Queen. The energy from his navitas blast was sucked into the Arch long before it reached its mark. Again the Dark Lord growled his displeasure.

From his dizzying height, with his dragon sight, Daelkay could see the entire battlefield. He shifted his gaze to the base of Mount Fairdra. There Sophia struggled through the frontline and ran toward her father. His connection to her was strong, growing- like a Bond? He felt her fear, but also her determination. Look out, a banman! His own heart skipped a beat. He started to dive, then pulled up, for the attack was already over. Thank Deus for that cheetatarah! The little Princess's fear pained him. Then there was a pang of pride, as despite her fear, she selflessly risked bodily harm to complete her mission. She placed the Onoxmon in her father's hands. Finally, a human he had not misjudged.

His evil master's thoughts crowded his own. Leamoldae had mounted Hellantae and turned to race up the mountain's slopes vowing to kill the 'infernal woman,' namely the Queen, with his bare hands. A deafening roar sounded behind the Dark Lord. Daelkay tucked his wings and dove.

Hellantae reared toward the noise. Leamoldae's mind was silent as he watched the dark wave of virtier rise from the battle field and sweep up everything in its path. It was coming right at him. Yet instead of turning to run away from the soil tsunami, as did the rest of his army, Leamoldae ordered Hellantae to run right at it. The equidae raced to cover the ground between them and the wave. He struggled against an ever-increasing uphill grade to reach the crest. The tumultuous virtier eddied beneath his hooves. It threatened to flip them backward into the turmoil below. Hellantae vaulted into the air. The crest curled and passed beneath. Hellantae rode the wake back down to solid ground.

Behind them the horde was battered and rolled and hurled and finally thrown right through the open Arch toward Exiltier.

Hellantae stood, sides heaving. Leamoldae tipped his head back to laugh in relief, stopping when a shadow crossed his fair face. He looked up to see the great purple dragon clasp the equidae and him in its talons. The dragon heard one thought race through Leamoldae's mind. Rescued!

The dragon's mouth curved up slightly with just a hint of satisfaction. Arrogance would be 'old moldy's' undoing. Instead of banking sideways or climbing hard, veering away from the gaping Arch, Daelkay leveled off. He flew straight in, taking his Dark Lord back to the Lower Tiers.

In the back of his mind he could hear the cry of a certain young Princess pleading with him to come back. She would be safe now. And he would take solace in the fact that Leamoldae's last look at the world above was through the iron bar talons of his own dragon. Daelkay knew he was sure to suffer greatly, but it was nothing he didn't deserve. The Dark Lord's screams of rage would echo in Daelkay's ears even after Alison collapsed to the ground, and the Arch snapped shut.

Chapter Forty-Nine
Drowning on Dry Land

Sophia gasped. It was hard to breath. The battlefield lay before them, silent and still. A thin haze of dust drifted above it. But no movement, no sound. Everything that had been between the King and the slopes of Drafair was gone. Daelkay was gone. Her mother, where was she? There, lying high on the slope. Was she all right? It was all too much. Too much to take in. Too much to think about. Her mind swam. She felt like she would drown.

The ground was back in place but appeared as though it had been heavily plowed. No visible trace of the army they had been fighting remained, except for those now cowering at the edge of the killing field or those who had fallen before reaching the plains. Even for the adults, this was clearly a sight hard to comprehend. Soldiers just stood there, mouths gaping. Others appeared to be moving so slowly it was like they were swimming. A moment before, where thousands had stood, now was nothing but dust and scattered debris.

The King pulled Sophia around from behind and hugged her. "You all right, sweetie?" It sounded like he was talking under water.

Sophia nodded numbly in reply.

"You sure?"

Again she nodded, but still felt as if she were under water.

"Stay here with Julia. I'll be right back."

From some depth beneath the invisible waves, Sophia heard herself say, "But Daddy, I've got to get back to V."

"Fine..." her father said. Even through the water, Sophia knew he was only half listening. His focus was elsewhere. He gave Sophia another squeeze, then rose. The King looked up the slopes of Drafair to where the Queen had fallen. Gallantae appeared at the King's side. Her father vaulted to his back, and they were off.

Clearing her head of the water just a bit, Sophia asked, "Is my mom going to be okay?"

"Yes, of course." Julia purred.

"You sure?"

"Yes, I'm sure."

"Well, then I need to get back to the cave- to Veronica."

From behind them Dalminyo said, "I'll take her."

Julia glanced up the hill from Sophia and back again. "Very well, the cave's a good place for you to wait... I'll be there shortly. I'm just going to go see if your father needs some assistance. Dalminyo will take good care of you."

Julia sprang forth. A brown and purple blur streaked across the valley and up the slope. She caught up to Gallantae just as they reached the perch on Mount Drafair where the Queen lay.

The Princess's mind was still swimming. Should she be worried about her mother? Julia said she was fine. Daddy's with her. What about Veronica? No one was with Veronica.

Sophia turned to Dalminyo and said, "Let's go."

Chapter Fifty
Fairytier

Veronica dreamt strange dreams of fairies. They were trying to nurse her back to health. For in this dream Veronica was ill, and everyone acted as though she were dying.

In another dream, Veronica watched Sophia playing in a big meadow with fairies dancing in the air all around her. It was beautiful. Evergreen trees surrounded the flowery meadow, and up in their branches, fairy homes glowed like natural ornaments. At the back of the meadow stood a castle. Its design was very organic, almost as if it had grown right up out of the ground. Coolly colored crystal and gem formations glowed and glittered, adding to the elegance. Hundreds of fairies zipped to and fro along its intricate causeways and through its elaborate complex. Veronica had never seen a more stunning castle on all the Tiers. Yet, somehow, Sophia seemed to be as tall as everything but its highest, most elegant spires. Was this the court of Allezell, Queen of the fairy realm?

In and out of dreams, Veronica drifted. Scoobee nuzzled her ears and neck. He lay by her side. She wanted to pet him, but could not. Again and again, Sophia looked down at her while a little girl fairy with long brown hair hovered about. Her sister was very fond of this fairy; she called her Parisia. Sophia looked so happy! Veronica wished to join them, but in this dream, as in all the others, she couldn't move.

Then her cousin Kara entered the dream, and spoke of taking them home. Veronica loved Kara. It felt good to see her. But home, wasn't she already home? She just needed to wake up. V tried to talk to Kara, ask her what was happening, but in this dream Veronica couldn't speak. Hadn't Mom said Kara and Aunt Vicky were working on something in the Upper Tiers? Or was that just part of this crazy dream? Oh, why couldn't she wake up?

Chapter Fifty-One
Sophia and Daddy

Sophia crawled into her daddy's lap. Since the moment she and Veronica had arrived back home through the Arch in Mount Grace, she couldn't get enough of him.

When the battle had ended it was Cordova who told the King and Queen the details of what had happened to their daughters. The little kangamou had been hiding in his tunnels paralyzed with fear when Sophia and Veronica first went through the Arch. He fretted in the shadows until Parisia returned with Sophia, and then stood guard with his Princess throughout the remainder of the battle. So he was there when Sophia came back on Dalminyo and returned to Fairytier with Parisia.

It wasn't fair that poor Dalminyo had been so severely reprimanded for his part in helping Sophia return to Veronica. Julia really should start speaking to him again–– after all, he is bound to help V. Dalminyo had told Sophia that when the King and Queen arrived, the kangamou was all too willing to throw him to the hobyahs. Cordova reported that as caretaker of Fairdra Court he had tried to stop the King and Queen's daughter. He questioned whether it was wise for Sophia to return to Fairytier, but Parisia had told him to mind his own business. In addition Sophia assured him that the King had said it was *fine* for her to return to Veronica. So what was a Kangamou to do? Sophia knew she had pushed her luck with that liberal interpretation, and under normal circumstances, she'd still be in trouble.

Sophia smiled as she thought about her daddy standing in Fairdra Court talking to a rodent! Surely he had wanted to scream and run from the cave. Mom was right. No matter how old you are, sometimes you just had to overcome your fears. Daddy did it with rodents, and she had done it with Tier-jumping.

It took four days for Aunt Vicky to gain permission from Queen Allezell for Kara to go retrieve the girls from Fairytier. By then everyone else had made it back home to Karta.

Mommy had wept when she saw Sophia, and Daddy seemed pretty choked up too. She'd never seen him like that before. Their relief that she was all right was such that they continued to smother her with hugs and kisses every time she came into their view. But her parents still had other worries.

Veronica remained unconscious. The days since she had blasted that he-byss back on Fairytier continued to creep by. Kids weren't supposed to be able to do that. They weren't even allowed to try until they were sixteen because it was far too easy to pass on your own essence, to drain your own life. Yet Veronica had done it to save Sophia; she'd done it out of love. If not for the fairies, she'd be dead. They didn't trust humans, hadn't let a human visit their tier in annuals. Yet when they found Sophia and Veronica at the Arch they helped them, used their magic to restore them. Parisia helped Sophia get the Onoxmon back to her father. Sophia could have loved them just for that, but there was so much more.

Her time with the fairies was like a dream come true and helped to block out all the ugliness of the days before.

She had never felt better really, yet a sadness weighed on her. Not really for Veronica, 'cause she was sure her sister would be all right. Queen Allezell had told her it would just take some time. Her parents didn't seem so sure, but the fairies would not lie to her.

He hadn't said anything about it, but Sophia knew her daddy had been through a terrible ordeal. So she stayed close to him. Even when he was being King, she would slip her hand into his and stand or sit quietly by his side. Daddy didn't usually allow this. He'd usually shoo her away when he had to talk to the generals or the like, but not now, so Sophia was certain he really needed her. His use of the Onoxmon was causing quite a stir all across the Tiers.

Now they sat alone in his study at the edge of the residence. The walls were paneled with dark black walnut and flames licked the low hearth of the fireplace. Daddy was leaning back in his big comfy black-leather chair next to the fire while it made shadows dance on the wall.

Sophia sat on his lap facing him. "Daddy."

"Yeah, honey?"

"What do you think happened to Daelkay?"

"Oh honey, don't you worry. That bad old dragon will never be able to hurt you again."

"Daddy, he never hurt me."

"Good... good." Dale gave Sophia a hug.

"He helped me."

Dale's brow furrowed. "Helped you how?"

"Didn't he tell you why he brought you back to Virtier?"

"What do you mean *back*?"

"Back from the Lower Tier where Lord 'Moldy' took you... to torture you."

"How did you-"

"Daelkay told me you were in a horrid place."

"That *miserable* beast."

"No, he's got good in him, Daddy."

"No Sophia, any good in him was eaten away annuals ago. He took you because of his hatred for me."

"No, Daddy, he doesn't hate you. He didn't want to take me. His master ordered him, but there's good in him still. I felt it." Dale shook his head, but Sophia continued, "He said he misjudged you. That he wished he'd never chosen to Bond with Moldy, but now that Bond is broken. That's why he let me find the Onoxmon. That's why he has a new master now."

"Oh really, who might *that* be?"

"Me! That's why he came for you, Daddy, because I asked him to."

Dale looked toward his daughter, but not really at her. She knew he was seeing something else entirely. He was thinking hard about something. Sophia knew because his lips moved silently. They did this a lot when he was working something out in his head.

"So see, we can't leave Daelkay down there with 'Old Moldy.' He belongs with us now."

Slowly Dale replied, "Sophia, the Arches on the Lower Tiers don't have Alistones, so they only work one way. No one is meant to come back."

"But you came back!"

"Yes, because Daelkay had the Alistone he'd smuggled in from Dragontier."

"So, that means he can use it to get back again?"

"No honey, he didn't have it with him. He had given it to your mom so we could make the Archway on the plain."

"Then why did he go through the Arch?" Sophia asked as her voice began to quiver. "Why would he choose to leave me?"

"Sophia, I don't think he chose to leave you. He did what he felt had to be done. Trust me, Sophie, that old dragon has done many things to be ashamed of that he's never tried to atone for. It sounds like you touched that stone that had become his heart. You made him want to try and set things right. Still, there are consequences for our actions even when we are sorry for what we've done. Daelkay finally stopped running from them and decided to meet them head on. He took Leamoldae through the Arch and back to the Lower Tier to protect us, regardless of his own safety. With that selfless act, maybe he hopes to find redemption."

"Redemption?" Sophia asked, a tear in her eye.

"Forgiveness in the eyes of the Pinn."

"Well, I forgive him and I'll pray that Deus does too."

"Well, that's a start."

"Can you forgive him?" Sophia asked, then as her daddy drew in a long loud breath added, "For me?"

"For you? For you I'll try," the King said, wincing as Sophia leaned on his chest to hug him.

"Oh, sorry, Daddy," Sophia said, drawing herself upright and pulling back his shirt to see the cuts and bruises beneath. "Oh Daddy, did 'Old Moldy' do that to you?"

"Yeah, 'Old Moldy.'" He chuckled.

She ran her fingers over a cut and her face hardened a bit. "Well, don't worry. I won't ask you to forgive him."

"Well good, because I don't plan to."

"He's going to try and come back isn't he?" Sophia asked looking for the truth in her father's eyes.

"He'll try. And if he somehow succeeds, we'll be ready for him. Now, why don't you go check on your sister. I'm sure your mom could use a little break."

Chapter Fifty-Two
Open Your Eyes

Veronica forced her eyes open. She lay in the middle of her parents' bed. Its massive size and soft inviting bedding made her feel safe and comforted. But wait, was this all just a dream?

"Oh, there you are, Veronica!" Sophia said sweetly from behind on the other edge of the bed. "We've been waiting for you. Mom and Dad are sick with worry. I'll go get them."

"Wait, don't go! Sophia, what's happened?"

"Don't you remember?" Sophia brought her sister up to date, talking as fast as she could, jumping from thought to thought. "Well, I did like you said and took the Onoxmon to Dad. Parisia helped. Mom made a Traveling Arch. Then Daddy sent 'Old Moldy' and his entire army back to the Abyss. It was scary! Way scarier than tier-jumping. Then I went back to Fairytier with Parisia. I think I'd be in big trouble for that if they were not so worried about you. The fairies took care of you. Parisia's mom saved your life. She's not as mean as she acts. Parisia and I played and played. It was awesome! Then Kara came, and we had to leave. I was so mad, but guess what? Queen Allezell said I can come back! Scoobee can't though, he's been banned for life. He shouldn't have tried to eat that fairy."

"Wait, then it wasn't a dream?"

"It was all really real, Veronica."

"All of it?" V said sadly, thinking of Zane. She'd stabbed him, and he had turned out to be a shape shifter. How could she have actually liked him? Dad was right, boys were nothing but trouble. She'd definitely be steering clear of them in the future, shape shifters too!

"Yeah, all of it, and by the way, thanks for saving me, Veronica." Sophia gave her sister a big hug. "Mom said you shouldn't have been able to do that." She thrust her hand in the air, mimicking the gesture Veronica had made. "The bright-light navitas thing... it could have killed you instead of the he-byss thing." Sophia stopped for a moment staring at her sister, then added, "Oh right, you don't know."

"Know what?" Veronica sniffed with tears welling up in her eyes.

"About Zane."

"What *about* him?"

"You didn't hurt him and he-"

"It's still alive?" Veronica exclaimed, sitting up in the bed.

"No silly, that he-byss shape-shifter thing wasn't Zane! Zane is here, and he's fine. You can't believe how the whole Kingdom's been celebrating, except for Mom and Dad of course. They've been really worried about you. Zane has been too. I think he really likes you, you know."

Tears filled Veronica's eyes. "I didn't hurt him?"

A voice from the doorway said, "Nah, I'm fine."

Leaning confidently against the door jam, he pushed an unruly black strand of hair away from clear blue eyes and gave her a crooked little smile. Alive. Not a monster. Just a boy. She leapt from the bed, ran across the room, and forgetting herself, flung her arms around Zane's neck and kissed his cheek. As she clung to him she whispered, "I thought I had stabbed you!"

288

Zane took a few staggering steps into the room, spinning slowly to catch his balance, so now he faced the door.

"I thought you were..." She couldn't bear to say it, she just hugged him. She closed her eyes and smiled as he squeezed her in return. His warm embrace enveloped her. For one brief moment she began to melt right there in his arms.

Then his body became rigid. She lifted her head to look at him. Zane's eyes widened as he looked over her shoulder. He released his embrace and actually pushed Veronica back. She turned to see what had interrupted- "Daddy!"

As she flew to him, a broad smile replaced her father's odd sneer, and he swept Veronica up into his arms. Sophia had run out to get their mother and now returned, dragging the Queen by the hand. A royal group hug ensued with lots of kisses and exclamations of happiness.

Through the encasement of their arms Veronica could see Zane watching with a broad smile. Then the smile faded, and a strange look she didn't understand came across his face. His hand stroked the back of his tousled black hair, and he glanced around the room in discomfort. Then he turned and walked out through the beveled-glass doors onto the balcony. From there Veronica knew he could see all of Karta laid out before him. The shine was dimming, and everything was awash in a vibrant warm golden light. She returned her parents' embrace. At this moment everything was right in the Land. She didn't know what tomorrow would bring, and it didn't much matter. Right now life was... well, as Zane would say, it was spectacular.

She looked out the window and saw a glorious red bird soaring overhead. She reached out with her mind until they connected, and felt that Zane was with Ember too.

She looked down at the city through the hawken's eyes. Ember swooped over the castle garden and saw Julia. The great cat looked up and knowingly streaked toward the royal residence. Next, Ember was above the stables calling to Dalminyo. With Gallantae at his side, the spotted equidae reared in celebration. Veronica was all right! His joy filled her heart. Ember climbed higher now and headed back toward the castle. She could see Zane on the balcony, with Mount Grace towering above. Then Veronica vaguely felt, and could now see her mom guiding her body to join Zane on the upper terrace. There they were, the King, Queen, Princesses, and Zane. Even Scoobee and Julia were now on the balcony. What an image. Oh yeah, only one word to describe it. Spectacular!

Epilogue: The Dark Crystal

Yorgide understands your desire to know more, but I am sorry to say this tale is at an end. Not to mention, I'm exhausted. Not just anyone has the Gift to use a cas to show and teach you this way.

Whether or not you will go home to earth now is one of the few questions I am afraid I cannot answer for you. I cannot tell you when or even how you might achieve this. All I can say is that you are very special, yes indeed. Travel between our worlds is rare. It does not occur often, but be it known or unknown, there is always a reason for it. Do not worry. Your path home will be revealed, but only once you have learned what you must from your visit here.

Of course, there are many other stories I could show that might help you learn what you must, but I thought we should perhaps save them for our next meeting. For example, I've taught you nothing of the dark crystal yet. After I have had a rest, perhaps a spa treatment, I'm sure there are more than a few lessons in that tale that could help you find your way home.

Oh... there, there, don't be sad. You are making Yorgide feel bad. You know, on second thought, I guess I could spare a little more time to pass along a story as important as the dark crystal...

So then, let me think about this a moment, where should Yorgide begin...

Glossary Of Terms

CAST OF CHARACTERS

Alison- Queen of KenKarta

Allezell- Queen of the Fairies

Aphina- the white dragon

Bella- a Unucornubelluacomis

Cletus- ruler in the Pringer Forest, ally of KenKarta

Cordova- a kangamou and caretaker of Fairdra Court

Cort Leamoldae- a Lord banished to the Lower Tiers

Daelkay- dragon Bonded to Cort Leamoldae

Dale- King of KenKarta

Dalminyo- equidae Bonded to the Crown Princess of KenKarta

Ember- a hawken

Gallantae- equidae Bonded to the Queen of KenKarta

General Fooney- trusted advisor to the King and Queen of KenKarta

Harold Plow- Zane's stepfather

Hellantae- equidae Bonded to Leamoldae

Julia- a cheetatarah and messenger for the Royal Family of KenKarta

Mira- Zane's mother

Norman- King of Brython, ally of KenKarta

Parisia- Fairy Princess, Daughter of Allezell

Rick- King of Askard

Scoobee- dog of the Royal Family of KenKarta

Sophia- Royal Princess of KenKarta

Veronica- Crown Princess of KenKarta

Yorgide- your narrator, cascader and guide

Zane- stable boy

PARTS OF THE WHOLE

Abaddon- Ruler of the Abyss, devil

The Abyss (Byss)- Hell

Deus- Ruler of the Pinnacle, God

Empty Space- the area that separates the Tiers

Lower Tiers- tiers located closest to the Abyss; place where those loyal to Abaddon live and to where those convicted of crimes on Virtier are banished to

The Pinnacle (Pinn)- Heaven

Upper Tiers- tiers located closest to the Pinnacle; places where Mythical creatures are granted Lands of their own.

Virtier/Center Tier- the largest of the tiers; remains stationary at the center of the World of Tiers; it is the Tier where most humans live

The World of Tiers- the world made up of the Upper, Center and Lower Tiers located between the Pinnacle and the Abyss.

PLACES

Askard- a Land located to the southeast of KenKarta ruled by King Rick

Bedforda- small community located to the far eastern edge of KenKarta

Brython- Land to the southeast of KenKarta ruled by King Norman

Casglen- an ancient gathering place located at the tip of the Pringer Forest

Chinja- Home of the Chinjana people; a large isolated Land located to the west of KenKarta

Exiltier- largest of the Lower Tiers; place where most humans are sent when banished

Inculta Moldea- desert area that leads up to the city of Moldea

Karta- the capital city of KenKarta

Ken- largest city in the Palousoa region of KenKarta

KenKarta- Land on Virtier ruled by King Dale and Queen Alison

Kief- large port city in the Land of KenKarta

Konakua- an island Land located in the western waters

Medius- a city of KenKarta located along the Alydon river

Mitigo Plains- the no-man's land of Virtier no humans are allowed to live there

Moldea- a Land to the northeast of KenKarta; home of Cort Leamoldae.

Mount Fairdra and Mount Drafair- twin mountains located on the eastern edge of the Mitigo Plains; an ancient gathering place of Mythical creatures

Mythscola- Prestigious school for the Gifted located in Karta

Pallatier- Lower Tier, home of the Pallamales

Palousoa- a land within KenKarta; the area where King Dale grew up.

Pringer Forest- a Land located to the east of KenKarta; home of Cletus

The Raknorock- the Mountains that surround all of Virtier; the edge of the world

Seatella- a Land located to the northwest of KenKarta.

Sparthena- the Land of men south of the Mitigo Plains

Yolnegue- the Land of men north of the Mitigo Plains

THINGS

Alistone- an Imperium Piece set at the top of a working Arch

Arch- provides the means to pass through Empty Space from one Tier to another

Arch Stones- the four Imperium Pieces, other than an Alistone, needed to make an Arch function properly

Bonding- a process where by Mythical animals choose to be permanently tied to Gifted humans

Cascade- a device used by the Gifted to transmit and sometimes create images; used mostly as a means of communications across the lands and tiers

Demogeron- old word used to describe nobles or the ruling class on Virtier

Firedancers- large red flowers with purple centers that grow on the Mitigo Plains

Ge-ims- images and sounds created and captured inside a geode

Geode- Imperium Pieces that look like rocks but are filled with crystals; used to operate cascades and capture ge-ims.

Gifts- abilities endowed by Deus that when mastered allow one to draw upon the power of Imperium Pieces

Imperium Pieces- stones or gems that contain and generate sources of power that Gifted ones can draw upon

Navitas- energy created by Gifted ones using various Imperium Pieces; forms include navitas-fluo and navitas-telum

Onoxmon- believed to be one of the most powerful Imperium Pieces on all of Virtier

Star of Grace- an Imperium Piece charged by Fairies: very powerful

Violaqum- purple clouds unique to the Mitigo Plains

CREATURES OF THE CENTER AND UPPER TIERS

Camallo- large animals often domesticated to be used as beasts of burden

Cheetatarah- Mythical dark brown cat-like creatures with purple spots; are faster than even the equidae, but at full speed their endurance isn't typically as good

Dragons- large winged creatures that hold Mythical powers including verbal and Gifted speech; most live on the Upper Tier of Dragontier

Equidaes- Mythical horse-like creatures that can run at great speed for long distances and speak to the Gifted; though they have been granted their own Upper Tier, many still prefer to become Bonded to humans

Fairies- small winged Mythical beings that have retreated to their Upper Tier of Fairytier to avoid contact with humans

Hawken- hawk-like birds that often display the ability to allow Gifted ones to see through their eyes

Kaboukaba- largest land animal on Virtier with the ability to communicate to Gifted ones

Kangamou- small rodent-like creatures often endowed with some Gifts

Unucornubelluacomis- a large Mythical amphibious creature with the power to heal injuries and alter moods

Zadeer- striped deer-like creatures that inhabit the Mitigo Plains

CREATURES OF THE LOWER TIERS

Banmen- humans banished to Lower Tiers

Cavevils- large vicious creatures banished to the Lower Tiers

Hobyahs- violent child-sized creatures long ago banished to the Lower Tiers

Pallamales- humanoid creatures that live on the Lower Tiers

THE OLD WORDS

Pilkraft-old magical word used to invoke an Imperium Arrow

Scutuma- old magical word used to invoke an Imperium Shield

Silex- old magical word used when turning living matter into stone

Sopor- old magical word used to induce deep state of sleep

View a list of vocabulary words and a lesson plan at **www.KenKarta.com.**

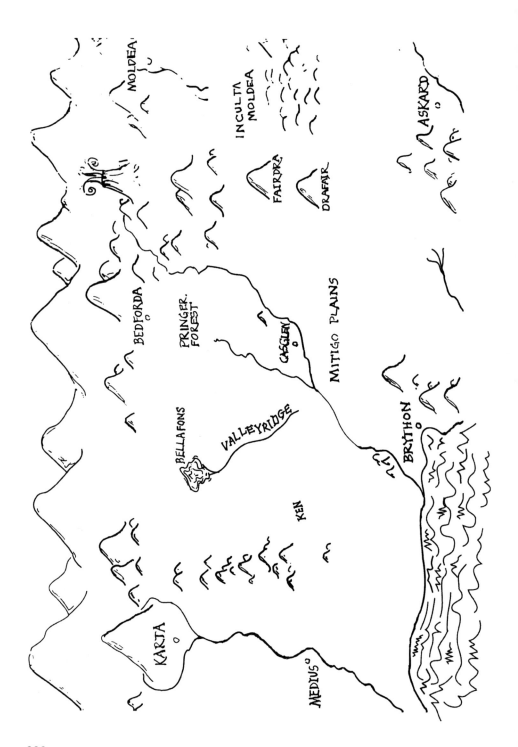

Acknowledgements and Appreciation go to…

My collaborators and muses, Veronica and Sophia. Try as I may, I love you both more than mere words can convey. Thank you for helping create not just this magical world to write about, but for making the one we live in magical as well.

Mrs. Sallee and her 2006-07 second grade class at Bower Hill Elementary. The interest and excitement exhibited while I read you the first rough pages are in no small part what encouraged me to put in the time and effort to turn that story into this book.

Gabrielle DiBattista and Olivia Nagel for being test readers. Girls, your enthusiasm was infectious, not to mention uplifting.

The ladies of DDHCS. Cathy and Becky, thanks for listening… and listening… and listening!

My friend Amy Harakal. Your thoughtful and straight forward analysis built the backbone of the glossary of terms and the accompanying vocabulary list found on the website.

Photographer extraordinaire, Leanne Collier. Thanks for making us look good!

My friend, sounding board, and head cheerleader, Jodi Lesniakowski! Your fearless editorial input and wonderful graphic creativity has helped bring this book to life.

Les Polinko. Your pen, paint and pensive talent drew these characters out of our minds and captured them on paper. Wow, what can I say? You are, "spectacular!"

Susan Mary Malone, for reading an early draft and seeing, not just where the story was, but where it could go. Thanks for then using your masterful editorial skills to provide me with the GPS coordinates to get there.

My publisher, Sherry Linger Kaier. Thanks for believing!

My husband, who day in and day out does the heavy lifting. Dale, your hard work allowed me the privilege of taking on this wonderful and fulfilling endeavor. I love you.

9 780984 316632